BUZ
AND STIF GO TO
COLLEGE

MICHAEL JOHNSON

BUZ AND STIF GO TO COLLEGE

iUniverse books may be ordered through booksellers or by contacting:

iUniverse
1663 Liberty Drive
Bloomington, IN 47403
www.iuniverse.com
844-349-9409

ISBN: 978-1-6632-0452-3 (sc)
ISBN: 978-1-6632-0453-0 (e)

Print information available on the last page.

iUniverse rev. date: 10/13/2020

Buz wanted to be an Air Force pilot. That was his first ambition. His father had been a pilot and his father had retired with the rank of Colonel and a good pension. Pensions and Colonelcies were a million years away for Buz, but you had to plan ahead if you wanted to get ahead.

There were a whole bunch of problems from the start when he decided to apply to the Air Force Academy. In fact, his dad was flattered that Buz wanted to fly in his footsteps, but even he wasn't sure it would get off the ground. For one thing, Buz's grades were not too great. He only barely kept off from flunking out of high school. The liberal grading policies at Drakesville High had finally passed him with a C- average. The only positive points to support his application were several letters from retired Air Force officers, his father's friends, recommending Buz for his "innate good character", "demonstrated leadership potential", and things like that. Then there were all those minor run-ins with the police when he was in high school. Really nothing but a bunch of DUI's, some vandalism and the time he broke into his girlfriend's parents' house while they were trying to sleep. Also, the Air Force had changed its recruitment rules. They had to have more diversity. This was understandable. You couldn't have all bleached out guys all the time. The policy had a negative effect on marginally qualified candidates like Buz. Buz received his letter of non-acceptance without surprise. It was nicely written, even friendly (We wish you success in your future life plans), but it was clear: thanks, but no thanks.

Stif got his nickname from his body shape. He was six foot three inches in height and thin. He was a top player at basketball, really good, voted second in his high school league. Drakesville went seven to two in his last season. Stif might be material for the major leagues. His coach said so. Later Stif found out that his coach said that to just about everyone. Stif was very good, but there were many high school players who were very good. The majors wanted only the exceptional players, and only the best of those.

"Flunk city". Buz and Stif were drinking beer in Stif's borrowed car just two weeks after both had barely squeezed a high school diploma from their less than mediocre academic records. It was early evening and they were parked on the side of a dirt road near the lake. "I flunked algebra twice. I passed it on the third try, though. I even got a C," Buz reminisced proudly. This showed that progress was possible. "But I'm really lucky I did damn good in history. How many guys can remember who discovered America? Right? Or who married up with Pocahontas? When they signed the Declaration of Dependence? Or who the Puritans were? I knew all that crap. I guess that's what got me through."

"Yeah. You lucked out on all the theory subjects. Back down on earth, the biggest thing you're ever gonna fly is a paper airplane." Stif laughed until he spilled half a beer down the front of his t-shirt. He didn't notice.

"You're a top comedian, man", Buz retaliated, "too bad you don't get that rank in pro basketball."

Stif crushed his empty beer can and tossed it into the back seat. "Well, at least I took off. I got ranked number two in the whole league." After a moment's reflection Stif realized that this was not exactly up to the image of himself that he dreamed of. "I had a chance at the majors."

"So what now?" Buz.

Stif opened another beer. His eighth for the night. He was cutting back.

"I thought so. You don't have an idea. Me, though, I've been thinking." Buz could have said twenty or thirty more things to cut his friend, to get even for Stif's put-down about the AF, but he knew they were in the same boat, buddies since elementary school and with basically the same problems, so now they had to row together if they ever wanted to get anywhere at all. Buz's father had said nothing when Buz failed his Air Force Academy application. He had seen it coming. He wasn't dumb. "My old man got to be a Colonel because he knew all this stuff that you have to study hard to understand. You wouldn't believe all the technical crap you have to learn to fly a plane, then lead your whole squadron and talk to generals and guys like that."

"Yeah. No. I get it. But all God's children ain't got wings." Stif shook all over as he laughed, but this time he held his beer can upright.

"All right. Forget that. But I got an idea that could just be do-able. It's got to do with hitting the books, like my old man had to do to pull ahead."

"What?"

Buz spoke slowly. He was three inches shorter than Stif, but he had a heavier build. "Okay. You know there aren't any jobs around this putrid burg except at fast food restaurants. We could go to the city, but even there we'd be worse off than we are already: it'd be harder to find a job, everything expensive as hell and all that stuff. Okay. What I was thinking was this. Why don't we go to college and get a higher education? With a college degree you can get a good job with great pay. The TV people talk about it all the time."

"Yeah, but it's expensive as shit."

"Hey! Cool the language. If you're gonna be a college student you have to talk correct. Correctly. What we do is take out a couple of those Student Loans. They're almost like free money. You use the loan to pay college tuition and living expenses and all that and you don't have to pay it back for ten years. By that time you're making a mint and it's not a problem."

Stif was impressed. He opened another beer. He had two open at once.

"Yeah. We apply to Peabody State University. You don't have to be an Einstein to get it in. Mr. Schoholy told our civics class that. He ought to know. He graduated from Peabody State." Buz.

"Old Piss?" Peabody State University was known

affectionately to students and to locals as "Old Piss", because of the first letters of the first two words of the name and because of the fact that it was founded back in 1931 as a junior high school.

"That's right. It ain't exactly Harvard or Oxford, but it's a pretty good school after all, even if everybody laughs at it. Lots of guys who go there end up working for big corporations or even having their own offices."

"Hmm. Maybe you're right. I guess anyway you can meet a lot of girls there." Stif.

"Hell yes. Millions of 'em. Mostly girls go there now anyway."

"Okay! You're on. Where do we sign up?" Stif found it easy to make major decisions after ten beers.

"Well, it's not exactly that simple. You have to fill out an application form for Peabody State, then you have to have your grades, your transcript, sent from Drakesville High to Peabody. Then you have to take a test called the SIT. You apply for a Student Loan with a form you can get through the mail. When you do all that and you pay your tuition, you're in. I mean, if you get accepted."

Stif stared ahead, expressionless. He was confused and discouraged. "There's got to be something easier."

"It's not that hard! You go one step at a time. First, you fill out your application for Peabody State, then you apply at the D High office to have your transcript sent there. After that you take the SIT test, and then you apply for Student Aid. Finally, with all that fixed, you get admitted to Peabody, unless you're really bottom of the barrel flunk material. College doesn't start until September anyway."

"Okay. I guess it beats flipping burgers."

Buz, the smarter one, knew what life was all about. That was mainly girls. The problem here was that girls didn't seem to like him. He wasn't fat, or too short, or ugly. His features were sort of—well, they were there, all of them more or less rounded and in the right place and not too big or small but … nothing else. His physical build answered to the same leveling mediocrity. He was not thin, but not really athletic in build either. He was into sports, sure, and he did all of them pretty well, although he couldn't hold a candle to Stif when it came to basket. He had a large gang of friends in high school. There had been no shortage of beer parties over the weekends or even during the week and after school. When it came to talking to girls he naturally emphasized the subject on which he was an expert: Buz. Buz's ambition to be a pilot, first of all. The problem was that girls seemed to be full up after ten minutes or so of Buz talk. They usually moved away.

But that was out now, the pilot idea. Along that line, he thought of all those things about life that were hard and not too cool, but that you had to get through to get to the real thing—to the girl. The uncool stuff started in grade school, then just built up and added-on until Buz could only try not to think about them in a clear way. His plan was to take one little piece at a time and see what happened. Going to college was a big piece of life, but you could start slow. Even Peabody State University would be a challenge, Buz knew it. But he was the guy who had wanted to fly for the Air Force and maybe someday take off in a space ship going to the moon or mars, who knows? He ought to be able to handle starting out at P.S.U. Peabody was only fifty miles from Drakesville. Easy trip.

Stif, of course, also knew exactly what life was about. He had a really clear vision of the whole thing. It was about basketball. Basket was great. That is, it was the real achievement that showed that you were special. Now, after the recruiters for the majors had turned thumbs down on him, he spent more time watching basket on the screen than playing it. He was still participating in a big way. Of course girls were just as important. In a way, girls were like basketball in the sense that they too were the goal. You had to get it through the hoop. Stif was sort of handsome in a way, with his thick red hair and fair complexion and large features that were more *romantic* certainly than Buz's. He could count on the effect of his long, but not too long nose that was also thin and pretty well adapted to his mouth and chin and eyes. Still, it was hard for him to get girls to like him—a point that made him sympathize with Buz, and vice versa--since, generally, for girls, ten minutes of basketball talk, like Buz talk, were about the limit of endurance. He had scored a few times with girls. What he wanted was to have a regular girl friend, or maybe two or three, and then to keep adding to the number and chalking up the experiences. Right now he was playing solo on the court, putting the ball every night through his own imaginary hoop. Buz told him they'd have to move to Peabody when they started college. That was okay. Every town was at least fifty percent girls.

Even though Peabody State students were generally low average in grade records and test scores, getting into Peabody was not that easy. It was a byzantine and labyrinthine process. Buz had learned these words in his senior English class at Drakesville High. They came in handy. First you had to fill out an application that was ten pages long. Besides names and addresses and dates, you were asked how you felt about certain things, the sort of things the news media talked about all the time. Then you had to describe your goals in life. The best thing was to put something like "helping humanity" or "making everyone equal in opportunity" or abolishing sexualism, the movement that kept women underneath some sort of glass roof. A friend from Drakesville High had told him about this. DiRoccio was already enrolled at Peabody. When you get there, Rocco added, just agree and do and say what you're told. That way you'd get through it, get your diploma, then you could forget it all. You'd be a college graduate with tons of job prospects.

After filling out the application you had to have your transcript, the record of the courses you took and the grades you got, sent from Drakesville High to Peabody State. Buz worried about this. He wasn't sure what his overall grade point average was, but he knew he had a lot of D's and three or four F's. He was maybe a low C average, if that. He knew Stif was even lower. Stif had spent too much time on the basketball court, and even from an early age he had been a devoted TV fan. His basket success made the teachers friendly when it came to grading, so he usually managed to squeak through with a passing grade, which was a D at Drakesville.

Then there was that big test, the SIT. It was almost all multiple choice questions, so you were guaranteed at least a 25% score by sheer dumb luck. Also, it stood to reason that you would actually know the answers to some of the questions even if, like Buz and Stif, you had hardly ever listened in class and rarely read a page in the textbook or turned in a homework assignment. Sometimes you learned by sheer osmosis. Buz remembered this word from high school biology. He wasn't as ignorant as he thought. Even the base bottom non-learners, if they were at least literate, had a chance to pass the SIT. Maybe the college bigwigs planned it that way, to get more Student Loan money.

That is the story of Buz and Stif, the story so far. But there is another story. The story of history Professor Hambrett Biggins of Peabody State University and his brilliant wife, Artesta Brackle, a hard driving, hands-on professor of sociology at the same institution. They had met in graduate school. Artesta had been impressed from the first by Hambrett. It was not that he was good-looking or athletic or that he had a fascinating personality. Ham, as his friends called him, was just the opposite. At twenty-six he was, well, not that much overweight. Only twenty or twenty-five pounds, but it was distributed in the most unflattering way possible, all in the butt and the belly. Where Ham excelled, where he really brought home the bacon, was in his doctoral thesis. Although, the thesis was actually very simple. Hambrett Biggins sought to *quantify* the relative victim status of various groups, historical actors in American History. This was the innovation called Quantitative Historical Measurement (QHM). The technique was to count up all the available historical anecdotes that argued for the victim status of a particular group, then to divide that sum by the total of all such anecdotes for all groups. For instance, Group C might tally 6,204 victimization anecdotes. The grand overall total number of all v.a.'s (victimization anecdotes) reached, at the time Ham's paper was submitted, at least 32,402. Thus, Group C earned a score of .1914696, which was rather impressive. The hard part had been to build up, that is, to write, the theoretical scaffolding behind Quantitative Doctrine. To do this Bigg, as his friends also called him, had to deal with, to arrange an enormous amount of research results. He had to bring in theory from half a dozen disciplines. Ethics, sociology, historicism, economics, psychology and philosophy were called on for building material. In the end, that is, when Bigg finally handed his finished thesis to his faculty advisor, Professor Bieberkopf, it was a document of more than seven thousand pages including illustrations and drawings. A very large part of it consisted of long, unacknowledged quotations. This was a trick Ham had learned in junior high, where he cribbed most of his writing assignments right out of the encyclopedia. Unfortunately, elderly Professor Bieberkopf succumbed to a massive stroke only two weeks later, before he had finished reading even a quarter of the paper. Rumored reported that total confusion and irritation about the thesis did old Bieberkopf in. Ham's masterpiece was accepted. No other faculty member wanted to try to read it. Now Ham was Doctor Hambrett Biggins Ph.D. But it was the thesis, not the seven thousand pages, but the Quantification idea, that had aroused the sexual concupiscence of Artesta Brackle.

Artesta was working in a different theoretical area for her doctoral thesis in sociology. After a decade and a half of research, her work would develop into the highly respected academic area of paleo-sociology called Castration Discourse (C.D. It's not what you think.

It's almost entirely theoretical). C.D. evolved from transgender studies, at the point where they intersected with biological research on the behavioral influences of hormonal secretions. It was a broad concept involving gender formation and the difficulties encountered by individual personalities as a result of the radically unequal nature of modern Western societies. Artesta and Ham met at a revolutionary film seminar. It was mutual sympathy at first sight (or rather, discussion, since Ham immediately started to tell her about his impressive development, which obviously could not refer to an anatomical feature). They co-habited from the start, although personal projects, including physical relations, could never have primary importance for two people so entirely committed to setting the world right.

How did the two super-brilliant doctoral students end up at Old Piss? It can be ascribed to their idealism and spirit of sacrifice. When they were in graduate school both Artesta and Ham joined a group that wanted to bring freedom, happiness and free sex to all persons. This was an organization founded in the sixties during the great freedom rebellion. It was called the Blizzardmen faction. The Blizzardmen intended to spread their doctrine of liberation as far as possible. Both Artista and Ham could have made it into the faculties of Harvard or Yale, maybe even into Oxford or Cambridge, or at least to one of the bigger and better known state universities. But the Blizzard faction already had many adherents at those places. In fact, most of their adherents were at those places. Central Direction decided that Art/Ham had a duty to the faction and to the people to carry the flame to lowly Peabody State University. They had to start the long slow march through the institutions at rock bottom.

Years later, the Blizzardmen no longer existed. Art and Ham were still stuck teaching a bunch of pre-literate hicks at Old Piss. Why? The answer must be sought in that same spirit that emerged during their early years of idealism and totally selfless sacrifice. An old comrade in the Blizzard front had become an informer for the FBI. He had given the FBI a complete list of Blizz operatives known to him, in order to receive better treatment on charges arising from the illegal possession of explosives and so be able to continue the liberation work *outside*. That, in any case, was what the Bigginses believed. They had been x-balled from the top university faculties because of their early involvement with a group reputed, without entire accuracy, to have engaged in terrorist activities (a few small and largely dud bombs, a bit of arson, some threats). That explained the fact that even though both were full professors with impressive publishing records, neither had been able to get a job at a more prestigious institution long after the fall of the Blizzard movement. At CUNY, for instance, or even at SUNY. Probably neither would ever reach Department Chairperson at Peabody State. But there were other reasons. For one thing, Ham kept trying to shove his seven thousand page thesis in the face of anyone on the Piss faculty (one curious professor had found a couple of pages on dog breeding copied from an encyclopedia at pg. 3048 of the thesis), or on the faculties of other schools, who could read. Artesta was suspected (there was no proof) of performing clinical ocular measurements on the crotch areas of male faculty members for some project related to her C.D. theory.

Her Castration Discourse thesis had been read and was widely feared even among the highly advanced group that constituted the P.S. teaching staff.

So. Hambrett Biggins today. Today Ham was fifty-five years old. He was a hundred pounds overweight. His build, as disloyal critics put it, resembled a washing machine roped to the fourth rung of a step ladder. A hernia, a loop of intestine that kept protruding into his inguinal area, had rendered him impotent for the past twelve years. A medical operation was out of the question because of his excessive weight. General anesthesia might depress his breathing permanently. He had a severe case of hemorrhoids. He was entirely bald. His facial features resembled a pumpkin three weeks after Halloween. When he lectured to his classes, and his class sessions were almost entirely lecture/cross examination, with only occasional brief periods for questions by students and no group discussions at all (Ham alone knew what had to be learned), he could not rest his physically stressing weight at the teacher's desk in the usually way, i.e. by sitting. His inflamed hemorrhoids made this very uncomfortable. To speak to his classes, he lay on his side on top of the teacher's desk, like a seal on an Antarctic beach. The women in his classes tried to look away. The boys laughed behind held-up notebooks. But! Hambrett Biggins was still devoted to liberation. If he was not physically attractive, if he suffered from several embarrassing maladies, so what? Was it not his love of humanity that mattered? Hambrett Biggins' long term bet was that it was. It was rumored that Artesta Brackle now found surcease from the terrible needling of her libidinous urges in same gender affairs, as well as in engagements with male faculty members not her partner. There was nothing wrong with it. In any case, rumors about faculty persons are unreliable. Most of those who dared express an opinion on the matter thought that Artesta was as much a victim as anyone.

Hambrett, despite his shortcomings, both physical and intellectual, was a very ethical man. He was entirely devoted to justice, as he knew that it had to be. There was one thing, though, that really grabbed his ass (his own slang expression, which dated from his high school days). He hated to see the way certain younger males, especially his students, were able to attract the interest of girls by their youth, good looks and physical potential. This was unfair. It was injustice. In a perfect world everyone would be equal in every way. Hambrett would be just as admired by at least some young women as the athletic young Adonises who strutted on campus. In the meantime you had to struggle on against injustice.

The SIT test was a real bitch. Buz and Stif had to sit at school desks for hours using little pencils to fill in the dots on their answer sheets. The multiple choice questions were easy in one way, because all you had to do was to guess and then mark your answer. The math section questions were harder, but you could skip the ones that weren't really obvious. Buz and Stif knew they weren't doing well. At one point Stif forgot which test he was doing. Was it English or History? In any case, the questions were, well, they were a question. What the hell were they talking about? If you could understand the question you'd be halfway to the answer, but you might as well ask for the moon. Stif knew they never had a lot of this stuff at Drakesville. What the hell was post-structural linguistics?

What the hell was linguistics? That was probably junk they taught to the rich kids at private schools. When the two walked, dazed, into the outside sunlight after four hours of test taking, Stif was sure he had flunked. He had done so badly that he was afraid they'd cancel his high school diploma in addition to crossing him off the college list. Buz felt somewhat better about it. "I think I passed. You did too, probably. Remember, you get an automatic twenty-five percent right just by sheer luck, since you only got four choices on most of the questions. Then you gotta know the answers to *some* of the questions, so give yourself another thirty percent. With luck, you can figure out another ten percent just by logic. So, that's a total of sixty-five percent. It's passing. What the hell."

"I dunno. What's extro-phyto-morphism?"

"What?"

"Extro-phyto-morphism."

"I must've missed that one."

In fact, Stif and Buz did not do as badly as they had a right to expect. They were informed by mail two weeks later. Stif scored 601 out of 1000 and Buz scored 610. They were below average, just a notch above flunk out. It was good enough for Peabody State. Letters of acceptance came in the mail.

The next step was Student Financial Aid. This was a Federal program intended to help poor but gifted students pay the high tuition costs that schools had to charge in order to keep up with research expenses and faculty and administration salaries. After they had submitted forms and documents testifying to family social status and income, they were informed that Buz qualified for a total loan of $45,000.00 and Stif a loan of $41,495.00. Why the difference? They finally concluded that the question was like the SIT test itself, incomprehensible but not important. With that kind of cash, Stif argued, why the hell did they need to go to college at all? Why not just buy a sports car and head for New Orleans? Because, Buz cautioned, for one thing, they didn't give you the money all at once. They just dribbled it out to you a little at a time. The university attendance office kept in close contact with the loan authorities. Most of the money would go directly from the loan authorities to the school authorities. They'd give you a tiny allowance to live on.

Stif's face registered deep disappointment. You could tell because the beer abuse circles under his eyes popped out. "Then why the hell are we doing this crap in the first place?"

Buz replied with patience and understanding. He had already explained it a dozen times, but he knew his friend was a slow learner. "Because, when we get to be college students and we keep whacking away at it, we'll eventually get our college diplomas. Then we can get good jobs with good pay and a whole lot of girl friends."

Stif nodded. "Okay." It didn't sound too bad when you put it like that.

They rented an apartment in Peabody. It was in a low rent area. Their Student Loans budgeted three hundred and forty-seven dollars per month for living accommodations. $347 each, a total of $694. The apartment was located in a neighborhood where old sofas and tires were piled on the street corners. Every second lot was vacant. The nearby grocery store was called "Abarrotes".

They moved into a unit on the ground floor. Stif

would have preferred the upper floor, because "he didn't like having people living on top of him". It was a small one bedroom apartment. It was in severe need of remodeling. That wasn't important. They were in Peabody to get a higher education. The unit had wall-to-wall carpets, but the carpet had been chewed up in about a dozen places. It was faded and stained. The kitchen had a refrigerator, a stove and a sink, but all in poor shape, with plenty of rust spots and ancient stains. The paint on the walls of the living room and the bedroom was peeling. It looked like someone had used a baseball bat creatively on the walls at several places. The bedroom window looked out into a yard with yellow grass and overgrown weeds. But the bathroom. The bathroom. Even Stif was shocked. Why the hell would anyone want to carve his initials on a toilet seat with a knife? And to add obscene phrases? The sink was largely black. A few patches of white enamel remained. The shower had no glass door and no curtain. You just turned the water on. The puddles from hundreds of showers had destroyed the bathroom floor, covering the ancient linoleum with large green and brown patches.

"Place stinks," Stif judged with unusual accuracy.

"Hmm. Yeah." Buz had to agree with the obvious. "Anyway, it's livable. We won't be here forever."

The apartment was rented "furnished", but the furnishings were limited to an old sofa and a padded armchair with no bottom in the living room, a wobbly table with three partly broken chairs in the kitchen, and a mattress in the bedroom. It was agreed that Buz would take the bedroom, since he was the brains behind the operation, and Stif would occupy the living room at night, sleeping on the old sofa. On their first night in Peabody they discovered that this arrangement was impractical. In late summer Peabody nights were hot and humid. The only air conditioning in the apartment was provided by an old but still functioning unit mounted in the bedroom window. It was impossible to sleep in the sweltering living room. Even after consuming a full six pack of sixteen ounce cans of ale, Stif couldn't manage to pass out. Besides, the sofa was full of holes in the fabric, where springs stuck through to gouge you in the ass. Stif drifted miserably into the bedroom at two a.m. Buz was lying on his stomach. He was not asleep. You could tell because he kept moving.

"I can't sleep on that broke down motherfuckin' sofa. And it's hot as hell out there." Stif moved close to the bedroom air conditioner, which was going full blast. "Pretty nice in here, though. Besides, the springs are comin' through on that old junk heap davenport. They jabbed me in the butt about a hundred times." Stif dropped his shorts to show his roommate the red marks. He usually slept nude, but he had worn his underwear since there was no curtain covering the living room window. The mattress was not a double wide, but it was more than a single wide. They could share it. It would be cramped, but you had to go all out for scholarship.

Buz was not stupid. He was actually very bright in a lot of ways. He knew, deep inside, which sort of things were "right" and which weren't. He had an inner vision of the "okay", the right, the good. Stif did too, but his philosophical conceptions were limited by the fact that his thinking never strayed far from basketball. "Sinking one" was just about the top you could do on his ethical scale, but there were other things too. Since they were there anyway, it seemed they ought to go to school.

"When's class start?" Stif was enjoying a can of ale for breakfast. He was actually eager to get on with this college stuff. The sooner they started, the sooner they would be finished with the whole load of crap.

"We're enrolled at Peabody, but now we have to register for classes. We have to register for at least four classes each, with three units of credit per class. If the loan guys think we're just goofing off, they'll cut off our cash. So like twelve units is the minimum enrollment for the semester. Anyway, you have to have at least ninety-six semester units in order to get your diploma, your Bachelor's degree, so we better start whackin' away at it." Buz showed Stif the PSU Course Catalog. It was about three hundred pages thick. Each page described a half dozen or so courses arranged by subject and level of difficulty. Not every course was given each semester. Some, for example Comparative Vertebrate Anatomy, might be offered only once in several years.

"You mean we have to take all of this fuckin' book crap?" Stif flipped through the pages of the catalog. He was incredulous, and angry.

"Hell no. Just a small part of it, a bit at a time. Only four courses in a single semester."

"I can't even read this catalog thing!"

"You're holding it upside down."

"Oh. Yeah. Sorry. Hey, here's one that doesn't sound bad. 'Women's Wrestling. An introduction to the basic methods and holds used in women's collegiate wrestling. Students participate in one on one oppositions after being fully coached in the appropriate techniques'."

"Funny. You're really cracking me up. But let's get down to the serious part. I looked through the catalog while you were swilling beer last night, and I found four courses that look like a pretty obvious place to start. First, American History I. It's a required course. You have to take it to graduate. Then, English IA. That one's required, too. You gotta take IA and IB in English if you want to graduate. Another one is Beginning Psychology. It tells you how your mind works and how your personality got all screwed up, that kind of thing. It doesn't sound too hard and it counts toward the total credits that you have to earn to graduate. Then there's College Mathematics. It's mainly the same old algebra crap we had at Drakesville, plus a bit of geometry. I don't think it'll be too much of a bitch. So, that's the courses I'm going to enroll in and I think you ought to enroll in the same ones, so we can compare notes and share books, buy just one book for both of us, because the books cost a mint. If you want to enroll in Women's Wrestling you better wear a cup."

"Okay. I was just joking. Although, it sounds like it'd be fun to watch."

"Keep on with that and you'll be on the sexist shit list. It explains that in the catalog, too." Buz took the catalog back and turned to the front of the book. "It says right here, in the Introduction, 'all varieties of sexist, racist, ethnic or gender insensitivity will be severely sanctioned, including possible fines, suspension and expulsion.'"

"Okay. I really think women and men are the same anyway."

Soon they were enrolled. Since neither Buz nor Stif had a computer they had to use a Library model to register for their desired courses and later for course work. (To economize on unnecessary expenses, Peabody Administration did not provide students with individual pre-programmed laptop computers. Instead, they offered the use of several dozen desktop computers located in the Student Study Space of the PSU Library). It took two hours to register, because Stif kept clicking on the wrong spot on the computer screen, then cancelling the page, then trying to bring it back up. He swore so much that he was warned twice by a librarian. Stif thought it was lucky the librarian happened to be a black man in late middle age, a Marine Corps veteran. He was actually very nice and even guided Stif's hand over the mouse a few times. It felt good.

At last it was done. They had even entered their Student Loan numbers into the computer so that PSU could collect the appropriate tuition fees directly from the lending bank.

"Whew! That part was a fuckin' bitch and a half, mother. I hope the rest of this college business isn't gonna be that hard." Stif was emotionally repulsed by commitments to book work. He had never even liked reading comic books. "I feel like getting fuckin' drunk till Tuesday."

They were outside of the PSU Library now, so the use of language contrary to the Code of Ethical Behavior was not "problematic", as Buz put it. He had picked up the word from the catalog.

They walked around campus for a while, then ended up in the campus cafeteria. Stif bought a large soda drink and a hot dog. They didn't serve beer. There had been too many incidents. Buz had a bottle of water and a cheese sandwich. He felt that he was developing scholarly traits already.

There was a large telescreen hanging on the cafeteria wall. They were showing a basketball game. Stif tuned right in. About a dozen male students were watching from seats close to the screen. Stif analyzed the game immediately. He could see what was happening. One team had a few star offense players but was weak on defense. The other team was hot on team play and defense, but couldn't sink the ball. He watched fascinated with the hot dog stuck in his mouth. Then he saw them.

There were two girls sitting at a table close by. They were really great, just the way Stif, with his habitual sexist patterns of thought and feeling, liked them. A little heavy, well developed in front and behind, blond with large features. They were laughing at him. They were even pointing and nudging each other. It took several minutes for Stif to figure out why.

"Take the hot dog out of your mouth, man. It looks like something obscene." Buz.

Stif followed orders. "All right. The game got me distracted."

The girls left. Stif watched their marvelous recessional, forgetting about the basket moves on screen. Yeah, he had goofed. He knew he had to have more couth if he ever wanted to get to the "goal" on campus. Women students here were sophisticated. He sucked from his soda drink. This was PSU. It wasn't Oxford or Princeton, but it wasn't a bus stop in east Drakesville, either. Stif went into a long study while he chewed on a piece of hot dog amply seasoned with mustard. He knew that some people— they could be called intellectuals (Stif knew the word and could fill in some of the definition)--thought that fans of professional sports, especially the more intense fans, showed poor taste and low intelligence. He himself belonged to this category, of intense sports fans, beyond any doubt. But he was intellectually (he had discovered very recently, in fact just today, that even he, even Stif, had an intellectual side, however rudimentary at this stage) and morally (not referring to TV preachers) certain that the evaluation of the smart and book-type people was not completely accurate. In Stif's view, the heroic skills demonstrated by professional basketball players and many gifted amateurs could lead to points other than through the hoop. The brilliant and coordinated drive toward a sink and the equally colossal skills exhibited by defense squads were proof of a capability that would serve in almost any area of endeavor. The spirit, teamwork and enormous talent of the players were the same as those that took the astronauts to the moon. So, if the astronauts could do it, why not Stif? He thought the two girls ought to have admired him. He had almost made it to the majors. Couldn't they guess?

Next step, the campus bookstore. This was alien territory to both Buz and Stif. Neither had ever set foot in a bookstore before. It was not a venue that could fascinate extreme and almost exclusive basketball aficionados or even failed candidates for Air School. Long rows of shelves loaded with stacks of books stretched in every direction. Each pile of books on the shelves was provided with a label that told the academic subject, the course title and the name of the instructor. Here was one for Electronics. Advanced Theory of Electronics. Gravney, Darvin. The label always gave the last name of the teacher first. It was sort of a tradition. Then there was English 207, Shakespeare as Feminist. Trubloff, Max. Spanish 01A, Beginning Tourist Spanish. Jones, Melford. You had to take other courses just to enroll in some courses. For instance, there was Sociology 313, a senior course entitled Castration Discourse and its Relevance in Contemporary Society (C.D.R.C.S.). Brackle, Artesta. "Enrollment may be concurrent with lab section. Without special permission from the instructor, enrolling students must have completed at least 12 units in sociology and psychology."

Stif picked up the text for C.D.R.C.S. He flipped through the pages. It was all writing, no pictures. "I don't think I wanna go for this one. Too freaky. Besides, how are you gonna get it on with a girl if you don't, you know, even have the equipment?"

Buz took the book from him and read a few lines. "That's not what it's about at all." He read aloud slowly, pronouncing the longer words with some difficulty. 'The therapies used to promote the gender adaptation of transex individuals in a largely binary world can also be effectively adopted to promote the integration of persons who, because of unresolved libidinal structures originating in parental repression of the child and prelapsing into adult age periods, demonstrate reactionary attitudes that often incent violently in areas of sex and gender. Transgendric therapy can promote understanding, treatment and co-recovery in these individuals.'" He thought about this. "I'm not exactly sure what it's saying, but I think it's pretty deep. Incisive, that's it."

"So you're gonna enroll in the course?" Stif was amazed.

"It's only for seniors. It says so in the Catalog. I looked it up. Unless you have permission from the instructor, Brackle. And she'd probably have to do some sort of examination first. Or unless you're required to enroll by the Dean."

"How come the Dean would want to make you to enroll?"

"I don't know. Maybe like if you were having a problem with your other courses."

They moved on. They were looking for the textbook for American History I, a required course. They found History, but not A. H. I. A clerk, a large woman, probably a part-time student employee, moved along the narrow isle that separated rows of course textbooks. "Hey, where's American History I? I don't see it anywhere." Stif looked at her while he waited for an answer. No. It was okay about her being big, but she just wasn't pretty.

"The course title has been changed. It's now called 'Native American Space after the Catastrophe, 1607 to the Present'." She lumbered off. She could tell she wasn't properly appreciated.

"Oh." Stif searched the shelves of Hist texts. "Catastrophe, catastrophe. Where the hell is it?"

Buz had better literacy skills. "Here it is. The little sign has the same teacher as the section we enrolled in on the computer, Biggins, Hambrett." He picked a book up and read the title aloud. *How White People Destroyed Eden and Everything in It with Their Big Evil White Feet.* That's the textbook. Looks kind of interesting. It's for the class we have to enroll in."

"Yeah?" Stif took the book from his roommate. The book was filled with pictures and drawing and diagrams. That part was fine. The less you had to read the better. The pictures seemed to be straight out of a horror show. Almost every page showed guys with wide brimmed hats torturing more or less naked people, burning them at the stake, whipping them, then sitting down to huge feasts at long tables. "People of conscience ought to be deeply ashamed of what was done by their supposed ancestors", read one caption.

Stif was getting tired of the bookstore. The place was crammed with heaps of books of every kind, but hardly anything else. He knew that somewhere guys were sinking baskets. "Let's get this over with. How much is the fucking book? The Evil People one?"

"Look at the price tag. You're not that illiterate."

Stif turned the book upside down, then front to back. "One hundred and fifty-eight point ninety-five. What? That's crazy. Maybe in pesos." The shock was a brutal rim shot at the end of a tight game.

"Textbooks are really expensive. That's why I thought we should enroll in the same courses. We can share the book. That cuts the cost by half."

Then there was English IA. You had to buy two books. One was a large but thin manual called *I Learn College Writing*. The other was a smaller but much thicker paperback. *Our Anthology of All the Diversities*. Buz opened *Our Anthology*. It was a collection of stories and poems and parts of novels. Each selection was accompanied with the photo portrait of its author. Lots of wide smiles of people who could have worked for the U.N. The two texts for English IA tallied at over two hundred dollars.

American. "You have to remember, though, that after the course is over you can sell 'em back to the bookstore for at least half what you paid."

"Half what the bank loan paid," Stif corrected.

"Yeah, but one of these days we're going to have to pay it all back."

At last the book shopping was done. Stif and Buz, each carrying a heavy load of ink smeared paper, barged up to the checkout counter. The clerk was a thin, short guy. He wore a blue sweatshirt with the Peabody State University logo, an alligator carrying a football and trampling several human players clad in jerseys and helmets. Stif thought the thin short guy must be a poetry major.

The poetry guy passed their books one by one over a scanner. It was okay to be thin, but you had to be tall, too.

"That'll be six hundred and thirty-seven dollars and sixty-two cents. Cash or credit?"

"You kidding? There ain't that much cash." The repetition of stock phrases gave Stif a feeling of emotional security, at the same time shoring up faith in his own intellectual potential.

"Credit," Buz stated. "Can you take loan numbers?"

"Sure can." The thin young clerk held his fingers over a number pad. He had dark hair but he looked like he hadn't seen the sun for years. Probably he spent too much time in the Library. "Go ahead." It was all automatic. Your student loan number paid for everything. The amounts were progressively subtracted from your remaining loan credit balance and you received a paper statement or an email each month telling you how much you had left.

Buz gave the number. "We'll use my loan for this one, then we can use yours for the other non-tuition costs this semester," he told Stif.

"What other costs?" Stif was alarmed.

"For one thing, tutoring. A lot of students end up

having to take a couple hours of informal tutoring every week, if they don't maintain a grade point average over 2.3. They usually get an older student to do it, but it's an extra charge, not included in the tuition Old Piss gets direct from the bank. I figure we can both sit in on the tutoring sessions and pay only one fee, if we have to do tutoring, since we're taking the same courses. I'll just say you're my retarded cousin on a visit from Minneapolis or something."

"Great. Why don't we say you're my grandma keeping a watch on me?"

"Funny. Anyway, that won't come in until near the end of the semester, and only if we're under a C average." Buz thought it pretty likely.

The thin clerk put the books into plastic bags. There were three bags full of books, plus *Our Anthology,* which could be carried under an arm. Stif and Buz were ready to walk out of the bookstore and head to anywhere more interesting when the clerk held them back, grabbing Buz by the sleeve and motioning with a finger to his lips for silence.

A strong, capable, but probably angry and aggression-friendly woman of late middle age passed in front of the checkout counter. Her facial expression did not tell of a happy moment. When she was out of sight the clerk explained. "That's Brackle from the Sociology Department. She teaches Castration Discourse." There was fear in his quivering voice. "If your Advisor or the Dean recommends it, they can make it a required course for you."

All that afternoon it had been difficult for Buz or Stif to make even eye contact with any college girls. They all seemed to think there was something wrong with the two. Every bright smile and direct look was met with a sneer or raised eyebrows. Buz took a good hard look at Stif. That explained a lot of it, he thought. It wasn't that Stif was a psycho or a real moron or a mental case or anything like that. He knew Stif would never hurt anyone and that he had an IQ well above eighty (maybe eighty-five). It was just, well, he looked like someone who would have to take a course in remedial English just to say hello. He was rough looking, not like a "tough guy" but like someone who might forget to take his shoes off before going to bed. But this, Buz told himself, was a problem that could be solved by education. Once Stif began to assimilate knowledge, he would be far less repulsive to women.

They were at a beer joint called The Peabody Suds Palace. It was only a few blocks from the University. Other students filled several tables. There were some girls, not bad looking, but obviously occupied.

"Hey," Buz raised a glass mug, "here's to a great and glorious academic career. We're on our way!"

"Cheers." Stif took a long drink. He didn't look happy. Of course, it usually took at least a six pack before Stif reached a stage of Nirvana, but it was probable that he had doubts about their progress so far. "What about that lady, you know, Blackley, the one the guy at checkout told us about? I'd hate to end up in a course about 'you know what' with a mean old schoolmarm like that."

"You mean Brackle? Forget it. Every university has lots of hard ass brainy types. You see," Buz drained a good deal from his mug of beer, "when you get that smart, you don't understand that you can't control the whole universe all at once. So you get real mean. I read about it somewhere. They call it post-brilliance syndrome."

"She's in the sociology department and she teaches a class about some type of surgery. That's what the short guy said." Stif brought his legs together and hunched forward as he sat at the table.

Buz laughed. "Don't freak out. That stuff is all metaphorical." He pronounced the word, an impressive five syllables, with pride. "The course name is 'Castration Discourse', but what it's about is totally different. It's like a sort of advanced Civics class, all about social problems and movements. The title's just a way of talking about things. Artesta Brackle is highly respected at all the top universities. I read that in the school newspaper when we were at the cafeteria. It said she invented a whole new theory on how women can break out of all the oppression and be free, you know, liberationed. Her only problem is she's too smart for all these average dumbbell guys, so she gets real pissed off at 'em. She's got all kinds of degrees and tons of prizes for her research papers and books."

"Oh." Stif motioned the waiter for more beer. "Two more. No, better make that four. These are real small glasses." He turned to Buz. "That makes some sense, her being mad at all the morons. I get that way a lot too."

"Yeah. And she's married up with the guy who teaches the history class we just enrolled in. That's Hambrett Biggins and he's got a specialty helping people stop being oppressed. He's always for the underdog. The same article talked about him. All the other history professors gave him a prize."

Stif drank off the foam from his third glass. "Just so

we don't have to wear our eyeballs out reading tons of shit. I read slow."

"Slowly. It's a adverb."

"What is?"

"You read slowly, so it's a adverb."

Stif shook his head. He held his mug of beer at a distance and gave it an odd look. "What the hell are they putting in these things?"

Buz laughed again. "You're a little bit behind in your schoolwork. You'll catch up fast, though, I know it. Any guy who can sink baskets like you did can't be a total idiot."

"Hell no. I was number two in the league. I might have made number one if I had an extra year at Drakesville High."

"You did have an extra year because of all your flunked courses. You graduated on the five year plan, remember?"

"I mean an extra year after that."

The next morning was the first meeting of their history class. It was scheduled for ten a.m. at Periwinkle Hall. If you didn't show up at the first class meeting you could be dropped from the class enrollment list. There were a lot of other students who would be eager to enroll in your place, since the course was required for graduation and Professor Biggins, the class teacher, was a nationally known figure. He was controversial, but highly respected. He might have won the Nobel Prize, but physics was not his field, nor was literature, and certainly not peace. He dealt with the facts of living in a highly flawed society. That he could easily become enraged, even verbally violent when recalling the past and present of oppression, was all to his credit.

BUZ AND STIF GO TO COLLEGE

Stif had stayed up late last night drinking beer and watching television on the small portable set he brought with him from Drakesville. And it was hard to get to sleep on the small mattress he was sharing with Buz. The alarm clock went off at nine o'clock, but Stif slammed the snooze button for an extra fifteen minutes of sleep. When they finally rolled out of bed, the two were almost late.

Stif went to the bathroom. Beer was an efficient diuretic. Buz joined him after a decent interval. "Hey, maybe we ought to shower together to save time. I heard that Biggins gets real pissed if you don't show him proper respect and you come in late. Also, they say he even shouts at his classes if they're too backward."

"Okay." Stif turned on the water in the shower and stood back as it started to flood the bathroom floor, since there was no shower curtain. "I guess we can shower together like high school boys, but let's not queer off like high school boys."

"Who the hell would want to queer off with you?"

They were in the shower stall together. Space was limited. Each had his own bar of soap so they began to wash their bodies, rotating with a certain discretion around the stream of hot water coming from the shower head. Each seemed to notice the other's body for the first time. Stif's penis was longer, but thinner. Buz's member was thicker, but at least an inch shorter. Tie game.

Spontaneous erections, unrelated to sexual feelings, occur in young men, even in group showers. They both knew this and paid no particular attention to the fact. Still, you had to scrub thoroughly, especially in those areas that will naturally accumulate greater odor. They ejaculated at the same time.

"I knew you were a fag. This proves it!" Pissed off, Stif was drying himself with the same towel he had brought with him a week ago from Drakesville.

"You're the fag. I was thinking about my last girl friend. It's not my fault you have skinny shoulders that look a bit like Darlena's. That's what I was focusing on. Who knows what *you* were looking at."

"I was looking at my fucking feet."

Buz might have made a remark involving the f word and the use that feet could be put to by an outrageous pervert, but he refrained. Peabody State had been his idea and he had to lean over—but certainly not in the shower—to keep the two together on their path to higher education and good paying jobs. Alone, each would have to work harder and pay higher expenses.

"This is it. 203 Periwinkle. Let's get in there." Buz had navigated their way to the right port. Stif had cursed and sworn all the way from the University parking lot that Periwinkle was at the other end of the campus, near the women's wrestling gym.

The classroom was almost full. They found two empty desks near the front.

It was five minutes to ten. Stif and Buz both slumped in their hard backed and hard seated desk chairs. They relaxed, caught their breath. Then Buz noticed that none of the other desks in the front row was occupied. Several of the other students were staring at them, grinning, joking to each other. Maybe it was a tradition to leave the first row unoccupied, out of respect for Mr. Biggins, the great Professor. "Suppose we move to some seats further back. Looks like Biggins may not like students getting too close to the front of the classroom, probably in case the newsmen come to take pictures of him or something like that."

"There aren't any other seats." Stif raised his arm and showed the rest of the classroom with a sweep of his hand. All the other desks were occupied. Then he noticed the pictures on the classroom walls. There was a big one of Che, the bearded revolutionary hero. Then there was Mao as a young man, a clear eyed idealist. Near the teacher's desk was a smaller picture. In this one Stalin shook hands with a bearded man. Trotsky? Bukharin? Kamenev? Stif had no idea. He didn't know any of these guys, except Guevara, who was supposed to be all right, and Mao. But after all, this was a history class and you had to expect all sorts of weird stuff from the past.

Then it happened. Professor Hambrett Biggins stepped into the classroom. Hushed and frightened silence throughout the room. Also surprise, because Biggins was dressed in a style unrelated to the sartorial habits of any known local professor. He wore a large, loose brown robe, a djellaba. On his head was a short white turban. Under his chin was a full black beard, not a real one. He wore sandals on feet large enough to stick out beyond the traditional skirts of his robe. Strung across his back and attached in front by a leather strap was an antique-looking rifle. Probably it wasn't a real rifle. This was forbidden by laws and regulations on a dozen levels of authority. A small paper notice was stuck to the rifle, near the trigger: "not an actual weapon".

Hambrett rushed, as much as he was capable of rushing while carrying a hundred pounds of extra body weight, to the front of the classroom. He turned and looked at the students with an expression of unconquerable contempt.

A hand made sure his turban was in exact position on his head.

"I hate Hate!!!" He twirled about in front of the blackboard. For a man nearing the morbid phase of obesity, he somehow managed steps that were almost those of a ballet dancer. "I hate Hate!!!" He did a little dance, probably an authentic tribal step. "I will destroy and kill it Totally!!!!"

The audience of students sat breathless and motionless. They felt like they were in a movie. A few looked toward the door. When did the other guys with guns break in and start firing? But most of the students understood. This was the beginning of Diversity Week at Peabody State and you were encouraged to imitate the dress and customs of other cultures and nations, although generally without armament.

Biggins tottered to one end of the front row of seats. Now he was standing directly in front of Stif and Buz. They had carelessly attracted attention to themselves by wandering into the Demilitarized Zone. Biggins stuck a finger close to Stif's face.

"You! Why do you hate Hate?"

Stif did not answer. He believed that it must be Halloween and that an aggressive clown had invaded the classroom. Then, for an instant, he became delusional. No. They were in a movie theater. This was some sort of spy science fiction war flick.

Biggins had a fish on the line. He reeled it in. "You! Why do you hate Hate?"

Stif came back to reality. Now he remembered where he was, but he had no answer. He went dry. Buz whispered in his ear, "because it hurts people."

"Because it hurts people, sir."

"Because it hurts people," Hambrett repeated in a tone drenched with satire. "You have no idea how much it hurts people. You know nothing of the hurt of Hate! You are part of the hurt of Hate! If you do not hate Hate as I hate it, if you do not oppose the full pattern of Hate, then you are part of Hate!"

Then to Buz, "you are a likely looking young gentleman. What in your over-protected, over-privileged, white middle-class background could make you in the least aware of the suffering of those who are victims of Hate?"

Buz was far more tuned in to what was happening than poor under-educated Stif. "Nothing, sir. I hope to learn a great deal about it in this class."

There was laughter on Mount Olympus. The gods thundered in hilarity. Hambrett guffawed and giggled until his vocal cords dried into a weird cackle. "Learn more in this course! You will, my hopeful young gentleman, you will!"

Ham lifted his djellaba in front, revealing tumbling masses of swollen flesh. From a belt that held up the ordinary trousers that he was still wearing under his robe, he extracted a book.

The students were still staring in disbelief at what they had seen the moment the djellaba rose. It was like something out of *Ripley's Believe It or Not*. "The One Thousand Pound Man". Hambrett held the book in one hand and raised it for the class to see. A number of students thought he had brought along a copy of the Koran as a prop for his Diversity Week outfit. "This is our text." Ham waited silently for at least five minutes to allow the total significance of this remark to sink in. "I wrote it. We will be using it throughout the course. Those of you who have brought your texts, open to page one." Hambrett lay sideways on the teacher's desk, depositing most of his rear on the surface. He read from the book, using a voice infused with hurt and desperate rage. "Killed! Killed! Killed! All killed! They killed all, they massacred from sheer love of cruelty! Their greed, their vicious desire to possess and then to destroy the world! Their evil hatred of everything they could not understand! Children, women, animals, Native Places of Sacred Oneness! Tribes of millennial traditions! Gone, gone forever and replaced with the putrescent garbage of your capitalist civilization of exploitation and degradation!"

After the class Buz and Stif walked away confusedly onto the open ground outside Periwinkle. Other students were equally dazed. They had expected to be emotionally knocked about, to be upset and to be shaken out of their complacency by the world-respected Biggins. But they had not been prepared for anything like the actual, awful presence of he himself. They recovered slowly, like people at the periphery of a large explosion. A few recalled the facts mentally. Professor Hambrett Biggins was known for his unconventional methods. They were harsh, sometimes actually brutal, but they achieved results. One hundred percent of those who passed his course ended by sharing his beliefs. They too became activists. Well, they were supposed to become activists, but few actually went to much effort. All the same, they were little Bigginses, enlightened students who would go on to spread the truth, the doctrine of Biggism throughout the land. Some would even write songs about "the new word" and sing them while accompanying themselves on the guitar.

"Wow! That was one hard ass dude!" Stif, not being able to analyze with the help of intellectual terms, was always thrown back on the lowest colloquial level.

"Yeah. He comes on strong. I expected something like that, just from what I read in the student paper, but he really pulled out all the stops. Too bad we couldn't have sat in the back of the class."

"Or in the hallway." Before the class ended, Hambrett made the students sign their names on a sheet of paper that marked with little squares the position of all the desks in the classroom. These would be their assigned seats throughout the semester. Ham said that he refused to be bothered with learning to recognize by sight students who were still enmeshed in the bourgeois imperialist worldview, so he would remember them by the seating arrangement. The first two chapters of the text were assigned for the next class meeting. (Native North American Space after the Catastrophe, 1607 to the Present. Biggins, Hambrett. M-W-F 10:00 a.m. to 11:00 a.m.)

Student rumor had it that, besides being a star in the constellation of advanced thinkers in the realm of history, Biggins had a personal animus toward young male students, particularly young, good-looking male students. Then why, Buz wondered, pick on Stif? Contrary to an opinion shared by a few in Drakesville, mainly Stif's mother, and she was probably lying, Buz had never thought that his friend was handsome. Buz scratched his head. He decided to put it tactfully. "They say he has it in for young guys who could be competition with him for the coeds."

"I guess that could include just about everyone, even you." Not at all smart in books, Stif could come up with a swift return from time to time.

"Thanks a lot. He probably noticed how skinny you are, and considering what an enormous fat slob he is, he felt envious and resentful. After all, he's probably six times the weight of a normal guy and most girls don't really go for that. You're gonna have to put on weight if you wanna get through the course."

"Maybe I could put a pillow under my belt, you know, like I was playing Santa Claus for Christmas. Maybe that would cool him off." Stif was piling up the jokes, probably to cheer the two up after a difficult class experience.

"It's worth a try. Also, try scrunching up your face a bit, like you were in a Frankenstein movie." Buz gave an example of the sort of thing he meant. "Not that you're good looking anyway, but with Biggins it's all relative."

It was diversity week, but nothing was very different. They were walking along a paved campus path with tall classroom buildings rising at intervals on either side. Every two feet there was a Diversity Week poster. "Help Diversity Week. Be Different from Yourself!"

"Oh yeah, that explains why Professor Biggins came to class dressed like an old lady from Arabia. We're supposed to be different this week." Buz.

"An old lady with a beard like Abe Lincoln?"

"Sure. Why not? I think old Abe would have appreciated it. Everybody has to get into freedom."

Buz and Stif were unaware of it, and they would not have cared anyway, but the student body of Peabody State University was composed of the following elements.

57% female students
28% black students
25.3% non-Hispanic black students
6% Asian students
5.8% non-Hispanic Asian students
12% Hispanic students
2% Native American students
1.7% non-Hispanic Native American students
.53% Native Alaskan students
.5% Native Alaskan non-Hispanic
.12 Eskimo students
.1 Eskimo non-Hispanic students
.35 Native Hawaiian students
.34 Native Hawaiian non-Hispanic students
3.2 Pacific Islander students
3.1% Pacific Islander non-Hispanic students
4% other non-Hispanic students
5% Middle Eastern students
5% Middle Eastern non-Hispanic students
4% Eastern Balkans and Caucasus students
3.99% Eastern Balkans and Caucasus non-Hispanic students
3% unclassified
17% two or more groups
12% two or more groups non-Hispanic

Peabody obviously had a long way to go to catch up in the area of fair admissions. The school Administration had already received official notification from the Justice Department.

Stif and Buz were walking toward the cafeteria. They thought they were walking toward the cafeteria. Their next class was scheduled for 2:00. It was Beginning Psychology, An Introduction to College Psychology. That is, Buz thought Psych was their next class. Stif argued for the idea that it was College Mathematics. They had forgotten to bring a list of their classes with them, probably because Stif was too emotionally upset about what had happened between them in the shower that morning.

"I'm sure the next class is Arithmetic. I know I saw it on the schedule they gave us. I didn't bring the schedule because you got me so twisted around in the head when you started queering off in the shower that I couldn't of remembered my own name!" Stif.

"You queered off, buddy. If you'd a tried to jab me with that long pecker I would've cut it off!"

"Just try it next time." Stif gave Buz a shove at shoulder level.

Buz shoved back. "Back off, buddy. I'm not playing around!"

They started to face off. It was going to be serious. They had come to blows before. All guys do it, even the best of friends. It was sort of what friendship between guys was about. Then they saw it. The misery and humiliation of Hambrett Biggins' class and the resulting ill humor was forgotten, as were their divergent versions of the shower incident and the disagreement about their class schedule. On the wall of the campus auditorium, normally used for gym classes in winter and large student meetings, was a huge banner with a message in black paint. "Kill All Racist White Scum!"

"What the hell …?" Stif's jaw dropped open and hung in space.

Buz stood gawking for several minutes. It had to be some sort of graffiti put up by juvenile delinquents.

Stif was quivering on his long, thin legs. In this condition, he couldn't have sunk a basket from a stepladder. It wasn't that he recognized himself in the highly negative phrase painted on the side of the auditorium, but he knew that in the new thinking you could get convicted by association. "Oh man! I suppose Biggins had it put up, to teach somebody a lesson."

Then Buz remembered. He laughed. "No. It's nothing to worry about. It doesn't mean a thing. My Student Advisor told me about it, but I forgot. The Justice Department is complaining that Old Peabody is doing all this discrimination in its admissions department, so the Administration decided to put that sign up to impress the Federal investigators when they come to campus to take a look."

"Yeah? Well, maybe they didn't have to take it all that far." Stif continued weak in the legs. Not that he had been afraid, he told himself.

"It's because these Federal guys are sort of thick in the head. You have to make a point the hard way if you want them to get it at all."

The two were back in their apartment in the late afternoon. The class after History had been English IA. A clerk at the Administration office clued them in. They argued about it on the way home from campus on Garvey Boulevard. Stif drove. He was the only one who knew how to keep the engine running on the 1986 Fiat, a long term loan car from his mother. The engine tended to die at every stop, probably because the carburetor was busted.

Stif argued while struggling with the controls of the old car. The day's experiences at Peabody had made them both ill tempered. "I was sure the next class was College Math. I saw it on the schedule they gave us."

"How come it turned out to be English IA?"

"Probably they switched it on us just to see if we could figure it out." Stif pumped the gas pedal of the car to distract from the argument with engine noise.

Inside the apartment, Stif immediately turned on the TV and opened one of the beers they had bought at the neighborhood store. He sat on the living room floor, resting his back against the front of the rotten sofa with its dozens of sharp, protruding springs on top.

"Go ahead and take a break," Buz commented, not intending a criticism of any kind. "Remember we have a lot of homework to do. We have two chapters of Hambastard's book in History and then that English class assignment."

The English class was almost a relief after the dramatic tension of Hambrett Biggins' version of History. Ms. Di Vaggio, a slender woman in late youth, seemed to be a kind, gentle type of person. She spoke in a soft voice. It was clear that this was to show at the first class meeting that she was non-threatening, non-violent and that she loved everyone, as everyone should. Although she acted like Miss Nancy from the kids' TV show, students reported that she was a real brain and that she had every move in her classes planned out philosophically and psychologically. Having learned through experience, Buz and Stif settled into seats at the back of the classroom. Professor Di Vaggio used a teaching method totally opposite to the famous Hambrett

Biggins blunt attack called "Historical Realism", so the strategic seating plan was unnecessary. Vaggy's style was known as "the soft soap". It was mild. If Vaggy did not like something you said she expressed regret and hurt through a certain contortion in her facial features and body posture. That told you that you were on the wrong track. She told the class about her experiences as a volunteer teacher in Soladan. It sounded like "Soladan", but Di Vaggio's gently persuasive voice was hard to make out from the back of the class. Near the end of the hour long session, which was something like an old Broadway show, *The King and I* ("Getting to Know You") or *People* ("People, People Who Need People") Di Vaggio asked the students to tell what country they were from. If they were born locally, then they should tell what ancestry they claimed. It was a Diversity Week exercise.

Stif had it figured out. When his turn came, he announced "Albania." He thought that being from Albania would make points for him, like a basketball free throw. He wasn't sure where Albania was, or what it was, but it seemed like the kind of place that would turn Vaggy on.

Professor Di Vaggio smiled. She liked liars. They were creative. They could lead the others into new ways of thinking about language, themselves and our society.

Buz answered, "Newfoundland." He was on firm ground here, even if it was a lie. His aunt married a guy from Newfoundland, uncle Neville, and he knew that you could be from Newfoundland and talk English and not wear any special head gear. It was exotic, but not something that you were obviously lying about.

The classroom exercise had been an enriching

experience. Professor Di Vaggio gave her comprehending smile to the classroom clock. Time was nearly up. "For the next class meeting, work through Lesson One in *I Learn College Writing*, 'An Introduction to the Noun', and read the short story in *Our Anthology of All Diversities* entitled 'When I Wishes I Been Blessed'. Quiz on Wednesday."

Following Peabody campus tradition, the students had massively rushed the door in a crazed effort to find their way out. Stif accidently knocked into a guy who looked like he played football and got ricocheted off the door frame. His shoulder still hurt an hour later. That was partly why he was now drinking beer while watching TV and leaning against the rotten old sofa. To soothe the pain.

Buz appeared in the bedroom doorway several TV programs later. "Okay. I finished Lesson One in *College Writing*. It's all about the noun. 'A noun is a name word'. You better give it a try. We have two more first meetings tomorrow, Psycho and College Math, and they'll hand out homework, too. This noun junk isn't all that easy. You see, you and me are nouns, we're things. Actions are verbs, it's totally different."

Stif nodded. It didn't sound easy. "Yeah, just give me half an hour more. I'm watching a killer comedy show on TV." Stif popped another beer open.

An hour later Stif wandered into the bedroom. Buz was lying on his stomach on top of the mattress studying the Introduction to Ham Biggins' *White People*. Stif read over his shoulder. His lips moved silently and slowly. The Introduction said, "Professor Biggins' epoch making social culture study examines history from textualities that are not within the transparent mass of conventional studies but are situated in a focus of locations that permits direct historical encounter. It is rooted deep within the tradition of cultural studies and reiterates the definition of culture as a contested terrain, a site of struggle and transformation". Stif blinked, shook his head. "Huh?"

After several minutes during which he failed to distract Buz's intensive studying, Stif asked, "anyway, you feel like taking another shower?"

Meals were a problem. They couldn't eat every meal at a fast food restaurant or even the Peabody cafeteria. It was bad nutrition, like everyone said, and it was expensive. According to their Student Loan counselor, they should budget no more than eight dollars a day, each, for food. When they stopped for beer on the way back from Peabody, they forgot to buy food. It didn't seem to matter at the time. Two hours later they discovered that the larder was bare.

A solution was found. Buz would walk to the corner store, called *Abarrotes,* and bring back some kind of food. In the meantime, Stif could study the lesson about nouns in *I Learn College Writing.* It was assigned for tomorrow, Wednesday. It would be Stif's job to do the cooking when Buz brought home the groceries.

Stif lay on the mattress struggling with noun theory. "I am a noun," he kept repeating to himself. Nouns were name words and all things had names, so every *thing* had to be a noun. But weren't running and jumping and sinking baskets also things? So why were they verbs instead of nouns? He turned the pages to scout out new territory in the text. Adjectives, adverbs, prepositions, conjunctions, articles. It wasn't just nouns and verbs. Each group had a definition, examples, clever pictures and drawings, and exercises. Stif turned back to nouns and stared at the page. The text was simple, but also confusing in different ways. He hoped Peabody English IA would turn out to be a course like the ones at Drake. If you showed up in class and didn't cause too much trouble, you passed. "I am a name word." He was still repeating when Buz came back with supplies.

"Here you go, chef." Buz tossed a small plastic bag on the mattress beside Stif's long, thin body. "Go to work on this stuff. I'm really hungry after walking all that way to the market, not to mention putting up with tons of bullshit at Peabody."

Stif emptied the bag. There were two items. A can of beans and a plastic sack of tortillas. "Okay. I think I can make something out of this junk, but it won't be turkey with all the trimmings. Anyway, you bought it. I would've brought back some TV dinners. They're easier to cook."

"This stuff was pretty cheap. We have to save money somewhere. Our loans just barely cover staying alive."

Stif walked to the kitchen. He was wearing underwear only, because of the heat. Even with the air conditioner going full blast, autumn days in Peabody could be uncomfortable. Okay. He looked around the kitchen. Now that he wanted to know how things worked, he felt like he'd never been in a kitchen before. It was true that his mom did all the cooking at home. He had often watched her, telling her about his basketball games while she expertly concocted delicious meals. Now Stif was the cook. He found out right away that they had no pots and pans and no plates or knives or forks. Improvise, his mind told him. There was an electric stove. He turned on several of the burners. In a minute they were glowing red. Then he used his pocket knife to open the can of beans. Now it was simple. He put tortillas on top of the burners and poured beans onto them. Soon they were sizzling.

"Hey, Buz! Come and get it! I got dinner ready. It was fuckin' easy!"

Buz showed up. He sniffed the air. "What the hell's burning?"

Stif showed him the tortillas. He pulled a half charred tortilla off the burner. "Ouch! Fucker's hot as hell!" Beans spilled on the kitchen floor. Stif bit into what was left of the tortilla. "Help yourself."

Buz used the tips of two fingers to pull a burning tortilla off the heating element. He took a bite. "Yuck! What the hell did you do to this stuff? Piss on it?"

"It's just like you brought from the store, only heated up."

The two other tortillas were burning. Flames rose from the blackened food material. Smoke was filling the kitchen. "Damn it!" Stif turned off the heat on the stove burners. It was too late. The top of the appliance was aflame. Stif used his cupped hands to carry water from the kitchen sink faucet to the stove top. Buz followed his example. After several water deliveries the fire was extinguished. Then there was a flash of light and the room went dark.

"Short-circuit," Buz explained. "Water will do that to electrical connections."

Stif was sitting in the darkened living room. "I hope that short-out didn't wreck the television. My mom gave it to me," he called out in the direction of the bedroom. Even without power, the refrigerator would keep the beer cool for a long time. He sipped and looked at the stars through the living room window.

The next day they telephoned the apartment management company office from a campus phone to tell them the lights were out in the rented unit. The receptionist informed Buz that "utilities are the tenant's responsibility." The receptionist hung up.

"Now how the hell are we going to study at night?" Stif asked. "Not to mention watching TV, in case it still works."

"I guess we can use candles."

"And what about the air conditioner? How are we gonna sleep in this fuckin' tropical heat wave? Last night it was like an Amazon adventure after the lights went out."

"Do what you suggested before. Take lots of showers." Buz made facetious jokes because his roommate, the author of the problem, seemed to whining a lot and not looking for solutions.

Beginning Psychology, Psycho, was the first class of the day. This was the first meeting of the class, so the instructor, Professor Talifa Greenleigh, introduced herself.

She was not short, although, as Stif noted immediately, she would not have made a good basketball player. She was thick in certain areas, the chest region in front, the derriere in back. She liked to stand and to address sitting students with a four foot height advantage, like most of the instructors. Probably it gave them a personal feeling of superiority. The Student Rebellion years were over, but you could never know when the "eager young minds" might try to slip out of control.

BUZ AND STIF GO TO COLLEGE

Professor Greenleigh had earned her Ph.D. in psychology from the University of Northwestern Alabama. Her resume was not exactly Ivy League, but she had certain advantages. She was a local woman who had done well. Her father was a popular Methodist preacherman. She was entitled to patronage at Peabody. For her doctoral thesis, she had studied lobotomy surgery and its effect on intelligence. She smiled most of the time and her bland expression translated her acceptance of theories of environmental determinism. Student rumor had it that she had had one herself. A lobotomy. She told the class that they were part of an historic culture of violence. But lobotomy, which had been used abusively at a certain period of history, was also a therapy that should not be rejected without consideration. It had an enormous potential to pacify patients with chronic tendencies to violence. It could result in individuals blandly accepting environmental determinism.

Dr Greenleigh's family was not just another group of old world peasants, either. She claimed descent from both Jefferson Davis and Frederick Douglas. And she was an internationally respected social scientist and intellectual. The teacher's desk in Psycho class was covered with piles of books and papers toppled into a single mass. Over her years at Peabody she had consistently argued that the school's formal Psycho curriculum, while naturally focusing on issues of equality in society, did not include an adequate account of the latest advances in sociology and psychology. Fortunately, Doctor Greenleigh was able to complete the curriculum and to fill her own students in on the new ideas. Like Professor Bigg, she had written a textbook. The sticker price at the Peabody

Student Union Bookstore, $178.00. It was the required text for her sections of Beginning Psychology. *Discourses of Domination and Discourses of Liberation: The Unequal Individual in Our Society* was an attractive publication. It had lots of pictures and graphs and little essays set off from the main text in boxes to explain particular subjects. You got a twenty percent discount if you ordered directly from the publisher.

"Sex can be a form of communication as well as a form of pleasure," Professor Greenleigh said. Stif and other students took notes. It was clear she knew what she was talking about. She wrote the book. "This is a principal theme of our study." She held up a copy of the textbook, *Discourses of Domination and Discourses of Liberation: The Unequal Individual in Our Society.* She held it up long enough for the students, most of whom had not yet come across with $178.00, to take in the cover design. In the center was a photo of Dr. Greenleigh herself, but ten years younger and thirty pounds lighter. On one side of the front cover there was a picture of student demonstrators holding picket signs that read "Free Dr. Greenleigh!" In the corners of the cover were smaller daguerreotype photographs of Frederick Douglas and Jefferson Davis. Next to the photo of Davis was an old picture showing groups of cotton harvesters bending to scrape up the precious fibers.

"The subject of this class is the working of the human mind and emotions. We will attempt to understand the nature of human sexuality and its varied structures and multiple levels of expression. Certain types of sexual expression have historically been criminalized for reasons of class, race and gender domination within society. We will join the movement to understand this domination and to reject and to end it. With our text, *Discourses of Domination, Discourses of Liberation*, we will study and become involved in the understanding of a vast spectrum of libidinal interactions. Anal, oral, genital forms of libidinal expression, as well others which cannot be characterized by brief descriptions, will be our themes. I want you to put aside whatever preconceived moralistic feelings and ideas about sexuality that you may have brought with you. I want you all to be ready to re-think, even sometimes to re-experience sexual existence. Fear is associated with the historic social treatment of sexuality. Fear has been used to prevent the expression of sex and to confine it to forms and venues that are useful to a certain class/gender/racial structure of dominance."

Dr. Greenleigh shook her head. "We are here to put off those layers of dominance and distortion. We are here to feel emotionally free, to think free, to be free. Free." Her head nodded deeply in the direction of her breasts. At the same time, she held the text even higher with both hands. The middle finger of one hand was extended in what might have been a colloquial gesture of contempt toward the photo of Jeff Davis.

It may have been just his imagination, but Stif thought that Professor Greenleigh constantly positioned herself to expose her breasts and buttocks to male students. She bent over frequently, ostensibly to point out passages in copies of *Discourses* open on student desks, thereby calling attention to her anterior and posterior attributes at the same time. Except for Stif, always alert to prurient interest, the students appeared largely indifferent to these maneuvers. Perhaps, to the extent that they were aware of them, the students considered these oddly prevalent postures a type of anthropology custom, like the Eskimos who were supposed to offer their wives to guests. But no one could ignore the challenge to ordinary behavior and social custom that occurred at the end of the class hour when Greenleigh lay down on the floor of the classroom in front of the blackboard. She looked at the ceiling. She pronounced, "I am the substance of my mind." She raised her arms and opened the palms of her hands in the direction of the classroom ceiling. "Take copies of the class syllabus when you exit."

"Hey, that old Doc Greenby was okay." Back in the dump, late that afternoon, Stif was again relaxing with beer in front of the television. "I think she's got it over Ham a million ways. I mean, they're both sort of heavy, but Greenie's got it better arranged. Like both front and back. What I don't understand is how Jefferson Davis could be married to Frederick Douglas."

"It's Greenleigh. And that marriage thing is what transgender theory is supposed to explain," Buz joked.

"Oh. Okay. I see." Stiff sucked a lot of foam from the can opening.

"No, you idiot. Jefferson Davis was never married to Frederick Douglas. It's their descendants who got into that transsexual stuff."

A friendly student at Peabody had advised them about the electrical problem caused by last night's tortilla fire. She said it was probably only a melted fuse and that all they had to do was to buy some fuses and find the fuse box in their apartment. She was right. Now the electricity worked fine and Stif could see that the TV had suffered no damage. The stove was beyond recall. It had all of this charred gunk on top and the burners would not work even after the power was back on. Stif did not consider this a major problem. You really didn't have to cook tortillas, he had finally discovered. You could eat them raw, and the same with a lot of other stuff. The doors and the windows of the apartment were open to vent the nauseating odor of incinerated tortillas and beans.

"Greenleigh really got like real weird near the end of class," Stif admired. "I guess she was goin' through some kinda ritual, you know, like a primitive tribe."

Buz was in agreement. "Yeah. It was like she was pretty smart and she was using all these half-dollar words and the class was drinking it in, but suddenly she thought she was an old Egyptian pharaoh or something inside a pyramid."

"Maybe she had a psycho-tropic moment, like she was talking about. You know, when you feel you just have to follow what your own brain cells tell you, no matter how crazy the shit seems." Stif.

"Could be. Anyway, I think it was just another 'pedagogic method', like Biggins' Historical Realism. Some students in Native American class were talking about Big and his method. Someone said he even got a whole write-up in *NewsTimes* magazine for inventing the last word in 'ultimate and totally effective teaching'."

"I think we learned a lot from Biggins." Stif opened another beer. "Even if he had to force fuck our virgin brains."

"Right. So maybe Greenleigh has her own system. Either that or she really is crazy."

That night Buz did the food preparation. Even with

the stove not working, Stif could not be trusted. He might try heating food with matches or burning old newspapers from the heap in the parking lot. Buz had brought a sack of groceries back from *Abarrotes*. A package of sliced salami, a large hunk of cheese wrapped in plastic and a loaf of bread. Total price, eight ninety-seven. They were pressing on budgetary limits.

The next day Professor Hambrett Biggins' class was on the schedule again.

Every Monday, Wednesday and Friday ten a.m. to eleven a.m. Both dreaded it, after their first experience, but they were considerably reassured by the description of "Historical Realism" that appeared in The Daily Peabody, the campus newspaper. It said H.R. was a teaching method developed by the prize winning Professor. The basic idea was that you had to shock complacent middle class white youth out of their ignorance about the way our society really worked and was structured. Sometimes Ham indulged in theatrics, even verbal aggression, but it was because he cared about his students. It was the result that mattered. Knowing this, Buz and Stif were able to assemble the courage to take their assigned front row seats in the class originally called American History I.

Professor Biggins arrived five minutes late. Head down, dressed in a wrinkled brown suit, he passed silently to the front of the classroom and stood largely blocking the blackboard. He looked out into the classroom. You could tell that he was not in a happy mood. He blinked behind the thick lenses of his wire frame glasses. The lines in his face displayed deep, pessimistic concern. Clearly he was not satisfied with the learning capacity of the class to date.

"How many in this class would be at all concerned to know that their ancestors were mass murderers?" He stared at the class. There was no response. Everyone seemed to be sitting still and holding their breath to avoid drawing the attention of the instructor. "If your ancestors came here in the last four hundred years and if you form part of the majority group, you are guilty of half a dozen mass genocides! Think about it. Please just think about it." Ham fell back into brooding silence. After a long moment of thoughtful pause he stalked toward the student desks. There was a slight sound of shuffling books and limbs. A few students were thinking about making a run for it. Ham kept walking slowly, slowly. His hands were folded behind his back. He stopped in front of Stif and Buz, the only students in the front row of seats.

Stif went off incontinently. "Yes, sir! I mean no. Or, or, I guess I do mean yes." He was ready to confess. Anything to short-circuit a brutal cross-examination.

Professor Biggins laughed. He turned on his heels and walked away. "How many of you have brought your textbooks today?"

An almost unanimous rise of hands. Except for Buz and Stif. They had forgotten to bring their book. This was probably the result of the beans and tortilla fire. A psychological traumatism can affect memory. Professor Greenleigh had confirmed that in Psych.

Ham strolled back toward the two in the first row. "Not brought our books have we?"

Stif wanted to explain about the fire being responsible for it, but he was too frightened to speak.

The professor's hands went to cover his face. A gentle laugh, then the sound of weeping. "You did not remember your books because you did not want to remember your books! Our text describes the historical guilt of dozens of generations. From the Mayflower and Captain John Smith, the beginnings. The Murderflower! They were the forefathers of you, of …" He consulted a list of student names on a paper drawn from his pocket, searched for a few minutes, then gave it up. He turned again to Stif and buz. "Whoever you are, and they exterminated the original peoples! So they could steal native land! Are you proud of this?"

"No. No."

"What are you going to do about it?" Arms akimbo, Biggins waited for an answer.

"I don't know yet what we can do about it." Buz spoke up. He felt he had to take charge. He knew more about the scheme of things than Stif. "Try to do something to change things, I suppose."

"'Try to do something to change things, I suppose'. Try to do something I suppose! After four hundred years of massacre you suddenly decide to 'try to do something, I suppose'! This is moral amnesia. This is moral imbecility. This is moral *evasion!*" Ham turned toward the rest of the class. "Is this what you want to be? Moral amnesiacs and morons?" Biggins walked away. He tossed the paper printed with student names into a wastebasket. Suddenly he rushed back. "How much money do you have in your pockets?" He addressed Stif. Tall people always attract attention.

"I don't know." Stif's voice trembled. "Not much."

"Whatever you have and whatever you once had was obtained by theft! Stolen! Stolen from the forced labor of slaves! Forty-five percent of the capital now existent in this country is derived from the expropriation of surplus value produced by unpaid labor. That is the source of finance for your college education and whatever else of value you have got your hands on." The other students looked suspiciously at Buz and Stif. *Those two* ought to soak up the blame. They did it. Even Stif and Buz knew that Professor Hambrett was right.

"Forty-five percent from unpaid labor, forty percent from land swindles, twenty-five percent through the exploitation of immigrant labor." The categories overlapped, so the total was more than 100%, as usual. "Without that stolen capital you would have nothing! You would be wandering naked in the forests back in Lincolnshire or Niedersachsen! I think there is little to be proud of in that."

Professor Biggins did a slow recessional from the two occupied front desks. Then he turned back once more. "When you are driving in your expensive imported sports cars with your young girl friends, I hope you have the decency to tell them that they are riding on theft and murder!" Murmurs of approval rose from the class. Laughs of cruel satisfaction.

Biggins had basically repeated the content of the previous class meeting. You had to repeat if you wanted to impress important truths on students of mediocre mental capacity. Now the real lecture could begin. The classes of Professor Hambrett Biggins contained no student discussions, no question periods. They consisted entirely of lecture. A rigid lecture format was appropriate, Biggins had often explained to fellow faculty, because students came into his classes with minds that resembled the famous Cartesian *tabula rasa*. They were utterly blank because our society had a vested interest in covering up its crimes. The students were willing victims of amnesia on the subject of historical morality. Ergo, there was no point in student discussions or in question/answer sessions, except in a very controlled situation.

Sixty minutes later, chastened students emerged into daylight. Stif blinked. He felt empty. His personality had been voided and cancelled. After he looked around for a few minutes and saw that the same buildings were still there and that the sun was still shining, he thought that he might have hallucinated the performance of Hambrett Biggins. What he thought he had just seen could not exist within a college classroom. The ranting, the grisly, detailed descriptions of axe and rifle killings, starvations, whippings and repressions without limit did not usually occur in college classes, did they? But one look at the faces of the other students confirmed it. Ham had brought hell to earth at Peabody.

Buz and Stif said nothing to each other. Each was being dragged in the psychological undertow. Stif's ears were still ringing. It was like coming out of a movie theater after the scariest science fiction film you had ever seen, multiplied by ten.

Finally Buz found some words. He was the smarter one. His brain was able to regain its habitual less than brilliant functioning sooner. "I guess we're pretty awful."

Stif nodded. "Especially raping pregnant native women, then killing them, then stealing everything they had, then …"

Buz held up his hand in a plea to desist. "I was taking notes."

They walked on. Now they were on the flatter area of

the campus. Probably through the unconscious influence of instinct they were looking for the cafeteria. There they could get cooked food without burning anything down. English IA was in the afternoon, so there was time for a lengthy lunch period. Maybe Di Vaggio wouldn't make such a big thing about forgetting their school books.

Old Peabody cafeteria food was really not bad at all. There were sandwiches in plastic wrappers, but there were also large hunks of warm meat bathing in juices. There were soft drinks and plastic cartons of milk. Peabody was moving toward an all vegetarian menu, but change had to be gradual, given the resistance of ingrained custom. Prices were close to commercial market levels.

Six dollars and thirty-eight cents and five dollars and ninety-two cents. The bills for Stif and Buz, respectively. They took their trays to a plastic and metal table. Stif drank most of his carton of orange juice at a single draught. He was dehydrated from last night's beer workout, not to mention the breathless hour with Ham.

Buz cut a morsel from his slice of roast meat and carried it to his mouth with a fork. It was pork, or maybe mutton. It might even have been beef that had been frozen for long years in a packing house, then auctioned to the highest bidder. It tasted okay, especially loaded with additional salt and followed with a chew from the stale bread roll. He was eating quickly and he was glad that Stif was putting his own food away head down on the plate without making any unappetizing comments about their adjourned Native American history class when it happened. Buz was hit on the back of the neck with a paper wad. Ouch! He turned quickly, then smiled. It was Davis!

"Hey, bleach-out! You doin' your major in cafeteria?

Just what I expected from you, man." Davis was captain of the school basket team. A tall, good-looking young guy with a very athletic build and a sense of humor.

"Hi, Dave. Glad to see you. This is Stif, my roommate. He's a history major."

Davis waved, then turned back to the large, noisy crowd at his table.

"That's Davis," Buz explained to his companion, who was still watching agog. "He's the head of the Peabody basket squad. He's pretty damn good, almost sure to be recruited to the majors." Then Buz lowered his voice. "He gets all A's and never has to go to class. He's on a total scholarship. That's what he told me. He'll probably be on a major league team by the end of the year. We met at Abarrotes two nights ago when I went to buy something for dinner. He was doing the same. Except he went mainly for the tequila shelves."

Stif looked enviously at the sports prodigy. There was no doubt Davis had that impressive aura, that special something that Stif himself had lacked during his meteoric sports career. Then he focused again on his plate, now almost empty. He had to admit that everyone couldn't be the most impressive. But it hurt that Buz would point out *someone else* as a top amateur basketball player. Finally, he spoke almost in a whisper. He couldn't suppress envy. "Black people aren't always all that cool."

"There's a rumor he's on steroids and maybe some other drugs, like a lot of guys on the team. But what the hell, it's no worse than swilling down tons of tequila."

Di Vaggio was already sitting at the instructor's desk in the classroom when they came in. They headed directly to the back of the classroom. Punctuality had always been one of Di Vaggio's principal virtues. Her pre-school teacher had been the first to remark upon it. Di Vaggio busied herself at her desk, shuffling papers and manuals.

Vag wasn't bad looking, really, especially for her age. She had to be pushing forty. Stif came to this conclusion as he stared at her from his seated position. He could form a good idea of what she might look like naked. He thought she was too thin. "She's sort of good looking," he told Buz. "But I think she's gotta be, like dieting a lot."

Buz nodded. "Maybe it's because of reading all that English literature stuff like in our text. It doesn't do much good for your appetite."

Di Vaggio was sitting behind her desk, but she was slyly keeping the two first year students under observation. Class would not start for another ten minutes. She pretended to read a copy of the latest edition of the Modern Language quarterly. There was an article about fricatives and sound-induced violence. Di Vaggio approached the study of English with a sociological method. The canon of "famous authors" like Chaucer, Shakespeare, Milton, Swift, Fielding, Keats, Dickens and all the rest of that tired group had long been tossed into the trash bin. Their reputations were based on the tastes and the points of view of the ruling classes of prior centuries. Modern literature studies held that it was equally valid for a literature class to study comic books or the writings of the students themselves or anything else or nothing at all. What was important, Di Vaggio had concluded during her years of graduate training and intern teaching at the University of Southern Tennessee, was the way the study of literature affected the student and the community of which the student formed part. To be successful a class must have an emancipating effect on the student. It would have to change the way the student thought and felt about fiction and poetry and the way the student thought about their own society and about other persons in that society. What a class should do is to inculcate the idea that persons were the same. Not equal, since equality was an illusion, a fiction transmitted by Western civilization in order to prevent rebellion against imperial control systems, but exactly the same. They were like pebbles in a stream bed or primeval atoms. Personalities were often in appearance sharply different, but this was a result of misinterpretation (misinterpretation, not misunderstanding, since persons were actually signifiers and not autonomous emitters of text) and retrograde cultural conditioning. The goal, then, was to make the students feel that they were the same. Once they were convinced that they were the same they could begin to freely develop differences based on a common understanding of the interactive cellular context of signifiers. That was the theory. (English teachers no longer condemned the splitting of infinitives, as in "to freely develop". They encouraged it as the new correctness).

Professor Di Vaggio identified Stif right away as a potential emitter. It was clear from his facial expression and general gestalt that he was not burdened to any significant degree by formal education (book-attached cultural conditioning). His face was relaxed and bland in a way that argued against heavy script-focused learning. This meant that he had escaped a certain negative cultural conditioning. Even though he was twenty years younger than she, it would be without consequence, since pebbles and primeval atoms are unaffected by chronographic measurements. Stif had very much the same basic body form as Professor Di Vaggio herself. They were both tall and thin. Perhaps they had other things in common. His lack of strong influences from discredited cultural sources should make him receptive to cultural retraining. "Cultural retraining" was a technique of deflating the dominant text of its control over lines of discourse present in the student consciousness. It was the antidote to reactionary systems of belief. It freed the individual to a capacity for autonomous emission (in a mode posterior to controlled emission under the societal rules of irrational systems and hence not contradictory to primeval language-evolved emission). Method was the theory.

Di Vaggio stood up and walked toward the two eager learners. There were still only a handful of students in the classroom, so the opportunity for individual learning encounters persisted.

Ah no, Stif thought, she's skinny as a rail. Too fucking bad.

Di Vaggio rejected "saying hello", the custom of greeting other persons within a communal environment before starting a conversation. Greeting was part of the rigid network of rules imposed by a hierarchical culture restrictive of individual initiatives toward open relationships.

"What are your impressions in regard to the context of sexuality at Peabody? Have you had experiences at this date?"

Stif's mouth hung open. Buz looked at his shoes. Things had really changed at Peabody! In Drakesville nobody talked like that outside the school restrooms, especially not any teachers. And now a teacher was asking them about their sex lives. Stif had never even imagined sex could have something to do with a context. What the hell was a context, anyway? The last time they had faced Di Vaggio in a classroom, she had been "Miss Nancy". Now she was on some kind of science and pornography research trip! Buz understood the question, but could not think of a polite answer.

"It's been a learning experience." Buz, after a long embarrassed silence. This was a safe one. It was used a lot in brochures and introductions. It meant nothing.

"A learning experience," Di Vaggio repeated. "Yes. Experience must precede learning. In that sense, we are all learners."

Buz stared at a particularly interesting area of his left shoe. Stif was being *cognitively* left behind. Vaggy ascertained that his molars were entirely intact, an encouraging sign.

"You will discover that literature engages with life at a multitude of facets. That is what this class is about, at its most intimate level."

After minutes of confused silence, at last making a rough guess about the conversation, Stif announced, "sorry, ma'm, we forgot to bring our books." He immediately received an elbow in the ribs from Buz. "I mean, we're starting to get into experiences." Vaggy must be up to some kind of pedagogic crap, Stif finally twigged.

Di Vaggio was smiling and the expression on her face seemed pleasant, actually friendly and encouraging, so probably she wasn't going to go into a shrieking banshee attack like Ham. In fact, she was interacting with an almost beatific look of pleased comprehension at the totality of expressed texts.

Stif was smart enough not to do what Davis and a lot of other uninhibited sports heroes might have done in the same situation, given the allusive question from Vaggio. He did not make a gross suggestion about starting a sex act as soon as possible. Something like, "hey, so why don't we get it on, just us two? Why not?" They were at Peabody U, an established and respected institution of higher learning.

"Excellent! I think you're both making progress. You're off campus?" She was wondering if they lived in a college dormitory or in private accommodations. It could make a difference. She had developed a scent for such things over the years. She could smell it. Poor hygiene generally meant off campus.

"Yeah." Stif could answer this one with no difficulty. "We got a place off Garvey Boulevard." He gave her a friendly look. She was pretty around the face, anyway.

"Near the Abarrotes store?" She knew the neighborhood because Davis, the basketball star, lived there. She had visited Davis at home several times. Tutoring had taken place.

"Yeah. That's right." Stif grinned. "It's kind of a dump, but it's home sweet home."

Professor Di Vaggio could visualize the living pattern. Davis had shown great promise as an unconventional but genuine student. He had proven that he was endowed with exceptional personal attributes as far as the area of gender identification, but their relationship had foundered as a result of the chronic misdirection of verbal texts. He had a dozen other relationships going at the same time. She didn't think that Stif and Buz were like that. They were timid, and they weren't campus stars.

"I sorta do the cooking," Stif explained. It was flattering that a professor would take a personal interest in him, Stif, a first year student. Although she was totally too skinny. Maybe he could feed her up with tortillas. "I'm into, like, Mexican recipes."

"That is remarkable. I believe you said on the first day of class that your origins were in Albania. It is marvelous that such cross-cultural influences have developed. How long ago did you leave Albania?"

Stif was going to say "ten days", but he reconsidered. "It must have been at least three years. Yeah." He counted on his fingers.

"What part of Albania do you come from?"

Tough one. Stif thought about it for a full minute. He wasn't sure what, much less where, Albania was. "Um. Central part, more or less."

The classroom was starting to fill up. Dr. Di Vaggio had to attend to her responsibility for re-forming the thought processes of her other students. "See me after class. I make a point of learning the impressions of foreign students at Peabody." It wasn't that she was so hard up for romantic partners, but her experiences so far confirmed the findings of recent sociological studies that had concluded that males over thirty years of age or belonging to certain advantaged social classes were overwhelmingly structured psychologically by our society's rigid hierarchical values, and hence were poor long term romantic material for those already liberated. Stif was about nineteen and unformed intellectually. He was virgin territory in that sense. Enough to be molded to the general advantage.

Vag walked to the area of the classroom just in front of

the blackboard. It was an excellent position from which to survey and analyze the students and to try to guess their inner thoughts and feelings. On the whole, they were a simple lot.

Man, she had thin legs. They looked like pogo sticks, slinking along without touching each other. You could tell she had real drive in the mental zone, though. She was a top-rate brain. Stif.

"Now you did it!" Buz turned on his roommate. He was mad as hell. Stif, with his hundredth percentile stupidity quotient had just about ruined everything! "She knows you were lying like hell about that Albania shit you were dumb enough to tell in class. Once she gets the evidence she'll get you kicked out of U, and maybe me too. Anyway, even if it's just you, I'd have a hell of a time meeting expenses just with my own loan balance."

"You're crazy. She likes me. She thinks I'm like, the Sheikh of Araby or Rudolf Valentino. She's got this idea I'm an exotic sex god."

Still pissed, Buz had to laugh anyway. "You! Maybe in the men's shower."

"That was your idea, faggot. I was thinking of something totally different when it just happened."

The class had started. Di Vaggio began talking. She spoke in a louder, stronger voice than on the first day class session. Maybe she just got over a case of laryngitis. She addressed the whole group. She was earnest, intelligent, determined. "In the short story, *When I Wishes I Been Blessed*, why does Loofie decide not to kill the exploitative landlord even though her children are suffering from malnutrition and her elderly mother has to sleep on the back porch even in winter?" *Wishes* was the homework assignment. It was generally considered a great work of literature. The author had won the Nobel, after all, and the Pulitzer, plus a lot of little crap.

A bunch of the smarter students came up with answers at the same time. "Because she knew the white people would call in the Ku Klux Klan and that they'd lynch her and leave her children orphans if she did anything." "She knew Mr. Harding carried a gun and he murdered a lot of poor sharecroppers before." "She thought she could appeal to his better self, 'his real inside feelins' as she called them since, after all, two of her children were his because of serial landlord rape." "She didn't do it because she thought it was wrong to kill people unless they were murdering children and old people." "That's just what Harding was doing!"

Professor Di Vaggio considered these responses. "All interpretations are equally valid, so I cannot choose between any of the proposed answers. I have my own version. I think that in the story Loofie does not kill Mr. Harding because she does not want him to escape the guilt for his actions by a possible expiation. Loofie is an uneducated woman, but she is very intelligent. She has an intuitive grasp of ethical implications. If she had killed Harding, it would in a sense have been appropriate revenge and hence a cancellation of the debt of his guilt. By letting him live she is preserving his moral debt and not putting paid to it. That, in her mind, is a more complete revenge, since she regards what she calls 'a great big stain on his soul' as the worst fate that could befall a human being."

The class stared. They hadn't even thought of that one. Di Vaggio went on. The student faces seemed receptive. The instructor admitted to herself that she liked to lecture. She was rescuing blank minds from intellectual death by a huge unfurling of her own erudition. Now she was going to conclude her explication of the short story by the direct narrative approach that she preferred. There was not enough class time left for question and answer, the "Socratic method", which was usually unsatisfactory at P-body anyway, and not recommended by departmental teaching guidelines, given the mediocre student material. "Loofie is an intellectually highly capable woman. She is an analyzer. Near the end of the story we learn that she was able to obtain a scholarship through home study, then finish her Ph.D. at Harvard and finally become a member of the Harvard faculty. There she discovers that she is still facing the same bullying tactics that Harding used against his tenant farmers. That is another important point of the story. The same system oppresses us everywhere."

The hour was over. Buz moved to join the swiftly migrating students in a precipitous flight into welcome exile. "Hey, wait on. I got to talk to Professor Di Vaggio after class, remember?" Stif.

"I'll wait out in the hall. Just don't screw things up. And don't tell her about the fire. She'd probably put you down for psychological evaluation." Buz knew that leaving his buddy alone, even for a few minutes, was a risky business, but the Prof was insisting. For a not particularly ill-favored woman still on the hopeful side of forty, she had to be really hard up to make a try for pathetic Stif.

"Don't worry. I'm a lot smarter than that."

Buz sat on the floor and leaned against the corridor wall at a spot about twenty feet from the door to the

English IA classroom. He didn't want to have to say anything to Vag if she came out with Stif after the "interview". It would be embarrassing. He felt lucky that it was his roommate and not himself who was the target of her interest. He imagined what might result from Vag's "cultural interest" in the "Albanian". He couldn't have done it himself in the dark. Darsellia was just about the same age as his mom and even looked a bit like her. It would have felt like incest.

Ten minutes passed. Buz checked his wristwatch. Then twenty minutes. He was getting worried. Stif would have sense enough not to strangle anybody, wouldn't he? Finally he heard the sound of talking in the classroom. Stif came out. He was smiling from ear to ear.

"Okay, wow, fantastic, Darsellia. Meet you there. Hey! Thanks really a lot!"

Buz stood up and the two walked out of the building, Communication Hall, headquarters of the English Department. "So what Happened? You didn't fuck her right there in the classroom, did you? I thought you had more couth than that."

"No. Hell no. We were just talkin'. Her name's Darsellia. I think it's Portuguese. Anyway, she's crazy to learn more about Albanian culture. She thinks I'm some kind of a goatherd or a mountain bandit."

Buz looked straight ahead. He wasn't smiling. "She just wants you to fuck her. She never fell for any of that Albania bullshit. She's got too much brains for that. She's a professor, remember?"

"Okay. Anyway, she wants to come by our place 'in the evening' and interview me about the bullshit. I told her the best time would be this Saturday since you have to go back to Drakesville for your sister's birthday party. I'll loan you the Fiat. Just put in the clutch and keep your foot on the accelerator when you come to a stop." Stif thought about Darsellia. "I mean, I'm game right now to get it on with her, but I think it'd be cooler on Saturday. Then I wouldn't have to rush through it."

Buz's older sister was a lawyer. She specialized in archeology law, that is, law suits that result from excavations carried out by archeologists. She was single and she always came home for her birthday. Maybe she wasn't the new Marilyn Monroe in looks, not even compared to Buz. "Fine with me. I just have one request. Turn the mattress over after you finish the 'interview'. I don't want to sleep on any nauseating stains."

"Don't worry about that. Probably we won't use the mattress. I told her Albanians did it standing up. She wants the interview to be 'an authentic ethnic experience', so I'm going to meet her at Abarrotes and we'll walk to the dump. That way she'll get the thrill of seeing the neighborhood up real close."

"Wow. She really does have weird tastes."

The Fiat was one of the last cars in the Peabody student parking lot in the late afternoon. At the other end of the lot there was a large group standing around a huge late model van. Buz and Stif could see Davis with a lot of other guys and some women. They were playing music on a portable machine and dancing while they held tiny hand rolled cigarettes in their lips and beer cans in their hands. Buz waved. Dave didn't seem to notice.

At home, back at the dump, Stif took his usual position in front of the television. He leaned in a relaxed way against the rotted sofa and opened a beer. He sucked down a lot of foam, then a run of liquid beer. "Looks like we're doing pretty damn good so far at Old Piss. It won't be too long before we're both Ph. D's. Or at least me. I'm highly beloved by the faculty."

"You're not going to get anywhere if you don't do the class assignments. Vag gave us another section of *I Learn College Writing*, this time on verbs, plus another short story, the one called *Mi Nombre es Oprimida* for the next class meeting."

"Don't worry about that. I got an automatic A in English. My assignment is gonna be to keep Darsellia happy. It won't be easy. I mean, probably at least it won't make me all that happy. Did you see those tooth picks she calls legs?"

"Yeah. But I've heard that sometimes women like that have other talents. You know, like oral."

Stif thought about it. "Sure. That's probably it. Or maybe she could just give me a hand job. Hell, it would be worth it for an A."

"Doesn't sound all that interesting. You're pretty good at that yourself. I'll make you a deal. You go to my sister's birthday party and I'll take Darsellia off your hands, or maybe I oughta say her hands."

"Thanks man, that's real cool of you, but I gotta do it myself. I mean, the date. It'd be too hard to explain the switch to Darsellia. Besides, you're from Newfoundland, remember? Wherever the hell that is. That don't interest her half as much as Albania. She likes goat country."

Buz drove back from Drakesville late that Saturday evening. The party for his sister had been a big success. Their mother was always happy as hell to throw a party for her smart child, Janet, the archeology lawyer. Their father had almost ruined things by going on all the time about his air force days, his test flights and all that stuff, but he finally shut up. For some reason, Janet looked depressed. Maybe she was having professional problems. She talked about a law suit involving Zuni and Pueblo ruins. Something about "priority claims" and "historic trespassing". She didn't say anything about her last boyfriend, Ignacio. Buz suspected he was transgender. At her last party Ignacio had worn a dress. Janet explained it by citing the notion of "joking identity", a concept popular among anthropologists.

"I'm home!" It was close to midnight when Buz walked into "the dump", the apartment that he shared with Stif. The front door was open. That was probably to air the lingering odors of the bean fire and maybe the bathroom as well. "I almost got killed driving that death trap you got from your mom! It broke down ten times on the highway from Drakesville." Then he saw it. Stif was stretched out in front of the darkened TV. A forest of empty beer cans surrounded him. He seemed asleep, but his eyes were open.

"I couldn't do it, man! I was like a nimpotent. Man, she got pissed out on me. I got kicked about six times before she left here. Stif pulled his jeans down to show a large bruise covering most of one buttock and part of the other. Shit, I hope I don't get kicked the fuck out of English."

It was a shock to hear that Stif's faculty date went off so bad, even though, sure, what else? Of course he had botched it. Stif botched almost everything. His last success had been that end of season high school basketball game when he sank three in a row. The crowd had gone wild. Stif, from that point on, had considered himself an achieved success in life, so he could afford to relax. But what had really happened between Stif and Di Vaggio? It would be almost impossible to find out. His roommate was inclined to misinterpret the most obvious events. "What happened? Did you try to do it Albanian style, standing up."

"I don't know. She asked me all these questions, then she explained the answers before I knew what she was talking about. I told her in Albania everybody just gets it on when they want to and it was no big deal. She said it was just like that in Samoa when this lady scientist did a study on it about a hundred years ago. So I was making points. She knocked down a couple of beers and she seemed cool, so I made a move. I got her skirt up and I took my pants off, but nothing happened. I never had no trouble before and I been on some real bad blind dates. I tried another beer. Then another. *Nada*. No go. I don't know why, but I got the idea that maybe she goes for the rear-end method. I heard like a lot of older women go for that. So I gave it a try. Then she starts screaming at me and giving me some good pointers in the ass with her foot. And man, she's got like really skinny legs, but you should see her feet! Size fourteen, I swear it."

Buz had met his sports hero/problem personality friend in grade school. Later, they were best buddies at Drakesville High. Stif was not without talent. Basketball, obviously, for one. And he had a relaxed way of dealing with things and people. His main flaw was that he was at least eighty percent lacking in normal intellectual ability, in mental capacity. Oddly, this was something that made their friendship more important to Buz. Stif was someone who needed protection and advice about anything more complicated than opening a can of beer. "He moves us to pity and fear". Aristotle.

"Then she shot out the door. She said she was going to Davis's place just around the corner and that he'd fix me fine. Davis never showed up, though. Maybe he wasn't home when Darsellia got there."

"Okay, so it looks like nothing happened at all, except a bit of bare ass tumbling around. Don't worry about it. I think Di Vaggio won't make any trouble. She'd hardly want to explain to the Dean what she was doing at a student's apartment late on Saturday night. Just keep going to English class, but keep your head down, maybe wear a cap, and sit way in the back of the classroom." Stif stumbled into problems because of his stupidity, but it was that same characteristic that saved him from the worst situations. He wasn't smart enough to get into really big problems.

"Yeah. But maybe I should wear a football helmet on my ass. Anyway, since I'm not going to get an automatic A in English, I guess I just gotta hit the books." He picked up the manual called *I Learn College Writing*. He turned to the assigned chapter. "Verbs ... Fuck is a verb. I fuck, you fuck, she, he, it fucks, we fuck, they fuck. Only sometimes ... nobody fucks!"

"You're starting to get the hang of it. Keep going. I'll try to figure out that short story, the one about *Oprimida*. We have to write an essay about why we think it's so significant and relevant for our society. I looked at the story and the idea seems to be that this girl Oprimida, sort of an illegal alien, works at a fast food restaurant and she has to ask every customer, 'want fries with that?' Only she can't pronounce 'fries' and it come out 'flies'. So she gets fired and she has to work the streets selling her ass to a lot of really insensitive slobs."

Soon it was Monday and that meant Professor Hambrett Biggins and his Historical Realism. Every Monday, Wednesday and Friday from 10:00 a.m. to 11:00 a.m. Buz and Stif dreaded it more than ever. What would Ham be up to this time? Even though the two accepted most of the big professor's history idea, there were a few details of the project they weren't enthusiastic about. Ham told the class that he would "drag them all screaming if necessary into accepting their total sinful guilt before all of history and humanity". It sounded like he might get up to something physical. Even if Ham limited his tactics to the psychological, to playing around with their brains, it could be a hairy experience, maybe worse than getting beat up or sat on. Class opinion was shifting toward total radical hamism. Already nearly half the class had taken to holding the text, *How White People Destroyed Eden and Everything in It with their Big Evil White Feet,* high above their heads when Ham entered the classroom, like the Red Guards used to do with Mao's little red book. This showed that they were with him one thousand percent.

The classroom door was closed and locked. A few students were standing outside in the hallway reading a notice taped to the door. A little guy with lots of long dark hair was in front of the others. He read the notice aloud. "The Monday meeting of Section 4 of Native American Space after the Catastrophe, 1607 to the Present, has been canceled due to temporary illness. Wednesday's class meeting will be held as scheduled."

"Ya hoo!" Stif did a little jig and hopped about as well as he could with his bruised and sore gluteus muscles. It was the best thing that had happened since he sank those three baskets for Drakesville.

The small student with long dark hair was not edified by this performance. He raised his textbook above his head in a gesture of solidarity with Ham. "Professor Biggins will have your ass on a platter before he's done with you, don't worry!"

"Um. I was just glad, man, because we can study up more for next Wednesday since we don't have to sit it out this time."

The small student made a curious sign, sticking his thumb in the middle of the four other fingers of his curled hand. He marched off. Stif thought that this was just some kind of advanced cultural stuff.

"Man, it's a bum trip about poor old Professor Ham. I mean, we've been learning a hell of a lot of important stuff in his class. What do we do now?" Stif.

Buz had a suggestion. "Well, figure it out. It's only ten o'clock. If we want to get good grades with old man Ham, we ought to go to the Library and do some more studying in his book. When he finds out we agree with him on everything, he'll have to give us good grades even though he hates our guts like shit."

They were sitting in front of a table in plastic, form fitting chairs located in the interior of the huge, impressive, glass and steel, multiform and unsymmetrical Library building designed by a world famous genius. The shared textbook lay open on the plastic table. Two heads pored over it.

"The Destroyers landed in what they considered to be the year 1607. The Native Peoples themselves did not define time by arbitrary numbers, since to them all of time was one and served to live in complete physical and psychic unity with the natural forces of the earth. Within months the invader began a thorough process of wrecking a civilization more advanced than their own, one that they were incapable of understanding. Understanding was not their mission, however. To steal and to kill in order to satisfy an appetite for greed was their only plan." Buz was reading out loud. Stif could have done it, but when he read aloud each word came out slowly and separately. It sounded like a first grade reading lesson.

A young woman stopped in front of their table in the Library Study Space. Stif caught a glimpse of her and turned away from *How*. She was terrific. She was just his type: tall, large breasts, ample hips, cute features and great hair. The *antinomy* of Darsellia Di Vaggio. "You two are from Biggins' section 4 class, aren't you?"

"Yeah. Usually. Only he couldn't make it today because he got sick or something." Stif. He put on his best smile, the irresistible one that had seduced Darsellia.

"I'm in the class too so I thought I'd tell you about Biggins, since I know he's been hard on both of you." She sounded very intelligent, like a straight A student. That was Stif's impression. "Biggins didn't come to class because he got beat up by his wife, Artesta Brackle. She teaches here too. He had bruises and cuts on his face so he didn't want to show up in class. He was afraid we'd guess what happened and it would be very embarrassing for him. A friend of Professor Brackle's told me the truth. Brackle's going to post a full account of it on the web. So

Ham will probably show up on Wednesday, even if he has to wear some makeup over the blue spots. Usually he puts on a little makeup anyway."

"Biggins uses makeup? Why?" Buz thought that naturally Ham would reject any idea of improving his own physical appearance. Just for step one, it'd be like a manned space launch to Mars.

"It's not that he thinks it makes him more attractive. His idea is that since some women wear makeup, at least some men ought to wear it, too. That helps equalize the sexes on the subject."

"Thanks a lot for telling us. I feel sorry for poor old Big," Stif was still smiling seductively. "I mean, maybe he did something to deserve it from Brackle, but even so, if he got beat up, we ought to do some sympathy for him." Stif wanted to promote a humanitarian image of himself. It added an ethical side to his obvious physical attractiveness. Anyway, it was the general custom at Peabody; it was correct behavior. "Why don't you join us? We can study together, just the two, or three of us. We're starting to take in the textbook junk on Big's course and it's real fascinating, all about how all the crap started out." Stif moved over to make room for another chair. He pushed strongly against Buz on his other side. "Then later maybe we could take a lunch break like together, just the two, or three, of us."

"Thank you, I have a class." She walked away.

It was the same thing every time. She had been friendly, she even felt sorry for them because of the way 'Brett had treated them, then, as soon as Stif turned on the seductive charm, she just shot out to no man's land. Stif was left once again wondering why the good looking women— not the intellectual geniuses like Vaggio—always left him wondering. Maybe he took too many showers. There could be a chemical smell from the soap and shampoo. "Do I smell?" he asked Buz.

"Hell yes. But that wasn't what scared her away. You should have let me handle it. Naturally she walked off when you were sitting there smiling like an imbecile and inviting her to study some dumb textbook. That's not the way to meet women."

"It worked with Darsellia."

"Sure. Darsellia's so hard up she would have gone for an eighty year old wino with gonorrhea if she thought she could make it with him."

Stif's eternal confidence drooped. Now he wasn't smiling. What if there really was something wrong with him? "How the hell would you do it?"

Buz sat upright. He focused and looked serious, like he was a professor talking to his class. "First, you have to show a definite interest. Ask her questions about herself. Like her major, or where she's from. Say you really admire whatever she does or is. Then, ask her to lunch, not in a dump like the Peabody cafeteria, but in a classy restaurant. Above all, you can't just sit there beaming like a big self-satisfied joke."

Stif thought about this. "You're crazy. Well, maybe I didn't handle it too well. Next time, I'll know better." In fact, he knew that Buz was really just envious about his handsome appearance. Then, "if she got mellowed out with a few beers, she'd probably feel different."

Buz ignored this. It was too stupid to merit a reply. "I'd like to know why Brackle beat the shit out of old man Biggins. He must have pulled something pretty lousy on her."

"Probably she just got tired of looking at his big, fat, ugly, obnoxious face. Anyway, isn't Brackle the one who teaches that weird class, Castration Discourse?"

"Yeah. Although I've heard that it's not at all what a lot of people think. It's all philosophical and social, that sort of thing. She doesn't actually take a knife and, you know …" Buz pretended to hold an object with one hand and to cut it with an imaginary blade held in the other.

Stif laughed. "Maybe not. Or maybe she already experimented on Big. It could be because of all that fat, but he kinda looks like a girl around the face. At the first class meeting I thought he was pretending to be someone called Fatima."

This is what really happened. Two nights before the brief meeting of Buz and Stif and a coed in the Peabody Library Complex (now called the Learning Interchange Center, LIC), Professor Hambrett Biggins had a disagreement with his life partner, Professor Artesta Brackle. It was late and the lights had been off for nine minutes in their bedroom. Ham got up from their shared bed and left the room. "Gotta check on something," he announced.

Everyone has *sexual needs*. It is the same for men, women and others. When those *sexual needs* are not adequately satisfied, the person concerned can become unhappy, depressed, and sometimes violent. This was the unhappy fate of Artesta Brackle. She was the victim of unsatisfied *sexual needs*. (NDLR: sexual needs are a social entitlement. They are not synonymous with Freud's *libido*.)

When Ham had not returned to their bedroom after

twenty-five minutes, Artesta began to feel uneasy. They had not had sexual relations for five and a half months and Artesta thought that it was about time to give it another try. She knew Hambrett's limitations, his disabilities, but he ought to be capable of something. She had already placed a flashlight on the small table on Ham's side of the bed, in case he needed help locating the crucial areas. She got out of bed. She always slept naked, unlike Ham, who wore a sort of cotton tarpaulin. I will include only the most cursory description of her body. Anything else would be a violation of her personal privacy and her right to be protected against ridicule, contempt and disesteem. She was skinny in the area from her feet to her crotch, then she expanded enormously over the lower abdominal region, only to shrink again in the chest zone. Her head. Her head was … it was equipped with the usual raised areas and orifices, but very little more than that, except that her hair was long and dyed blond. From the back, or even from the side, she appeared more enticing.

Artesta was afraid that Hambrett, somehow sensing that the usual five month terminus for their relations had come round at last, might have returned to the refuge of television, a return that he would later excuse by claiming an attack of insomnia. Although they were intellectuals who wrote books as well as articles for professional quarterlies and who engaged in academic discussions with many of their former Blizzardmen associates now teaching at top universities, as well as with other Peabody faculty members, Artesta and Ham watched a lot of television. They did not read many books. At a certain point in their mental development, after reading thousands of the things, both had realized that books in their respective fields were really a lot of repetitious twaddle. The writers played with the same concepts, repeating them, rephrasing them, turning them upside down, inside out, but without adding anything of significance. Anyway, no texts of any real significance were even possible. Poststructuralist and postmodernist philosophers had established this conclusion in many long abstruse pronouncements.

The living room vision screen was black. Artesta immediately noted the light in the kitchen. She advanced, knowing what was going to happen and not regretting it, actually feeling happy about a physical contact that would, for her at least, be almost orgasmic. As she suspected, feared, and in a certain way hoped, Ham was standing in front of the open refrigerator. He was systematically devouring its contents. Weighing in at three hundred pounds, he was as big as the refrigerator, although much shorter. This was the last food that he would ingest for the next thirty-six hours, with the exception of some miserable broth and dry toast.

It was an uneven battle. Artesta was highly motivated. Hambrett was ignorant of the causes as well as the approach of the attack. He engaged in weak defensive maneuvers, such as covering his face or his genitals with small hands attached to disproportionately short arms. Ham was a very big and very slow moving target. Before he could utter the words "what the hell!" he had already received powerful and painful blows to the stomach, face, buttocks and groin. Arta could move fast, using her bony and sinewy arms and legs as flying weapons.

Hambrett Biggins, whatever his faults and shortcomings as a human being, was a victim. He deserves our pity and sympathy. And, frankly, whatever the theoretical justification—Artesta would have been capable of writing a thick volume of philosophical desiderata on the subject—no one should be subjected to the sort of physical abuse suffered by Professor Biggins. Afterwards, he crawled and was dragged back to the bedroom and rolled onto the mattress. He spent the night almost motionless.

In the morning Ham would not speak to her, except for the phrase "fuck you", repeated a dozen times. Artesta could not avoid thinking with a bitter smile that the incident had been caused exactly by the lack of that.

"So we gotta do Vag and English IA?" Stif was resigned to the experience, but unhappy about it in view of his failed encounter with the Professor over the weekend. What if she was still way off pissed? It could be heavy. They finished lunch in the cafeteria, where Stif had ordered an enchilada and a big soda drink, plus some chips and fries. He really was getting into Mexican food. Buz had a salad with some sort of processed sandwich stuffing shredded on top, all of it covered with a pink dressing that had a lot of little dark pieces of something mixed in. This was obviously healthier fare and better for the environment.

"Don't worry. Darsellia's not going to give you another kick in the ass right there in the classroom. It's against human rights." Buz.

"I don't know. What if she thinks it's a pedagogic technique, like that Histerical Realism business?" Stif.

"I really doubt it. Anyway, if she tries anything, I'll be on your side, I'll cool her down. Just sit next to me on the side away from the aisle." Buz was feeling more protective about poor Stif every day. Probably because Stif was showing himself to be increasingly inept and vulnerable.

The class was almost full when they arrived. This was reassuring, since it provided more witnesses in case Darsellia suddenly found herself a victim of uncontrollable yearnings for revenge. They slipped unobtrusively to the back row.

Professor Di Vaggio was seated at her desk in the front of the classroom. She looked peaceable enough. In fact, she had noticed Stif's slinking entry. She would ignore him. He was beneath contempt.

Di Vaggio started her class talk *in media res*. "I want everyone to think of three verbs. I want everyone to think of a transitive verb, an intransitive verb and a separable phrasal verb."

Consternation. Few in the class had read the assignment in *I Learn College Writing*. Grammar was dull stuff. Nobody but the dreariest grinds would bother with it.

Professor Vag walked down the aisle separating groups of desks. She stopped in front of a large but quite attractive young woman with a shaved head and neck tattoos. "Give me a transitive verb."

"To eat." The young woman was still chewing.

"Correct. 'To eat' is a transitive verb because it requires a direct object, as in the sentence, 'I eat a lot'. Now give me an intransitive verb."

The young woman—her name was Kalli, although few in the class were aware of it, since they couldn't see the large tattoo on her buttocks—was stuck. Kalli didn't remember that part of the text, about the intransitive verbs, not exactly, probably because she hadn't read it. "To regurgitate." She didn't like Professor Di Vaggio. You can't trust skinny people. They were always trying to beat on you.

The buzzer went off. "Wrong. 'To regurgitate' is a transitive verb. It requires a direct object. You have to regurgitate something. You can't just regurgitate."

Wanna bet, Kalli thought.

Di Vag moved on. Teaching at the university level was a thankless sacrifice, but it was one to which she was committed, so she had to carry on, fulfilling her duty to the ignorant through endless rounds of difficulties. One of a dozen students might show promise. Unless education was transformed in the way Professor Di Vaggio and others had written about in *Line of March*, people would never change and society would never change. It would never become an evolving social network of relationships that maximized ongoing innovation especially in gender and sex interactions. Teaching was the real revolution.

Vag stopped two rows from where Buz sat. Next to him was someone who wore a visor cap pulled down over his face. She knew that someone was Stif. She was determined to ignore him. It was a question of self-respect. "What is a phrasal verb?" she asked a boy who looked like an athlete, although not a particularly intelligent one. His expression continued blank.

"A phrasal verb," Vag repeated.

"It's a verb that's going through a particular phrase."

Professor Di Vaggio laughed. She liked to show that she really was good humored and tolerant. This section was a slow group, even for Eng IA at Peabody. "We're obviously not in a grammar mood today. For the next class meeting read the section on verbs again as well as the section on adjectives. This is a general assignment. There will be a quiz at the start of the next class period. How many of you have read the assigned short story, *Mi Nombre es Oprimida*? You can be honest. I'm not an educational ogre. I understand that sometimes students might not feel like reading a particular assignment."

Stif thought nothing. She might be able to read thoughts.

A dozen hands went up. This was a showing sufficient to justify a class discussion. "Good enough for now. In the story, why does the protagonist adopt this descriptive term as a name? *Oprimida* means 'oppressed woman' in Spanish, in case you didn't know."

A hand. "Because they fired her when they found out she couldn't speak the oppressor's language properly."

"That's accurate as far as it goes, but it still does not explain why she would drop her original name in order to assume a sobriquet that implies low status."

Another student tried. "Because after she leaves the fast food place she can only find a job as a sex worker and she thinks that type of job really sucks because she's always getting prostituted by a bunch of losers." The class broke into laughter.

Di Vaggio was still smiling with the minute of hilarity. "That's part of it, too, although I think it might have been expressed differently." The Professor was silent for a long moment while she appeared to reach contemplative levels of consciousness. There were no other takers on the question. No one wanted to be the next to be shot down. "Oprimida accepts a name for herself that identifies her as a marginalized person because she is alienated from a dominant society that does not recognize her as a human being but forces her to satisfy the needs of the privileged for sensual gratification. By assuming an imposed identity, she is pointing to her own victimization."

At least one student was confused by this explanation. "At the end of the story she kills a drug dealer and takes his money and his supply of drugs. They're in this alley and she kneels down and kisses this ring on his finger before she walks away from the body. How does that make her a victim?"

Vag looked at the class. "Would anyone like to answer that question?" It was a hard one. No hands went up. Professor Di had to take it again. "My interpretation is that this event at the end of the short story only reinforces our perception of her as an oppressed person. She began to use drugs as an anodyne to the suffering that society imposed upon her, using her low social status to reduce her to an even more humiliating and dehumanized condition. Remember, she has had sexual relations with the dealer on a more or less voluntary basis. By killing him and taking the drugs she is adopting the methods that society has taught her. In the wider society violence and theft to obtain temporary personal benefit are an accepted form of behavior, but they are legal only for the rich and powerful. When she kisses the ring of the murdered drug dealer she is not triumphing over a dead adversary, she is recalling a relationship that had human aspects, including affection and attraction on both sides. She is refusing her own dehumanization."

Stif whispered to Buz. "Wow. I wisht I'd read that story. Sounds like a killer."

The hour was coming to an end. Professor Di

Vaggio gave a little salute that was characteristic of her pedagogic persona. She raised a hand to eye level and then swept it forward toward the students. "Those of you who have completed today's assignment, please turn in your responses to the essay question about *Oprimida* before leaving the classroom." Di Vaggio went back to the teacher's desk. She had a lot of paper to shuffle through.

Stif held the palm of his hand in front of his mouth. "Shit! I forgot to write my homework essay question. You got yours?"

"Yeah." Buz waved the single sheet of paper with some complacency. "I told you it was time to get serious if you want to get your degree at all."

"I'll remember next time. Couldn't you, like, write both our names on the paper and say we discussed it together and hacked out the same answer? I can't talk to Vaggy after that Sunday night thing."

"I don't think she'd go for it. She hates your guts now and she's not all that stupid."

"Just give it a try, man. I'll do the same for you some time. If I flunk out of English IA, they'll cut off my loan."

"All right. Wait outside the class. I'll talk to her when everyone else is gone."

Now Stif sat on the hard floor of the hallway. It was uncomfortable. Skinny people are at a disadvantage when it comes to resting their asses on hard places. Finally Buz came out of the den of education. At one point Stif thought he heard dull sounds like a desk moving or heavy sacks impacting on a surface. He followed Buz to the main exit of Communication Hall.

"Don't worry, man. I got it all fixed for you. We both

get credit for the essay answer. She's not really pissed at you anymore about what happened Saturday night."

"Thanks." Stif was dazzled by the good news. "How the hell did you manage that?"

"I told her you're a fag."

"What! You fuckin' prick! You're the fag!" He grabbed Buz by the shoulder. "Get the hell back in there and tell her it's a lie or I'll bugger your ass!"

"Relax." Buz shook his buddy's hands off. "That's not all I did for you. I had to fuck her, too."

"Oh." Stif didn't know what to say. That made a difference.

"It wasn't all that bad. I just closed my eyes and imagined I was on a Pacific island with a bunch of young wahines."

Fall was finally coming after the long, hot, pecan summer at Peabody. The nights were cool now and the only heating in "the dump" came from a gas fueled heater attached to the living room wall. In the bedroom you had to sleep close to keep warm. This led to some inconvenience. Buz's thicker frame was constantly rolling against and partly on top of Stif's thinner and longer body.

It was an anxiogenic night. The next day was Wednesday and that meant another session (Monday Wednesday Friday 10:00 a.m. to 11:00 a.m.) with the idiosyncratic but brilliant and effective Professor Hambrett Biggins (See Timesnews article, March 2030). Last Monday's meeting had been cancelled due to Ham's "illness", but the Wednesday meet was full on, as far as anyone knew. His classes were always an ordeal, but some days were worse than others. In a previous meeting he had required the entire class to chant "I am an imperialist fascist murderer" at top volume for fifteen minutes. Even fellow faculty in adjoining classrooms had complained. In another session, he had declared "Proto-Cuba Day" in which the students dreamed aloud about how it would feel to live in a society that was not run purely for the profit of some of its members. Then, in yet another attempt to imprint improved social attitudes on the brains of his students, Ham had ordered all of the "white" students to sit in the back of the classroom so that they could obtain a physical understanding of the effects of segregation. This exercise was not unpleasant in all of its aspects. At least the back seats were sheltered from the typical Hambrettian hectoring.

Buz and Stif arrived at the History building classroom ten minutes late. Ham would certainly have something unpleasant to say as they took their non-segregated seats at the front. It was Stif's fault. He was taking an unusually long time to shower every morning and he insisted that Buz stay in the shower stall with him. He felt more secure, he said, by imagining he was back in high school locker room days at Drakesville.

As they got close to what was formerly called the AH I classroom, they could see that there was a crowd in front of the door, like at the last meeting. Maybe Ham was still out sick. Old Artesta probably gave it to him worse than anyone thought. A faculty type person was talking to the students. Her nametag/badge said that she was a Psychological Counselor, a professional whose job was to help students overcome debilitating emotional trauma. The roommates moved into the crowd, getting closer to the talking faculty type. The incredible news was that Hambrett Biggins was dead!

He was dead, the victim of an assault of criminal origin that had taken place last night in the campus parking lot. The P.C. (Psychological Counselor) was encouraging students to make appointments for individual therapy sessions and to visit the campus clinic to receive anti-anxiety medications.

At first Stif and Buz experienced this news as a relief. When the general attitude of sorrow and loss became clear, they changed.

"Wow. That's really too fuckin' bad! I wonder who the hell did it." Stif.

"Yeah. I know he didn't like us all that much, but, anyway, you feel all awful about it inside." Buz.

"It's a bummer. Even if he could get up kind of a mean streak. He had a lot of real good things going for him too. Like he knew tons of stuff about history."

The sense of shock and mood of deep mourning spread across campus. Students left flowers outside the History Department offices. That night there was a candlelight vigil. Hundreds of students gathered in remembrance and regret. A group from the Music Department played parts of Beethoven's Ninth symphony, including the Ode to Joy. Stif and Buz now genuinely participated in the mass feelings. Stif's eyes were full of tears as he deposited on the History building steps a tiny bouquet that he had pulled out of a campus flowerbed. His voice broke with emotion as he uttered solemn words of requiem. "Here's to you, old pal." Buz used his shirtsleeve as a handkerchief when the chorus intoned "*O Freunden ...*"

Two days later there was a noon hour memorial service for the defunct Professor Biggins, non-religious and informal. Guitars were strummed. Protests songs were taken up by amateur voices. There was improvised memorial expressive dancing. Artesta Brackle did not attend. Even so, her efforts relating to remembrance were perhaps more effective, certainly more time consuming. Professor Brackle circulated widely via internet, by a letter to the campus newspaper, through talks to small groups of students, and by word of mouth relayed even more widely by associates, her felt position that although she experienced the personal loss of Hambrett very deeply, her philosophical line, firmly rooted and long-held, was that since no afterlife or anything vaguely like it existed, and since tribute to non-existent individuals was futile, it was a better homage to Ham to use the "space" occasioned by his end to work harder for social change. After all, when your Line of March was over, that was it!

After the noon "Memorial Sequence" (Artesta's suggested expression) the two roommates passed star athlete and admired black activist Davis on a path leading to the campus cafeteria.

"Hi Dave, man." Buz.

"Fuck you." Davis plunged by them on the path, his tall, heavy frame bouncing at each step to demonstrate indifference to the greeting. Although they didn't know it, word was getting around Peabody that Buz and Stif had had it in for Professor Biggins. Probably they were the ones who did him in, or at least, maybe they were involved in the plot in some way.

Stif brooded over a cup of coffee and a burrito at the spotless cafeteria table. "I guess we shoulda have been nicer to old Ham while he was still alive. It won't do any good now."

"Right. We didn't respect him the way we should've. I mean, we could have tried to understand what he was all about. All that shouting and accusing was just his way of trying to make us think for ourselves. He even told us so." Buz swallowed half of his candy bar at a bite. Funerals always made him hungry. After his grandfather's interment he had eaten three slices of cake and a dozen cookies.

"What he was really trying to say, as much as I can make it out, is that we're all responsible for everything. Not like just you and me, but the whole big group. So that if we start feeling guilty about it, well, at least that's a start." Buz again.

Stif looked dreamily into his plastic cup of coffee. Truer words were never spoke. "Even when he was tearing into you, pulling your answers apart and laughing at them, you got the impression that he really cared about you." This part was certainly not true, but Stif felt that way at the moment.

On the cafeteria wall there was an enormous photo portrait of Hambrett Biggins over the message "Rest in Peace". It was an especially flattering photograph of the deceased historian. It must have been taken fifty years ago.

Buz was emotionally plastered. He buried his head in his folded arms. From a distance it looked like he was worshipping his cola drink.

Thinking that his buddy was overcome by grief and had lowered his head to hide his tears, Stif patted him on the back. "Don't take it so hard, man. I know he was like a father to us, but life has to go on."

Buz was wide awake in a second. He had covered it up because of the universal mourning, but now he had to let it out. It was time for emotional release. The sorrow of mourning often opens the door to anger. "That's not what's grabbing me. It's tough about old Ham, but I'm getting over it. There's something else that's been wearing me out for weeks." He looked at Stif with a plainly hostile expression. "I can't keep fucking Darsellia for you! It's just sucking me dry!" Buz had stayed that extra half hour after class for weeks. During the last after class session he had suffered from erectile insufficiency. 'Darse' had laughed it off. She was a tolerant person in general and she had observed this phenomenon in her partners many times. Her standards for romantic partners were highly egalitarian; that too must be said in her favor. "I mean, I can't go on with it. I'm becoming prepotent. You saw it in the shower this morning. When I do it with her I feel like I'm disrespecting my grandma's whole generation!" Buz.

"Okay. She ought to be happy with the fling you gave her already." Stif counted on his fingers. "It's been about four or five weeks."

"I know her better than you do by this time. She's gonna be forty-two next month. She hasn't had a regular boy friend for about six years. She's not going to find one soon and she'll be mean ass pissed."

"So? Can't she be, like, celebrate?"

"You mean celibate. No. She's not the type. She told me she had to live life 'to the full, to the end stop'. Kind of like Davis, but without the drugs. Can't you try it yourself again? I mean, you probably had a bad day at it that Saturday night at the dump."

Stif was starting to shake from anxiety. "How can I, man? You told her I was, you know ... one of those guys."

"That wouldn't be a problem. We just tell her you're really bisexual or transsexual, something like that. She's way into sociology and psychology, so she'd understand, she might even like it better. Anyway, it wouldn't matter, just so you got it to her."

Stif shook his head. "No, dude. It wouldn't work. I'm too psyched out on her."

"And I'm too fucked out!"

The two sat in silence for a full ten minutes. Suddenly, Stif had a brilliant idea. "Why don't we get your friend Davis to sit in on the next class meeting with us, and then, you know, 'stay after class' with her?"

"Dave's pissed as hell at me. I don't know why. You heard him when we passed him on the way here."

"I thought that meant he was friendly."

"No. He's got something against me, against both of us. Maybe it has to do with poor old Hambrett." Buz looked at the wall photo of young Mr. Biggins. "Besides, he got it on before with old Vaggio. He doesn't like women who are like, out of his generation span. He told me. He's into, sort of, enjoying his youth days."

Beginning Psychology was a much easier course than either English IA or Native American Space, the former A.H. I. Dr. Greenleigh was a natural teacher. Since she was a psychologist, she understood how the young individual mind was programmed by society to carry certain expectations about money and sex and, at the same time, a large number of prejudices. Still, change was possible. The student brain was far more flexible now than it would be in later years. This was the time to strike.

The assigned textbook chapter on "Sexual Relations in a Changing Culture" had been interesting to the students, and not least to Stif and Buz. It almost seemed to them that they had written it, or at least inspired it. Professor Greenleigh gave a short lecture summing up the principal concepts and locating them within the context of general educational psychology:

"Societies develop rules to control the sexual behavior of their members and those rules vary enormously from one culture to another, so that it is impossible to speak of a single norm or general human standard, such as was claimed by Europeans of the Victorian era. Margaret Mead confirmed this during her field expedition to Samoa almost one hundred years ago. Malinowski and Boas made similar discoveries in the Trobriand Islands and Baffin Island, respectively. Nineteenth and early twentieth century Western societies had insisted that monogamy and non-promiscuity were universal norms that could not be questioned. Deviation from those strictures was considered abnormal, pathological, or vicious. In fact, Western societies had adopted those rules relating to sex and marriage as a prop to political, hierarchical and capital property structures that developed during the late medieval and early bourgeois periods of European history. Today the situation has changed, at least in part. It is now widely accepted that the primary goal in sexuality is the satisfaction of the individual libido. If the libido, or sex drive, is repressed because of imposed rules based on religious beliefs or concerns about lineage or economic status, neurosis and sometimes physical illness can result.

The current widespread indifference to traditional beliefs and concerns about sexuality has improved conditions in societies once severely afflicted by sexual repression and patriarchal family organization. Much, though, remains to be done. Perhaps formerly repressive cultures have advanced half way, achieving a stage where sexual relations are no longer considered taboo because of conflictive marital, genderal, age or ethnic rules. The last half of the transformation will be more difficult. The ideal must be a universal village resembling closely what Mead found already in place in the Pacific. Individuals should choose partners on a basis of personal inclination, and only for short periods. This is the only arrangement that does not represent an arbitrary and broadly harmful imposition of repressive norms. All sex is equal. The choice of individuals must form the culture of societies, not the reverse."

When her talk ground to an end, Dr. Greenleigh invited questions from the students. This was only a formality, because, really, all they had to do was to read the book, her book, to find answers to any possible questions.

A young woman with short hair who wore glasses raised her hand. Stif and Buz tuned in. Maybe she would be interested. In them. "Then sexual morality rules are a sort of sexual oppression? Is that the point?"

"Repression is the usual word, but I think 'oppression' is equally accurate. All engagements in sexual expression are legitimate. The individual must satisfy their biological needs. That is primary. We should remember this and sympathize with all efforts at fulfillment of the individual libido."

Stif nudged Buz. "You hear that? Everyone's like supposed to get it on."

"Yeah. Sounds great. Maybe I'll like pump Greenie for more facts after class. See if see knows any girls who are, like, having problems expressing their libido and that stuff."

Another hand went up. "If all sex acts are acceptable and equal, doesn't that mean that bestiality and homosexuality are as valid as marriage between a man and woman?" This guy wore a white shirt and tan slacks. His short blond hair stood out like a sore thumb. Obviously a "reac". Stif and Buz craned their heads toward the questioner. He was an ugly mug, but, yeah, he raised a point.

Greenleigh focused her competent mind on the question. "Your question seems to consider bestiality and homosexuality as equivalents. Homosexuality is a normal variant of human sexual expression. Bestiality, that is, sex acts performed by men upon animals, while not actually objectionable in itself, is almost always the result of sexual repression that denies other outlets to the persons involved." Shut him down cool.

So much for that one. It didn't really get very interesting. "I heard about a guy in Drakesville who tried to do it with a chicken," Stif whispered to his companion.

"Probably because he couldn't get a date."

"Yeah. Anyway, it's cool if two girls like make it together, but I can't understand two guys doing it. I mean, what could they do?" Stif.

Now Professor Greenleigh finished giving her students the further benefits from her years of study and research on sex themes . "The study of the customs and beliefs of various human communities is properly a subject of anthropology, but sexuality in general is a basic area of psychology. The diversity of approaches to human sexuality proves that no single variant, for example that of the Puritans, can claim universal validity." Greenleigh took a pause. She sat down on a sort of table that usually held informational pamphlets about sex counseling. The table bent noticeably under her weight.

"I mentioned the general objections to psychology and anthropology raised by post-structuralist and post-modernist philosophies at an earlier class meeting. We will discuss their relevance in the coming weeks. Follow the reading assignments listed on the course syllabus."

The classroom emptied. "I'll put it to her," Buz said quietly.

"You mean right now? Like you did to Vaggy? That's kind of risky. What if the department chairman or the dean walks in?" Stif.

"No, you moron. I mean, I'll ask her if she knows any girls who are like, you know, suffering a deprivation, as far as their libido and that stuff."

"Oh. Okay. Good luck. Ask her if any of 'em have friends. I'm kind of deprived of sex rights myself."

Stif was the last to leave psych class, except for Buz and the teacher. Dr. Greenleigh was gathering notes and books, bending over at her desk when Buz approached.

"Ms. Greenleigh? I have a question that I didn't want to ask during class." Buz stood just behind her. Just behind her comfortable behind.

Talifa guessed the sort of thing that was in the offing. A guy surreptitiously asking for a date with her. "Shoot," she said without looking up.

"Well, it's like this. I was really fascinated by what

you told the class, about sexual repressions and that type of thing. There's a lot of it going on in Drakesville, that's where me and my buddy come from. We're both students here. What I was wondering, was, if you knew any ..."

"You want me to make a general evaluation of the current status of taboos in contemporary local society," Dr. Greenleigh interrupted, "during a private tutorial?"

"Well, sort of. What I meant was ..."

"This society—I should say, 'our society'—is really not different from many evolving cultures. Perhaps it is only less honest about the facts."

Buz didn't know how to get on with it, with the question. About the girls who might also be suffering from libido expression deficiency. He didn't want to be, you know, like brutal, and ask too direct about meeting other women, since he could see that the Professor had some sort of interest in him beyond the simply pedagogic. She kept staring at him in a certain way, like she appreciated his attributes. In the meantime he started to study Professor Greenleigh. She really wasn't all that old. She certainly had better angles than old Vag. She was fuller, with a totally complete attraction in the breast area.

"If you're interested in pursuing the study of this subject, there is a very highly rated documentary film that is being shown at the Peabody Art Cinema this Sunday, on the subject of sexual customs among the last uncontaminated cultures of rainforest Africa, interior Asia and the Amazon forest. I plan to attend."

"Hey, wow, why don't we like make it a date? We could go in my car." Buz kept looking at those complete attractions. He forgot about other dates, at least for now.

Social relations between faculty and students were

forbidden by the Peabody Code of Ethical Behavior, except at a casual level. Exceptions could be made, Dr Greenleigh knew. The Dean was not insensitive. Dr. Greenleigh did not consider herself a person with exceptionally developed libidinal needs, but her last divorce was two years ago and there hadn't been much activity since. The faculty males were not exactly satyrs. They preferred books to boobs. That was their right. But meanwhile more somatic persons had biological needs. Normally, Dr. Greenleigh would have rejected the concept of a "date" between herself and a student, but in this case there were special circumstances. She saw an opportunity to bring a poorly prepared student into the academic world of study and research.

Of course, the idea of a "date" would be purely notional. Dr. Greenleigh would have preferred to provide her own transportation to the cinema, although she was opposed to the automobile on principle, and in this she followed the Faculty Line of March. Cars harm the earth and endanger its many highly diverse peoples and species. If combustion engine vehicles had to exist, they should be for collective use, as buses, trains, tractors and large airplanes. For professional purposes only, e.g. showing visitors from other universities around town and campus, she kept a late model Mercedes Benz sports car. Unfortunately, it was now in the mechanic's shop for repairs. An engine part had been ordered, but the car would be off the road for at least two weeks. "I think we could go to the film showing together, since I am presently without means of transportation."

"Great! Just me and you. Why don't I pick you up early and we could go for a burger or something first?"

"That won't be necessary." Faculty rules. Any

extra-campus contact between faculty and students should not be of a social nature. It was essential to prevent any hint of scandal before it got started.

"Okay, then. I'll just pick you up at your apartment." Greenie really had some breasts, even if her protruding rear wasn't exactly Buz's cup of tea.

Greenleigh lived in a five bedroom, three bath house. She was the only occupant. In Peabody the price tag of a small palace wasn't all that high.

"Sure you can use the Fiat." Stif was sympathetic to the opportunity that Buz had stumbled into. He was jealous, too. Why did Buz have all these faculty women falling for him when Stif himself, a much more attractive guy, was entirely left to his own private libido expressions? Except, of course, for that bungled attempt with Di Vaggio, which didn't count. "Maybe I ought to come along just to drive the car. It's a tricky old junk heap. Remember what happened to you on the way back from Drakesville. You broke down about a hundred times."

"This is gonna be, you know, real personal. Three's a crowd."

"You don't got nothing to worry about as far as that stuff. I'll drive in the front, and you and Greenie can do whatever the hell you want in the back seat. I won't turn around at all. And it don't got no rearview mirror, so I couldn't even be a peeping tom; the rearview got knocked out in a accident. I'll be just like the chauffeur in one of those old movies. You know, like, 'home, James'."

"Okay. But don't say anything at all after she gets in the car. Because I'll have to talk her around a lot before things really start between me and her. She's into incest taboos and tribal orgies, that's what turns her on. It's what the movie is about."

"Great. I'd really like to see that movie. It sounds almost like porno."

The late seventies Fiat drew up in front of Greenleigh's house. It was a large two story house with attractive design features. It had a Spanish tile roof, several balconies, half a dozen small turrets and towers, and a three car garage. "Wow! Professor Greenleigh sure isn't doing too bad for herself." Stif. "Looks like one of those places in Beverly Hills that they show on TV programs."

"It's pretty great". Buz surveyed the house. "Dr Greenleigh is really famous in her field. She's 'highly respected'. Vaggy told me that and Vaggy's not that easy to impress. I mean, as far as professional stuff. Dr Greenleigh's probably pulling down six figures a year from Peabody State."

"Yeah. Real thrill. But, hey, see if you can, you know, after the date, pump her for a few bucks to pay for the gas." Stif was envious about the palatial estate. This was a normal reaction from a peon.

Buz went to knock on the door. In his hands he had a small bouquet, gathered from a campus flowerbed, just like the one they used for Old Hambrett. The door was large and heavy-looking. It was made of dark wood and was equipped with a bright bronze knocker and a matching doorknob and lock plate. He stood waiting for several minutes, rocking back and forth on his heels. Then the door opened.

It was Professor Greenleigh, but transformed! Her face

looked younger, smoother. Her eyes were redesigned and now featured longer lashes, thinner brows and a bluish shadow underneath. She wore a tight red dress with low *décolletage*. She was fantastic. Buz dropped the flowers on the doormat and hugged her. He kissed her neck, her cheek, her mouth.

"Hold it, Romeo!" Dr Greenleigh pushed him away. "This is just a ride, not a honeymoon." The Peabody Code of Ethical Behavior was very strict and often enforced. She had dressed in style for a big date, but that was just because she wanted to conform to *our society's* particular ritual taboos. It was almost an experiment on the subject of traditional mating behavior.

"Oh. Oh. Sorry, man. I was just, like, overwhelmed." Buz felt momentary pangs of conscience about violating sex taboos, even if they were arbitrary and archaic. "You look, like, almost, really beautiful."

Greenleigh craned her neck toward the car parked in front. "Who's that in the old jalopy?" She feared a sex ambush. Malinowski's study on the Trobriand Islands mentioned such incidents.

"That's just Stif, my roommate." Buz turned back to the teacher after a dismissive hand gesture. "He's the only one who can drive that tricky piece of junk. It really belongs to his mother, but she lent it to him permanently."

Greenleigh was having second thoughts. "Perhaps I should call a cab."

"Oh no." Buz was shocked. "By the time they got here the movie'd be half over. We'll be okay. If there's one thing Stif can do, it's drive the Fiat. Let's get started."

Dr. Greenleigh descended the porch steps with the aid of Buz's arm. Stif was wearing a visor cap so as to resemble a chauffeur. On the cap was a logo with the words "Fast

Lube". He nodded to the teacher. "Hi! Buz asked me to give you a ride. But I'm sort of fascinated by cultures and their sex rules myself, so I really want to see that movie."

"I can see you two are deeply immersed in themes of psychology and anthropology." Even Stif caught the ironic tone in Professor Greenleigh's voice. "I suggest you both take notes during the film and use them for your course projects."

"Sure. I even brung a pencil." Stif showed the stubby chewed end that he retrieved from his pants pockets. He always tried to carry something to write with, in case he had to note down the license plate number of a hit and run driver.

"Let's get going." Buz looked at his watch. "The movie starts in forty-five minutes and we want to catch the whole thing from the start."

The Fiat cranked over and took off with a lurch. "You wouldn't believe it," Stif turned around to face Dr. Greenleigh. "This wreck cost almost five thousand dollars new."

"Your momma got taken."

Whenever he had to change gears, Stif pressed on the gas pedal with his foot. Otherwise the engine was likely to stall. "She bought it at this Italian dealership." Stif pronounced it Eye-talian.

"Hey! Watch out for the traffic!" Buz. They screeched to a stop just in front of another car.

Driving with his head turned front to back, Stif had almost run into a huge pickup truck piloted by some redneck. A sticker on the rear bumper of the truck said, "Guns Made America Great". Blasting horns and obscene hand gestures sealed the incident.

"Sorry, man. I got carried away. I guess I'm too much of a conversationalist."

In the back seat, Buz had his arm around the shoulders of Talifa, that is, of Dr. Greenleigh. "Hey, you feel like something to eat? There's a burger joint with a drive-through on the way to the movie house. It won't take hardly any time at all."

"I think we should go directly to the cinema." Dr. Greenleigh used a cold, prim tone of voice. But, if she wasn't interested in some action, why the hell did she get herself all duded up?

"I could use a bite to eat," Stif put in. "Driving always makes me hungry. They don't have anything in those movie houses except popcorn and candy, maybe a hot dog."

A short drive through an expensive residential neighborhood brought them to Forrest Drive. Downtown Peabody was only a few minutes away. Buz gave Dr. Greenleigh a squeeze around the shoulders and chest. "I really enjoy your class."

The Fiat pulled into Peewee's Peabody Burger Stop. It was simple at the order window. "Three cheeseburgers. No fries." Stif.

At the pay window things got more complicated. "Damn!" Buz shouted. "I forgot my wallet at home!" The bill came to eight dollars and eighty-seven cents.

Stif checked his cash. He pulled a five dollar bill from his pocket. "I could use this, but I gotta save something for the movie ticket."

Greenleigh paid the bill. She took the change from a twenty.

Stif parked the Fiat in Peewee's parking lot while they

ate. He used the back of his hand to wipe burger juice from his mouth. Buz, more attuned to social requirements, used his shirt sleeve. Dr. Greenleigh took careful, modulated but not exceptionally small bites.

"Peewee's doesn't give out paper napkins," Stif explained, turning around to look at the professor again. "That'd take up half their profit margin."

Dr. Greenleigh fixed her makeup with the aid of a compact mirror.

"Okay, let's get going." Buz. "The film's on in less than half an hour."

The Fiat started up after half a dozen tries. The battery was losing its charge, probably because the alternator only worked half the time. They were off in a cloud of black smoke. "Hey," Stif put in, "I know Peabody pretty well by now. I've been driving around this burg for a couple of months. There's a short cut we can take so we can get to the movie with plenty of time to spare."

They turned down a side street. Soon they were in a back neighborhood. It was almost dark. The City of Peabody really cheaped out on street lighting. There was only one streetlamp every three or four blocks. "I think we turn next street." Stif.

The little neighborhood houses, dating mostly from just after the Civil War, to judge by their appearances, were set a fair distance back from the street. Dim light from television sets provided the main illumination. The Fiat's engine went dead just after they turned the corner. Stif guided the car to a curb. He tried the starter six or seven times. "Guess I'll have to look at the engine. Maybe I can fix it quick." Stif looked behind. Buz and Dr. Greenleigh were lying flat down on the backseat.

He had her dress up around her neck. He was really taking her to town, working top and bottom while she groaned and murmured in satisfaction. Stif turned away and faced the car hood. But why should I, he thought, get left out all the time? He hoisted himself over the seat and took the horizontal alongside Buz and Professor Greenleigh.

The next morning, Monday, the two students had to catch an early class. They were showering together, as usual, in order to save time and water, and also to maintain that camaraderie and social coherence that they had known in their high school gym classes. As usual, Stif began soaping himself from the top down. When he got to the middle zone he noticed that his member was smeared with some sort of caked on brown material. "Hey! What the hell!"

Buz laughed. "Why so surprised? You did her up brown last night. Don't you remember?"

Stif shook his head. "You mean Professor Greenleigh? You're wrong. You were working on that end. I was front to front."

"Then why's your prick covered with you know what? Look at me." Buz's virile member was clean. He balanced it with one hand.

"I guess it was hard to tell anything in the dark. I sure thought I had it right end up." Resigned to a regrettable admission and dangling his head in shame, Stif started to give himself an energetic wash up with soap. He had to massage it vigorously to clean off that caked on stuff, which led to the inevitable result. "Ah ah ah! She was so ... oh hot!"

Buz went through the same maneuvers, but without any commentary.

"Anyway, all sex acts are equal. Dr. Greenleigh taught us that. I mean, in class."

The Fiat just made it to the campus parking lot, thanks to Stif's engineering skill. The roommates jumped out and ran to the classroom. They were already late. It was 10:10 and it was Monday. Their Native American Space class had already started. It was now under the direction of history grad student Jasmine Peacefield, an intellectually brilliant young woman who shaved her head, wore plugs in her ears and a pin through one nostril. She did not follow the brutal Historical Realism method creatively pioneered by the dearly departed Hambrett Biggins. She knew how to control a class by using a very different approach. Her belief was that women teachers in particular had to keep their classes under direct, albeit benign control, otherwise the students, especially the men students, would follow a natural inclination to take advantage of a perceived weakness and would just relax and waste class time by turning a teaching space into a social event.

They were walking quickly along a campus lane on the way to Peacefield's Native American class when they passed going the other way a guy they recognized as one of Davis's friends. He turned to them and shouted, "bunch of faggots!"

Buz and Stif stopped and turned around with gaping mouths. What the hell was this about?

"Yeah, I know you two. Everybody says it. You're together all the time and we know what that means."

"You're crazy." Buz delivered this rebuttal, then he

grabbed Stif by the arm and led him in the direction of Peacefield's classroom. Davis's pack of friends were a socially cohesive group, something like what Greenleigh would call a hunting band, and it was best to avoid trouble with them if you valued your physiological condition.

Heading up to the quad area, Buz ventured a comment. "We only did it together once anyway, and that was a long time ago when we were real young."

"It was three times." Stif had to work harder on mathematics, so he tried to be more exact. "But we were drunk. At least I was."

Native Space went on without any big problems. Jasmine Peacefield was not a violent teacher. She did not put her students through humiliating ideological gymnastics, brow beat them or try to trip them up with clever cross-examinations. She did like to cry a lot. Every page of the class text was devoted to the tale of a brutal victimization, so she had a lot to work with. When she got on a real crying jag, she grimaced and pulled on her ear plugs. This brought half the class to an advanced lachrymose state.

After class, possibly because of the emotional workout, Buz had to use the rest room. "I gotta make the john," he told Stif. "Wait up and we'll hit the cafeteria for lunch and study for the next class."

In the men's room, Buz was surprised and at first ready to take a physically defensive posture when he noticed that the guy standing in front of the next urinal was Jay J. Jay J was buddies with Davis. It was he who had used the "Fag" word about the two that same morning.

"Hey man, sorry," Jay began as soon as he noticed Buz, at the same time checking out the other's equipment.

"I didn't really mean to hurt you all's feelings. I don't care what nobody does with their own space."

"You were clear wrong, dude."

"Okay. Just like you say." JJ was tall and big. He could easily have occupied two urinals at the same time, although that would have presented substantial water direction problems. "Anyway, I'm sorry for it. But there's one thing I want to let you in on," Jay went on, at the same time shaking the last drops from a member that had to be extendible to at least two feet. "It was Davis who took Hambrett out. A lot a people here think it was you and that other guy, but Dave got on him with some pals. That's 'cause he wouldn't come through with no spare change. It's all past and over, but I just thought I'd clue you in, you know, in case you got into any problems on it. Dave ain't a bad guy most of the time, but he dished me royal on a hash deal and that just burns my ass."

"Thanks." Buz looked concernedly at his own appendage, which, although respectable by normal standards, could not have been half as long as Jay's. As far as Hambrett, murder was murder, even if the former Professor wasn't the most likeable guy on campus, but it was a job for the authorities to handle. No need for any amateur detectives. JJ was a cool guy to let him in on the secret.

In fact, Peabody Administration authorities had already come to a similar conclusion. They had interviewed students who were at least circumstantially involved and had looked at the video recordings from security cameras operating in the parking lot. The film showed that Davis had assaulted Biggins and knocked him down, but the crucial event, the coup de grace, was unclear, because the fallen Biggins was surrounded and hidden from camera view by a number of students engaged in what should be called a gang beating. When the students left the immediate scene, Biggins lay motionless on the ground. Perhaps the academic prodigy had by chance suffered a cardiac emergency partially induced by the dramatic events that were concurrent? A decision was reached by University authorities to terminate the inquiry on the grounds of insufficient evidence. There had been no autopsy because Professor Brackle had ordered a cremation before anyone thought about "forensics". The police and District Attorney were willing to go along. It was the Dean who made the significant point. Davis was a sports hero at Peabody; he would soon leave for the major league teams and would be a success story that the college could point to with pride and write up in its brochures and internet advertising. Davis would help attract more students to Peabody and, of course, more diversity and more funding, thereby benefiting the entire community. Davis should be left alone. If charges had been made, half the Peabody Law School faculty would have provided a free legal defense for the wayward student, who had never been adequately accompanied as a poor and socially disadvantaged student.

Artesta Brackle had seen the videos and read the interview evidence, but she rejected the notion of homicide. She thought that Davis was as much if not more of a victim as Ham. Our society was to blame. The long historical context and precedents were clearly the real culprit. Anyway, prosecuting a socially marginalized student would not bring Hambrett back. Assuming that anyone would want to bring him back.

BUZ AND STIF GO TO COLLEGE

Professor Greenleigh devoted her next class lecture to the subject of anal intercourse, an area of study that the previously assigned textbook pages dealt with at length. There was a deep prejudice in our society that stigmatized and condemned persons who engaged in this form of sex, Doctor Greenleigh told her students. Traditional belief associated it exclusively with male homosexuality. In fact, it was a practice that was commonly found in many societies and among all groups. In a few cultures in certain tropical and mountainous areas, it was fully accepted and even valued above genital intercourse. Clearly, societies appreciated the fact that it resulted in reduced population pressure in regions that were already pushing against subsistence capacity. Sexual satisfaction derives principally from psychological factors. Physiologically and psychologically, anal sex could be as pleasurable to both (or to all) participants as genital intercourse. Biases derived from cultural and religious taboos continued to influence popular beliefs.

Stif looked at his desk. He pretended to follow in the text. He thought that Professor Greenleigh was trying to catch his eye, but he refused to make contact. He was still highly influenced by cultural taboos. He glanced obliquely at Buz, to try to make out Buz's take on all of this. His roommate's opinions were a point of reference for Stif, due chiefly to the fact that he himself was slow on analysis and even comprehension. Buz seemed to be looking at one of the classroom walls and taking notes.

His head still focused on the text and not at all on the lecturing teacher, Stif had a few thoughts about what actually happened the night before. Probably, Greenleigh had really dug it. That is, the rear end job. Otherwise, why would she be humping away on the subject now? As for Stif, he had been disoriented in a spatial sense at the time. It felt about the same as the other way to him. He had to be honest with himself, though. His catalog of experiences was limited. Was it four times, including Greenleigh? Probably. And maybe the tussle with Greenie didn't really count, because it was backwards and Buz was working on her front-wise in the classical method at the same time. When the hour ended, Stif shot for the classroom door. He was the first out.

Grades. So far, and the semester was almost half over, Buz and Stif had reasonable grades. These had to be reported at short intervals to the bank that carried their Student Loans. Buz was pulling at least a C- average in his courses and Stif was maintaining a D+, which was not bad at all for him. At Peabody, anything above a D was passing. The grade point average for the total Peabody student body was 2.3. It would have been even lower without the scores of a few dozen over-achieving exchange students from Asia and the Middle East. They usually managed a 4 plus. Drakesville High School had not emphasized academics. Buz and Stif could console themselves by remembering this fact. At Drake, probably even half the teachers were at the 1.9 level. The favorite subject of the Drake faculty was television appreciation.

English IA was not going well. Professor Darsella Di Vaggio was increasingly prone to turn her class lectures into dramatic and vigorous commentaries on contemporary social problems. In a way, this was understandable. Many severe problems existed in our society, and not only in the political and economic areas. No one questioned the accuracy of her claim when she said that, as regarded patterns of sexual behavior, males in our society demonstrated an historic tendency not only to abusiveness, but also to sexual indifference and frequently even to impotence. Their indifference resulted from changes in social attitudes that often prevented them from obtaining outright domination of their partners. They failed to adapt psychologically to a more egalitarian arrangement of libido context. Impotence naturally resulted from this psychological failure. It was really a form of denial and fugue.

The class listened obediently. A few of the students were upset by Di Vaggio's description of the sexual dysfunction problem of "our society", since they didn't have a problem, but you didn't dare challenge the Professor's version. For one thing, she could verbally floor you without effort. Her verbal skills were highly developed. She had read a million books in the areas of gender studies, the sociology of sex, and literary theory that focused on the gender factor in fiction and poetry. She could redirect a question by skewering it according to any of a number of currently popular psycho-sociological theoretics.

Now the class was waiting for her to explain how this analysis—the impotence and indifference flaccidly raging—related to the last reading assignment, which was a short story entitled, "Git It Up and Git It Off: Gittin' Down". Vaggy finally established the connection. The story concerned the experiences of an inner city woman who supports her boyfriend financially because of real affection and desire, but who gradually becomes estranged from him when his sexual prowess wanes as a result of drug and alcohol excesses and involvements with other partners, including one who necessarily prefers the anal approach. In the end—a better description would be "in the front"—she is forced to castrate him. She has "removed" an oppressive situation but she will carry for the rest of her life the mental scars that arose from an act that our society and her own former boy friend had forced upon her. The analysis of "Git" followed a pattern similar to that of the previous homework short story.

It was Buz who kept his eyes on the text this time. It was now two weeks since he had stopped his after class activities with Professor Di Vaggio. Vaggio must be feeling it. It was human nature. Everyone has sexual needs and Vag had to be pretty hard up by now in the boyfriend way. Probably she was not yet ready to move on to a radically different solution, such as the "intra-gender approach" suggested by their text. Buz absolved her from blame for the collapse of their intimate relations, but, after all, he wasn't guilty either. He just couldn't get it on with her anymore. He was, like, sucked dry. She was almost as old as his mom. At least, she looked it. Anyway, it was our society that had created the problem by imposing its taboos and conventions and stuff, right? Unfortunately, Vag was probably not the type who would go for the anal approach. Too skinny. If she were, he could have talked Stif into doing her up brown. That seemed to be his style.

Stif looked at Vag and then at Buz. He was trying to guess what sort of psychic energy might be going on between them. Buz had helped him out by taking Vag off his hands, but then Buz had dropped out because of what he claimed was sheer physical lack of endurance. Stif knew that Buz was now getting poor grades on his weekly class theme papers, even when he put in stuff like "men are natural castrators of those whom they dominate. They render their victims powerless in order to prevent resistance to their psychologically inflated need for ego imperialism". This was nearly a literal quotation from one of the essays in a reference work recommended for the class, a piece written by a highly respected Ivy League professor with the title, *Gender, Sex, Oppression and Resistance: Gorilla Warfare in Our Time.* Di Vaggio herself was one of the co-authors of the book. Stif hoped that maybe he could get Buz going again, and so keep Vaggy from being forced to react aggressively. More shower exercises might help by wanking up his libido.

Vag. "When sex is reduced to a subject/object opposition, with the losing individual being reduced to the status of submissive object, it is transformed into a weapon of domination."

The big girl with a shaven head and plugs in her ear lobes raised her hand. "Doesn't that also mean that the subject is transformed into a weapon so he can maintain the dominance? He becomes a phallic weapon. That's almost as bad. He's an object, too."

Vaggy looked at "Dumbo", as she had privately baptized this student who frequently asked irrelevant questions. "You are moving into the area of Freudian symbolism. I think we are indebted to Sigmund Freud for important basic discoveries in the area of sexual psychology, but the point I brought up is sociological, literary and, above all, political. It is more about the way our society is arranged than the way our libidos work."

Dumbo looked defeated but she was not ready to give up yet. "I think the reading assignment reinforces what I just said. We are all victims of our society's domination, of the way it imposes its class and gender based sex divisions and represses us."

Vaggy looked at the classroom ceiling with its pitted acoustic tiles. She looked at the floor with its scuffed plastic tiles. She inhaled and exhaled deeply for a good five minutes. "You raise some interesting questions. The idea that I am trying to convey, however, is that the oppressive situation that is described in the story we read is not entirely cultural and social and political. The gender attitudes that are described in 'Git It Up' have deeper sources. A large number of studies in the past few years have confirmed that the male dominant aggressive/passive sexual pattern is in fact rooted in neurophysiology and neurochemistry. Testosterone, the male sex hormone, induces bullying behavior that has as its inevitable counterpart an indifference to the well being of the other. The male ego, exalted by overwhelming biochemical excretions, dismisses the human reality of the penetrated partner. It cannot focus outside the context of a glorification of its sexual triumph."

The hour was up. The students again rushed to outside territory. It wasn't just a reaction to the usual class time boredom. Di Vaggio was getting really weird. Maybe she was heading toward some sort of mental crisis. Student rumor had it that her personal libido problems were working to the surface of her admittedly very large brain and threatening a violent outcome. Sure she was right in her gender/sexual analysis, but that look in her eyes and the sound of her voice reminded you of Jack the Ripper in the movie. A few recognized that she had borrowed many of her ideas from Artesta Brackle's Castration Discourse theory.

In the hallway outside the class, Buz caught Stif by the shoulder as fellow students ran out. "Man, you gotta give it another try, even if you got to use the rear end method again. Old Vaggy's about to flip her libido. Go back in there and give her some good lovin'."

"But I can't!" Stif raised his arms in emphasis of the futility. "It's no good. I can't get it up with her so she'd be even more pissed than ever." There was desperation in his voice. "Why don't *you* try it again? You were doing damn good for a long time after I petered out on my home date with her."

"Yeah, but that's passed. She reminds too much of my old lady, and that's sorta like incest. No. I gave it my best shot, but I'm fagged out, honest. It's no go."

They stood facing each other in the corridor, each aware of the explosive potential of the developing situation. Di Vaggio was an intense and powerful personality. In her own mind she dominated the world through her mastery of language. In fact, she had succeeded in establishing an imperium over her immediate "context", her classes. Now she had to be propitiated, like a volcano goddess, or else. Both thought of the situation in these terms, although they were unaware of the stylistic problem of mixing metaphors.

"Look," Buz tried again. "You did it pretty good on Greenleigh when we were going to that movie. Go back in there and try the same method on Vaggie. That stuff turns you on."

"You mean the anal business? That was a mistake. It's not my thing at all."

"Just close your eyes and dream. That'll take you through. You'll be saving the whole class, and especially us, from 'aggression rooted in the perversion of the natural libido resulting from the pressure of oppressive class interests'. That's a quote from our book." Buz did not want to argue around too much with his buddy. Excessive debate could weaken Stif's already fragile libido, but the situation was too serious. He did think that Stif was into "doing it up brown". Hadn't he even taken the bottom role himself a few times? "Give it a try with Vag now. What do you have to lose?"

Stif was tired of arguing. Buz's superior verbal skills gave him at an advantage. Stif hitched his jeans up around his waist. His crotch showed an angular enlargement. "Okay. I'll give it a go. Tell my mom I died a hero." He went in. To the classroom.

Minutes passed. Buz looked at his watch. It was now at least seven minutes since Stif had "entered the dragon". More time went by. Muffled sounds came from inside. Then the door flew open and Stif ran out. His face was drained of blood. It was as white as parchment. At the same time an alarm sounded. This was the emergency buzzer that had been installed in each classroom at Peabody in order to counter the threat of violent attacks by armed psychotic students. In case of need, a teacher could press a button that would alert the whole school of imminent danger. It was a loud and high-pitched noise, like an air raid siren.

"Scatter!" Stif shouted.

They ran down the hill to the campus parking lot. Stif was too nervous to drive. Again, Buz had to get behind the wheel and pilot the wrecked old Fiat. After a few blocks, Stif was calm enough to attempt an explanation.

"I tried it, man, like you said, but she just didn't go

for that reverse entry business. When I went back in the classroom she was real friendly, so after I made up some bullshit question about the course, I kissed her a couple of times, but when it got down to the nitty gritty she pushed the panic button. I ran out of there. I didn't really want to do it anyway. Especially that way. It's perverted. It was your idea."

Buz guided the Fiat in the direction of the dump. He had to concentrate on controlling the car while at the same time monitoring Stif's distracted behavior: Stif kept shifting his weight on the seat and leaning out the car window. There was something wrong with the Fiat's steering. It was always trying to veer to the left. Probably due to a severe front end alignment problem, plus mismatched tires. Finally they drove into the parking lot of the rundown four unit apartment building. Stif ran inside and collapsed in front of the television. He was almost comatose.

"Get me a beer, dude, please!"

Half an hour later, Stif was in better control. There was something very relaxing about the moronic daytime programming. He took a long drink. He managed to talk. "See, I must've hit her off center or something, so it was real painful. Anyway, it was plain it wasn't going to work. I got my pants back up and I was heading out of the class when she pressed the button, the one the teachers are supposed to use in case of those terrorite attacks."

"I should have known you'd botch it. You didn't handle it right. You gotta know how to go about these things."

"Now you tell me. Anyway, I suppose the cops will be here any minute. I'll be lucky if I get off with twenty years. They're real severe about student attacks after all the stuff they show on TV. Get me another beer, will you? I'm gonna be dry for a long time in the joint."

Buz came back with two cans. "Here. This'll cool you down. Don't worry. We'll get you the best lawyer in town. They all take a few charity cases."

Stif nodded. He drank deep from his second beer. "Okay. I thought it out. I think I got the answer. I'll throw myself on the mercy of the court. I'll plead guilty. I'll say I really love Vaggy and I want to marry her and do it the right way up."

"Exactly." Buz. "And I'll tell them all about your weak mentality and neurotic psychology. That ought to help. Vaggy's a hard woman, but I don't think she's merciless. She might forgive you if you say you did out of real love. Then, you could cop for one of those voluntary castration treatments." Buz looked at his roommate to check his reaction to this proposal. Stif was asleep. His mouth was open and he was snoring. It was all the stress and shit.

The afternoon wore on. Stif woke up and tried to focus on the TV. Some sort of game show was being broadcast, but he couldn't tell who was winning and who was losing. It was four-thirty. Buz was still sitting there and he was on his third beer, a rare indulgence for him. He handed Stif a fresh can. The police were really slow on their reaction time. They ought to have been pounding down the front door long ago.

Buz opened the apartment door and walked into the parking area. He looked around. No sign of a squad car. In the distance, he could hear a siren, but it was getting fainter.

"What class do we got for tomorrow?" It was nighttime and Stif was drunk but not incoherent.

"Beginning Psychology with Doctor Greenleigh. You do the assignment?"

"Yeah. We were supposed to describe a primitive society where the sexual customs are not the same as our own. I lived it out."

"You have to put it on paper."

Stif picked up a pencil. He wetted the lead end on his tongue. He grabbed a blank page from the floor. "Living in a Wild Tribal Zone", he wrote at the top in large letters. "That's why I love Professor Greenleigh," he said. "At least she knows what end is up."

Dr. Greenleigh was more impressive than ever when the session of Beginning Psychology started. She wore a patterned dress with Egyptian motifs, most of them showing female pharaohs with quite adequate breast development and facial features resembling the famous bust of Nefertiti. She had a good deal of make-up on, which she usually did not use for class meetings, with a lot of henna and kohl around the eyes, plus artificial eyelashes that swept the space in front of her vision. She announced the subject of her lecture. "Anal Intercourse in Multi-cultural Comparison."

Before giving a summary of this educationally and socially significant lecture, it is necessary to provide the student/reader with an outline of the discoveries of poststructuralist linguistic philosophy that have had such an important influence on contemporary thought, since they had greatly influenced Greenleigh's own thinking and behavior. First, the enterprise of teaching and communication at the university level has been enormously improved by the doctrine, now virtually unopposed within Academia, which holds that language is meaningless. Language is meaningless, but it is not quite as simple as that. Text, that is, a message of any kind, whether written or spoken, or even through any other means, has no fixed meaning. Its meaning is composed within the head of the reader or listener, the receiver of the message. Each receiver forms a different version of the text, and all of those versions have equal validity. It follows that any statement, but particularly those impinging on the areas of sociology, history and political science, can be taken apart and shown to be biased, arbitrary, ambiguous and meaningless. This method of smashing syntax and vocabulary is called Deconstruction and it is considered to be the most advanced theory to hit campus since 1917. It is a way of showing that any running of words by mouth or print or by electronic media is inconsequent, since void of fixed sense and significance. The only activity that is beyond criticism is the enterprise of critiquing language and showing it to be null in all aspects.

Greenleigh was an academic psychologist. She had her doctorate. She had studied and ingested the many theories, methods and schools of thought that had emerged since Freud. She was also aware of the body blow that Deconstruction had launched against the traditional system of psychology. At first Greenleigh opposed the new theory on the grounds, simply, that it destroyed all grounds. Now, she herself was an enthusiastic adherent of the method (Deconstruction). But at the same time she was not. And the reverse. It was complicated. Complication, reaching ever higher levels of abstraction and contradiction, was the only defense against linguistic attack. This was the famous *flight in advance*. To Talifa, though, one thing was beyond quibble. Entry level college psychology classes ought to be enlightened about a phenomenon that many Peabody students obviously misunderstood.

"Anal intercourse." Greenleigh faced the class. "Anal intercourse. What connotation does that phrase invoke?" Greenleigh waited for hands to go up in the classroom. There was confusion on student faces. No hands were raised. Greenie rather expected this. She decided to bring up the topic in class because it was obvious from essay papers submitted so far that the explanation in their textbook had not properly *penetrated* the student brain. She veered to another angle. "Is anal intercourse a synonym for homosexuality?"

Stif nodded from the back of the class but he didn't dare say anything. For one thing, the police could still be working on the incident in English IA with Di Vaggio, even though it didn't really count since he hit way off target. But Greenie was probably into the anal business. That must be why she kept bringing it up all the time. On that night of the date with Dr. Greenleigh, he got it right, bull's-eye, and that's why she really dug it. Even so, his ideas on the subject were traditional. Yeah, butt-fucking was the same as being queer. That time with Greenie was only a mistake, a *spacial disorientation* (Stif was really getting the hang of the vocabulary). He couldn't see which end was up when he parked the car on that dark street. With Di Vaggio it didn't count, since, as he recalled constantly to himself, he never even got past entry level. She shouted at him and hit the classroom panic button before he had a chance to give it a try.

"Is anal intercourse accepted in some cultures? Is it condemned by our culture?"

The class was not comfortable with this subject. That was another reason why Dr. Greenleigh had chosen it for her talk. You had to shock them out of their complacency or you would never be able to enter the tight orifice of their minds.

"It's considered to be perverted and sick by most people." A girl spoke. She was good looking, at least in Stif's estimation. In Stif's estimation almost all women under the age of sixty-eight were good looking and even some of the guys. "People who did it used to be burned at the stake by the Inquisition," she added.

"But what about our society today? Is anal intercourse more tolerated? Is it practiced exclusively by homosexuals?"

Stif nodded again. He almost raised his hand. Yeah. Only queers did it. Who the hell else would want to?

Buz, sitting in the desk next to Stif, was reading the text assignment for the class right now. Even though he had written his paper, he had failed to read completely through the assignment last night, what with having to deal with Stif's attempt to bugger faculty and his heavy drinking. The assigned chapter was called "Sex, Society and Culture: Introducing Perception into the Maze of the Human Eros".

A big guy with a beaver beard raised his hand. He had a deep voice, sort of like those football players they interviewed on TV in the middle of the game. "I think differences in sexuality are more tolerated today. It's not like it was twenty years ago when lots of people had a real religious outlook. Male/female couples engage in it. It doesn't appeal much to me."

Laughter from the class. Fag, Stif thought. You probably bugger your old lady.

"Hostility to anal intercourse is a result of the homophobic nature of our society." A small brunette woman spoke. Her name was Lena Zarankowski. She had transferred to Peabody after flunking out of CUNY because, instead of studying, she spent all of her time marching in protest picket lines. She was obviously a lesbo. This was Stif's evaluation. Most New Yorkers were Lesbians. Or at least half were Lesbians. The other half were fags. Stif leaned toward Buz. "I'm sure that Zarandouchi girl's a dyke," he whispered.

"Would you shut up?" Buz whispered to his pathetic buddy. "You really are dumb. Why do you think she's a Lesbian just because obviously she read the text assignment, where they talk about homophobia a lot? If you'd done your homework, you'd understand some of the basic ideas."

"Is anal intercourse inherently repulsive?" Greenleigh aloud to class.

Stif nodded his head repeatedly and stamped his feet. Hell yes, he thought. It was disgusting. You only did it when you didn't have any other choice. He squirmed in his seat and made faces.

Professor Greenleigh looked directly at Stif. She pointed at him. "You seem to be having quite a reaction. How would you characterize anal intercourse?"

Shitty, Stif thought, but he didn't say it. "I don't think it's as normal like other types of sex." Greenie was giving him some sort of look. There was something in her eyes, in her voice, in her facial expression. Now he was sure she had been aware of it that night in the back of the Fiat, and not totally distracted by what Buz was doing in front. Even though it was just a mistake on his part. But obviously she got a real thrill out of it. A lot of people were weird. Anyway, he would be glad to oblige her again, although preferably in the conventional style and on a regular bed.

Buz finally twigged to the whole scene. It was clear to him too that Greenleigh had chosen this crappy lecture subject as a result of her backseat date experience. It probably meant that she got a bigger bang out of Stif's perverted performance than out of his, Buz's approach, which was the normal front method. From what he remembered, it wasn't at all certain that she had an orgasm with him. He heard her make some little noises like "ooh-oh". Maybe she was faking it out of politeness. He resented the fact that she favored the pervert back entry method for which Stif was so justly infamous. And now she was devoting a whole lecture to it. Maybe she was frigid, so she had to do the rear approach. He had read about that in some magazine, although their class textbook didn't mention anything about it. Professor Greenleigh hadn't got the sort of thrill out of her experience with him that Buz had a right to expect.

Doctor Greenleigh turned to Buz. "What about you, *Mr.* Miller? How do you view anal sex? Are heterosexuals equally concerned, or is it only for homosexuals?"

"I think it's inferior to genital/genital intercourse," Buz said, using a phrase that he had just read in the text. "Because the lack of face to face contact limits intimacy." The text talked about this, using the exact phrase, but rejected the claim as an example of anal-phobia.

Greenleigh returned to the front of the classroom. "What about oral-anal sexual contact? Is it condemned by our society? For what reason?" Stif and Buz both drew a blank on this one. What the hell was oral-anal contact?

The lecture went on and on. Greenie was really driving hard in an attempt to liberate minds that had been stunted by a purblind middle class environment. To Stif, this was all book talk. It was correct, of course, *intellectually*, but it wasn't the sort of thing normal people went for.

After oral-anal contact, Greenleigh discussed oral-genital contact, then mutual masturbation, then exhibitionism, then voyeurism, then sado-masochism. She was full of ideas. Maybe she had tried them all and found the anal approach more to her liking. Buz thought about it. No, he wasn't ready to give it a try. He wasn't that desperate yet.

Finally she was winding down. Impotence, she said. Was it widespread in our society? What was its cause?

Stif was interested in this one. It was a problem he had never had before that time with Vaggy, except once or twice when he was doing it solo or in the shower with Buz. Probably other guys got that way because they couldn't face the fact that they were losers. Deep down maybe they were afraid of trying to give it to their old ladies and finding it didn't work. That was it. Stif raised his hand. "It happens when guys are afraid of being ... you know, not too potent. Maybe that's why they try that anal stuff." He stared at Greenleigh and grinned. That, he knew, would never be his case.

"You believe that anal intercourse is associated with a fear of impotence? Let's analyze the conceptual structures ..." Greenie trailed off, at least as far as Stif was concerned. He wasn't listening anymore.

BUZ AND STIF GO TO COLLEGE

Buz looked at his roommate. Never before had he realized that Stif was so stupid and so awkward. He had utterly no couth at all.

At last the classroom was emptying—Buz and Stif were prevented from being in the vanguard by a really slow moving fat guy. He blocked their access to the aisle that led to the door. Greenleigh took advantage of this configuration to approach the roommates. "If you two are interested," she smiled in a way that Buz thought provocative and Stif interpreted as romantic, "another documentary film is being shown next weekend at the Art Cinema. The subject of this film is anal intercourse among cultures inhabiting the New Hebrides archipelago. It was filmed on site." She winked. "We can take my car this time. It's a sports model but it can fit three." It would be safer. No room to maneuver.

Buz climbed over a back row of seats while the fat guy was still getting his various folds and areas together for the final push. "Sorry, Professor Greenleigh," he said. "I gotta study for my math class." He didn't want to be faced with a situation that would probably develop into that butthole stuff. He was still traumatized from the last time, although he had only watched Stif at work.

Stif followed. He also climbed over the backs of the rows of desks. The fat guy looked like he was finally ready to launch, but it was uncertain. "I'm sorry too, Mrs. Greenleigh. I'd like to go, but I can't leave Buz alone. He has some really bad psychological problems. I'll try to talk some sense into him." It sounded like an invitation to a great party, but he wouldn't dare go alone. He needed Buz to point him in the right direction.

"Why don't you want to go on another drive with Greenleigh? She's a good looking lady and it's obvious she wants it bad." They were back at the dump. Stif brought up the subject while he cracked open another beer. It seemed like a great idea to him.

"I'm not into doing anyone up brown. It's just not my thing. Go ahead, if that's what you want to do."

"It's not going to be like that again at all, and it was just a mistake. We can take turns front-wise. She'd get a double thrill. She doesn't look half bad for her age."

Buz thought about the new terms of encounter. No, it wouldn't work, not even guaranteed full front-wise. Too messy, too complicated. "She's almost as old as my parents. I couldn't do it again. It would be too close to incest." The first time hadn't worked all that well. He got a good pop out of it, but it just didn't play, since Greenleigh wasn't up to her part and she probably even faked an orgasm. Buz could not take a chance on a second blow to his self-esteem.

To put an end to the discussion, Buz left the apartment and walked to the mail box. He left Stif to his television viewing. He was already at work on his fourth beer at 5 p.m.

There was a letter from the Peabody State University Administration, the Dean's Office. It was addressed to Stif. Buz tore the letter open.

Mr. Snedley,
A complaint has been lodged against you by Professor Darsellia Di Vaggio. She has charged you have engaged in sexist behavior in her presence and that you have committed acts of sexual aggression of which she is

the victim. Her statements have been confirmed by the testimony of several student witnesses. As a result, you are suspended from the class of English IA in which you were enrolled. You may be eligible for reinstatement if you choose to appeal this judgment. You are allowed two weeks to file an appeal. If you choose to appeal, a hearing before a disciplinary committee of faculty members will be held within a delay of three weeks.

Additionally, you are hereby formally offered enrollment in a course designed to de-program sexist behavior and attitudes. Castration Discourse taught by Professor Artesta Brackle is a six week lecture/discussion course with associated lab section that offers three units of credit. Successful completion of Castration Discourse will result in an automatic re-enrollment in English IA. If you choose not to enroll in this therapy course, your behavior will be reported to police authorities.

Buz walked back to the dump. Wow. Stif really got himself into trouble this time. He tried the back entry method with Di Vaggio and she ratted to the Dean. Now they wanted him to take the dreaded Castration course. Poor Stif. He was an imbecile, but he had some good qualities. For instance, he was loyal. And he was easily led. That was about it. He wasn't too bad looking, with his large but regular features and his thick red hair, at least according to some.

"I thought you'd get in trouble with that butt fuck stuff. Look at this!" He pushed the open letter in Stif's face.

Stif took a good fifteen minutes to read it. He was a slow reader. They had enrolled him in a remedial reading course in fifth grade, but it hadn't helped. He was just slow in the reading department. Then it took Stif several more minutes to try to understand what it was about. Finally he twigged. "Hell no! They're not gonna cut off my balls! Forget it! I'll just take a withdrawal from old Vaggy's class. It's just a bunch of bullshit anyway."

Buz nodded. He sympathized. "I see your point of view. You're right. What I've heard, though, is that Brackle's class, Castration Discourse, isn't that sort of thing at all. It's just reading and some counseling sessions and some sort of touchy-feely games."

"Well they can take that and stuff it up the back method!" Stif swallowed half a beer in anger. He burped. "Fuck em!"

Buz gave him a comforting pat on the back. "Don't take it too hard. They put a lot of guys through 'the method'. But really, it's no worse than most of the other classes at Pee. And it only lasts six weeks and you get three units, just like a full semester course."

"No way, man. I don't wanna end up doin' a floor show in San Francisco. That's what happens to trans-, trans-, trans-whatever they are."

Buz laughed. "You really got the wrong idea. It's only an intellectual theory. At least think about it. Because if they drop you out of English IA you lose three units on your enrollment and that means you'll get your Student Loan cancelled. You'd only have nine units left, history, psychology and math, and you have to have at least twelve in a semester to keep your loan going. If you take the C.D. course, you're back up to twelve. Then, after you finish C.D., you can transfer back into English IA for the rest of the semester and get full credit, like the letter says."

"I don't care. They're not going to cut off my you know whats even if they give me a Ph. D."

Buz laughed again. "That shows you have the right spirit, but it's not what C.D. is about at all. Besides, it says that if you don't enroll, they go to the police about that incident with Vaggio."

The theoretical work that was the basis of what we now know as Castration Discourse was largely done by Artesta Brackle as part of her doctoral thesis. The basic idea of C.D. was that male chauvinism had in effect castrated other persons and had left them powerless. Other persons had been transformed into eunuchs. C.D. was a socially engaged method that aimed at restoring full power to non-male persons. The goal was to *reverse* castration, not to carry it out. That was the theory. In order to carry out this goal it was sometimes necessary to retrain the attitudes of machist men, to teach them to restructure their thinking and behavior, to abandon their culture and biology determined drive toward domination and sexual aggression. This was for the good of all persons. Professor Brackle had developed the process, which utilized various unconventional methods, but certainly nothing like the "castration" of legend. Buz explained this to Stif after he had checked it out in the college catalogue under course descriptions.

"I've heard a lot of guys even enjoy the course. It has a certain erotic angle."

"I don't know, man. What if they slip up and actually

do some cutting?" Stif looked toward his waist. "Then I couldn't get it on with nobody, not even with old Vaggy."

"You don't have anything to worry about. You'd have nothing to lose by taking this course." Buz realized that this statement was a double-entendre. Anyway, he still thought Stif had certain tendencies.

"I don't care. I don't like the idea one bit."

"I'm only asking you to think about it. If you drop out of Old Piss, that puts me in a tight situation, since I'd have to pay a lot more expenses just from my own loan, for rent and textbooks and transportation and everything else. And this is your last chance to save your college education. If you drop down to nine credits in a semester, you lose your student loan and you can't go on. If you take the course, you stay on track and you can get your diploma and a good job and lots of girl friends after you graduate."

It was true that since Stif arrived at Peabody he had been batting zero in the girl friend department, if you left out Di Vaggio and Greenleigh, and they didn't count since they were way too old to be serious girl friends. Even though he was tall and slender and not bad looking, girls at Old Piss seemed to sense that there was something wrong with Stif, something missing upstairs that made him poor boyfriend material. He usually tried a direct method, a real strong come on that had often worked at Drakesville, but was pretty clearly a no-go at sophisticated Peabody. Maybe C.D. could help. It might give him ideas on a 'soft approach', since it was supposed to educate everyone against "aggression". "Okay. I'll enroll in Brackle's course. But if there's anything like in a doctor's office, I'm outta there."

"That's the spirit! I'll help you along. I'll go to the class with you and wait outside. If you think you need help, just yell."

"Thanks, man." Stif finished his current beer. "Old Vaggy really got pissed off. But it's her own fault. She gave us this idea she was a real free spirit, what in her class discussions and all. How was I to know she's more fucking puritanical than a Lutheran minister?" Stif's father had taken him a few times to a Lutheran church on Sundays, but that was when he was about five years old, before his dad cut out for good. His mom used to belong to some other group. He couldn't remember which one.

Buz relaxed. Stif was really an easy going guy. He had to be argued around sometimes, but he almost always gave in. Probably the course would do him some good. Maybe after they rearranged his brains for him, he'd cut out all that stuff in the shower, and even at night, on the mattress.

The next day's mail delivery held an even more disagreeable surprise, at least for Buz. Greenleigh had fingered *him* to the Dean for sexually aggressive behavior—referring to his role the backseat incident, even though it had been the frontal approach, not Stif's sort of thing, and voluntary for both. He too was offered an enrollment in C.D. to make up the credits that he was losing due to the expulsion from Greenleigh's Beginning Psychology course. He passed the news on to Stif, who was, as usual, relaxing in front of the TV with a few beers after a hard day of classes. "I just got the same letter they sent you. Greenleigh has it in for me. She complained about me to the Dean."

"Damn! Too bad! Fuckers got you too. Well, I guess we're both doomed now." He didn't look very upset about it. "I told you we should have gone on another ride with Greenie in her little car, 'cause that would have cooled her down, and she was like in heat or something. When you turned her down, she got so pissed she made that complaint to the Dean's Office. I think you were really too macho to go for it, two guys with an old faculty woman, even though you said it was because she reminded you of your mom. Anyway, I asked somebody in Native American class and she said that course, the Castration thing, even makes some guys more macho. She had a boyfriend who took it and he quit school and joined the marines."

Buz was not completely convinced, despite the fact that this was exactly what he had tried to make Stif believe just a day before. He was nervous. The rumors that you heard about Brackle's course, as far as accuracy, were really anyone's guess, whatever the course catalog and some students said. You couldn't be sure what sort of bizarre antics the C.D. professor and her assistants—there were about a dozen of them—might be up to. "I don't know. I've heard Brackle is a hard nose taskmaster. She can even tell what you're thinking. She learned how to interpret facial expressions during her psychology research."

"Naw." Stif took a long cool suck from his open can. "That girl in Native told me Brack's really a nice lady and totally easy. She's cool with the students and the whole course is really just something got up to show how advanced Peabody is."

"Brackle was married to Hambrick Biggins," Buz

recalled. "They say when he kicked, she didn't bat an eyelash."

"So? That just goes to show she's relaxed and mature and not a big blowhard type like old Ham."

"Okay. But I'm going to wear a cup supporter when I show up for class."

Stif thought about this. It couldn't hurt and it would be extra protection. "I guess I will too. And I'll get some metal foil and reinforce the inside."

Castration Discourse was scheduled for Wednesdays, 4:00 to 5:30 p.m. It went on later than most daytime classes. Sessions would be held in the Psychology Clinic, which occupied the basement floor of the Psychology Department building, Sigmund Freud Hall. Even though Freud was now considered to be old hat and his theories largely inaccurate, he was still honored for discovering many of the basic features of modern psychology. In particular, he had been the first to promote the idea of the importance of castration anxiety in the human psyche (it does not involve males exclusively by any means). Castration anxiety is the basis of the psychological structure of male domination, since to ward off fears about their loss of the over-valued organs, men are driven to try to control those around them.

Anxious and uncertain about what was to come, despite constant mutual reassurances, Stif and Buz walked slowly downstairs from the Freud lobby. They found the clinic door.

"I think I gotta go to the bathroom," Stif said.

"Later. We don't want to be late for the first class

meeting. That makes a bad impression and they could add on extra stuff because of it."

Soon they were sitting in an ordinary classroom with half a dozen other students. Four of them were males, one was a woman and the sixth was probably a member of one of the trans-, trans-, trans-groups, as Stif would have put it. Some of the students were there on a voluntary basis and not because of a threat from the Dean's Office. On the classroom walls were pictures of Susan B. Anthony and Eleanor Roosevelt. Everything was completely normal.

Stif recognized a couple of the other students. The trans- trans-student and the woman student were in their Native American class. This thing was going to be all right after all. Stif was relieved. He waved at the two classmates. "Hi! You guys don't got anything to worry about with this castration thing," he yelled. Neither reacted in any way. Stif only wanted to reassure them that they had nothing to fear, that the rumors about "castration" were way off base and it seemed that the class would be entirely lecture.

"They're probably volunteers," Buz explained. "So they think you're one of the enemy, like me, sent here by the Dean to be deprogrammed."

"Naw!" Stif had talked before with Tril, the transgender person, and he thought that Tril was nice and sort of cute. He stage whispered to the two students. "I'm on your side. I'm in favor of Castration Discourse. I think it's cool."

"Shut up! Are you nuts?" Buz.

"We gotta cooperate. That's what you said." Stif spoke in a low voice. "We just get through this stuff, then we get our diplomas."

Buz was about to say, after three and a half more years

and a hundred and five more units, when she walked into the room. Impressed silence ruled.

Artesta Brackle. She seemed totally normal. She was dressed in black slacks and a red shirt and a funny hat that resembled something people wore in movies about wizards. She must have been about fifty years old or something like that. But she wasn't all that dried up, especially her cheeks and forehead. They could have belonged to a forty year old. But her neck was bright red and sort of wrinkled like she could play a turkey in a Thanksgiving pageant. She smiled. The bottom half of her face smiled, although an opinion in bad faith might have called it a cruel smile. The top part of her face was frozen into an expression of anger and resentment. And why not anger and resentment? She was the victim of systematic mistreatment. She thought so. And her husband had been murdered by your society.

The class stood up. She motioned them to take their seats again.

"Well, we have a fine group here for the first meeting of section one of Castration Discourse. I see that we have people of all kinds, of all genders, all classes." This wasn't true. All were white and six and a half were guys. She paused, then let out a special announcement. "I am Artesta Brackle." It wasn't that she thought that any of the eight could be unaware of that fact, but she wanted to reinforce the point. Her *persona* as a forceful and *cutting edge* teacher was part of the pedagogic plan for the class. Not that she was egoistic, but she recognized the importance of *transference* resulting from her reputation as a leading C.D. theorist.

She looked squarely at the class. "First of all, I want to say that if any of you, at any time, for any reason, have a complaint or a concern about the way this class is being conducted, I want you to come to me. We will work through all legitimate criticisms of this C.D. class. This is your class. You are in control. I want only to be an advisor and a source of information about the theory."

The students applauded. The six guys seemed relieved. "I told you so," Stif leaned forward and told the two other students from Native. "Nothing to worry about."

"What is Castration Discourse?" Artesta put the question to the class. "What is Castration?"

Stif started to raise his hand but was blocked by his buddy. The other students all knew the answer, but they were still embarrassed by the subject matter.

"Castration is the removal of personal power and individual autonomy from someone within the framework of a society." Artesta had answered her own opening question. That was always the case at the first meetings of her classes. It was planned that way. Otherwise, the whole class time would be wasted on guessing games. "It is what happens when a human being is deprived of full membership in the community, when a human being suffers removal of rights and opportunities. Then that person becomes a social, cultural, political eunuch existing entirely for the advantage of others."

Stif sat smiling to himself. See, he seemed to say to himself, I told you so. It's all just a bunch of word junk. Like the rest of the crap.

"Who can give me an example of an individual who was forced to exist only for the advantage of others?"

"Harriet Tubman," was one response.

"Susan B. Anthony," said another.

"Me," said the transgender person.

Stif wanted to say "Attila the Hun" but he knew that Buz was watching him closely.

"The literal definition of castration is removal of the male genitals. Its fuller and more complete meaning involves removing the right of access to power from any individual within a society. The fact that the word has historically been reduced to a question involving the *testes* supports my initial statement in our text. Historically, societies have defined power in male terms. It was assumed that no other individuals could be involved. When the research that I conducted as part of my graduate thesis revealed that this was an almost universal trait in Western societies, I began to develop the theoretical framework of Castration Discourse. Castration is the condition of non-male persons within most societies." Artesta paused. The smile on the lower half of her face wobbled, then turned to a grimace. "It is not males who have been castrated. Males have castrated *others.*"

Stif watched fascinated. Yep. Just what I thought. He nodded to himself. You tell 'em Arty.

"The purpose of this class is to discover how we may reverse the effects of castration. We will use several methods. Class discussions such as we have just begun will be an important part of our procedure. We will engage in reading assignments. Our main text is called *Castration: Ending Male Domination* by Artesta Brackle. How many of you have already purchased your textbooks?"

Two hands went up. The transgender person and one of the guys.

"Good. The others will find it available in the campus bookstore, but I suggest that you buy your books now. There are a limited number of copies. The price is reduced, since this course is councilor required. By the way, I receive no royalties or commissions from purchases of this book. When you obtain your textbooks, read through to the end of chapter four. This assignment will provide a background for the discussion of the anatomical and physiological bases of some of the problems of gender."

Stif tried to read over the shoulder of the guy who already had his book. It was opened to a page of print. "It is a vitally necessary societal goal that each person feel satisfied and fulfilled within their sexuality," Stif read. The last doubts vanished. Artesta was totally okay. The class was going to be about learning to feel happy with everyone and fucking off all that sex anxiety stuff. Stif had nearly reached Nirvana.

Like the other teachers, Arta began to focus on Stif. He twigged to this. She kept giving him a sort of *intrigued* look. It might have been because of his bright, thick red hair. That always attracted attention. Also, his large, regular features often interested women teachers. Oh sure, he was good looking. Stif knew this because his mother had repeated it a million times when he was a kid and in high school. There was something else, too. Probably women digged him for his intellectual capacity. They could read it in his face.

"The third method of our class will be clinical therapy. Not all students will participate in this method. It will be conducted in the lab area." She looked toward the back of the classroom, where there was a door with a small, wire reinforced window. The class turned to follow the direction of her gaze. "Individual students will be helped by one or two assistants."

So great. Stif was so relaxed that he wished he had

a beer or two in his hands. Now they were going to get some sort of massage therapy too.

Artesta went to the blackboard. She drew a picture in chalk. It looked like a tower with a sort of cupola on top, like the pictures of churches on postcards from Central Europe. Professor Brackle turned to face the class once more. "Phallocracy. The rule of the penis. It has penetrated our society since the coming of Patriarchal culture, which in late Neolithic times overthrew the peaceful reign of matriarchal culture. Villages in Europe, the Middle East and Asia were ruled by male chiefs, almost never by females, from approximately seven thousand BCE. Even now, our culture has barely begun to change." She walked with militant step toward the small group of students. She launched on a different tack. "Do we want our culture to change? Do we want our culture to erase the legacy of gender domination?"

Nine hands went up. Stif raised both of his. This class was really going good. It was almost like first grade all over again, except they didn't all have to go to the bathroom. Stif's first grade teacher, Mrs. Donariatti had told his mother that he was a bright boy. Donariatti didn't talk much about penises, though. They had to wait until fifth grade for that.

"Gender domination is a principal way oppression in our society is organized. It is not strictly a matter of male and female. Gender domination also prevents some males from developing alternate aspects of their personalities. It oppresses gays. And it dehumanizes transgender persons. It forces true hermaphrodites into the shadows. How many of you have read the novel *Dinglebelle*, the story of a hermaphrodite who grows up among the Eskimos?"

No hands were raised. Stif usually didn't read too much, especially during Christmas. He was too busy celebrating something. Buz had heard about the book. It got great reviews. Something about a guy in Canada who had the genitals of both sexes. Weird but fascinating. Eventually (s)he becomes a Montrealer.

"Look it up in the library computer." Now Professor Brackle, her arms folded behind her back in a way that emphasized her actually quite moderate breast development, walked up and down in front of the occupied desks. "On the whole, I think this is an ambitious and very advanced class section. We have a lot to learn, though, all of us. What I hope we will learn is …" Professor Brackle stopped talking. She rushed back to the blackboard and drew a large X across the tower with cupola. "… To ban from our minds any notion of the connection of sexual anatomy with personality. There is no necessary link. Only the historically rooted oppressive tendencies of our culture have imprinted this notion on our psyches."

Stif started to rub himself between the legs as he sat at a back desk seat. No one could see it except Buz, who immediately jabbed an elbow into his ribs.

"Beyond anything else I hope the students of this class will learn to rediscover their true humanity. I hope you will learn to think of yourselves as persons and nothing else, except what you desire to make of yourselves. You have the choice of all alternatives." Arta stopped for a minute. There were tears forming in her eyes. "Read the first four chapters of *Castration* before the next class meeting. They were cut short during the process, I mean of editing the second edition."

That was it for now. The students filed out. Maybe I

should wait around after class, Stif thought. This could be like English IA. He held on to his seat.

"Let's go," Buz said. He was eager to get out.

"Don't you think I should stay after class? I think Brackey likes me."

Buz grabbed his friend's arm and pulled him up. "Save it for something else. Don't get into that sort of thing again. That's how you always land in trouble."

They walked up the stairs to the main lobby of Sigmund Freud Hall, then out into the fading sunlight.

"Looks like everybody was real wrong about Castration Discourse," Stif pronounced again. This was such a psychological relief that he enjoyed repeating it. "This is going to be a fun course. Arty is a real nice person. I can tell. I don't know how she got married up with old Hambrick. That guy was so screwed up."

"They weren't officially married. They were just living together for a long time. In fact, from what I heard, Dr. Brackle hated his guts, and he had a lot of it to hate. When he wasn't browbeating his students he was eating. He must have been two hundred pounds overweight. That's why he died of a heart attack or some kind of stroke or something."

"I thought he was killed by some guys in the parking lot."

Buz thought about this. "Yeah, that's right. But if he didn't get worked over a bit too much, he would have had a heart attack pretty soon anyway."

"So she's probably looking for someone else to fuck her," Stif concluded. He saw his chance. "All these intellectual Ph.D. people got strong sex urges. At least the women do." He had learned something from his class hours already. "Hey, maybe it's because she's not getting fucked enough that she got into all this castration crap."

Buz looked contemptuously at his philosophically underdeveloped roommate. "It's a lot more complex than that. Anyway, she's way past forty. Probably once a year is all she needs. She must have a lot of brains, though, because she invented this C.D. theory and it has a lot of backers in colleges and with people who write books. It's a new area of psychology and it explains why our society is so messed up."

"Yeah, it sorta makes sense when Arta explains it. So at least, when we understand all about that C.D. stuff, they won't have to cut anyone's balls off." The two were in the parking lot now. As usual, a large group was partying at the other end around a huge four-wheel drive van, shouting, laughing, drinking beer. Davis was there. He was the leader. He was doing some kind of a dance to music from a player, twisting around with his back on the ground while still holding a beer can. The whole group seemed to get off on it a lot.

Stif unlocked the driver's door of the Fiat. The passenger door didn't have a lock. "I got it down about old Arty now. She's not exactly a nympho. But that doesn't mean she wouldn't get a thrill out of romance."

Later that night, Stif was still drinking beer in the living room around midnight. For dinner they'd had a do-it-yourself pizza that Buz brought back from the little store. "Hey Buz," Stif asked from a sitting position in front of the TV. He was dressed only in his undershorts. "Do you think guys who get their balls cut off can still do it? I mean, can they still fuck women?"

"You gotta take it easy on the brew, buddy." He looked

at his friend, who had obviously been rubbing himself quite a bit, and at the disorder of empty beer cans around him. "From what I understand, they become women."

Since the class suspensions, Stif couldn't go to Di Vaggio's class, English IA, and Buz couldn't go to Greenleigh's class, Beginning Psychology. Now they were separated for several hours each day. Stif could still go Pysch and Buz could still go to English.

Unaccompanied in Psychology, Stif kept staring at Professor Greenleigh as she gave the group a talk down about ego development and the role of the individual in society. The ego, when hypertrophied, interfered with the integration of the individual into society. Instead of fitting in as one amongst many and working for the betterment of the physical and emotional experiences of all persons, the hyper-ego is caught in a closed pattern of narcissism. This pattern works toward the dysfunction of society and of the person concerned. Therapeutic methods had been developed. But often the hyper-ego rejects therapy because within the closed pattern of his emotions and thoughts, he cannot accept the possibility of his own imperfection. Greenleigh walked back and forth at the front of the classroom as she talked. She turned frequently, displaying her well-developed rear, clad as it was in a bright yellow dress. Stif couldn't stop thinking that he had been in there just about three weeks ago. Of course, he thought he was at the other end. She must have liked it, though, otherwise she would probably have bucked him off. That is, if she was aware of it, given the front end distraction that Buz was providing at the same time.

Finally Greenleigh finished with the ego. Now she was

talking about something called "co-experience of shared feelings". That was sort of about how everyone shared the same patterns of emotional experience, although they might develop differently in each "feel-way", something like that. Stif was still stuck on the question of whether she remembered that night and their front-rear coupling. For some reason, he was enthralled by it. Greenleigh seemed to avoid looking at Stif, probably because of her official complaint against his roommate, Buz. She used to sort of like him, Stif. At least he thought so. After all, his huge mop of bright red hair was unusual and attractive and he was really handsome.

Now that Buz wasn't there, he felt free, like an "autonomous individual" as the class text put, although this was a characteristic associated with the hyper-ego. He could even ask questions in class, if he wanted to, the sort of questions that Buz thought were dumb and likely to get you into trouble.

"Ms. Greenleigh?" Stif raised his hand. "Is anal intercourse part of the ego thing you were talking about?"

Greenie stood silent for several minutes. Even with her Ph.D. and with Frederick Douglas and Jefferson Davis prominent among her ancestors, she was confused and upset by this complete non-sequitur. Finally she put a finger to her mouth, chewed for an instant, then spoke. "What does this question have to do with what we were discussing?"

"I don't know. It's just that, if it were something that bloated up your ego a lot, I guess you should try to avoid it." Stif smiled. The other students were staring at him, probably because of his bright red hair.

"See me after class." Greenleigh went on. She was really good at doing lectures and she didn't even need any notes. Even though she probably invented all the stuff as she went along. Now there was something called "reactionary cultural survivals". And there was the "resistance to full group integration". It might not be severe enough to force therapeutic methods, but it was a real drag for everybody anyway.

Then the class hour was over. The usual student rush to the door began. Stif stayed, cramped into a desk-seat designed for someone much shorter than his basketball height. He thought he had been invited. When the last student left, he started to unbutton his trousers. This would speed the experience along. Greenie probably had another class later in the afternoon to impart knowledge to, so they wouldn't have unlimited time. Dr. Greenleigh walked slowly toward him along the isle between the rows of desks. Like Vaggy, she really wasn't that bad looking at all, considering her age. All those freckles were sort of sexy, if you thought of it that way. She had large breasts, and of course that highly developed rear end. Her stomach had a bit too much padding. He might mention it to her later. She could enroll in one of those health and exercise groups open to students and faculty, where you stretched and then ran in place in the gym, then stood on your head and worked your legs in the air. As she came close Stif stood up, not because of the dating customs of an outmoded bourgeois culture, but just to get things started sooner.

"I had to complain to the Dean's Office because of your friend's behavior. It was sexist and aggressive beyond any allowable point. And I have bent over *backwards* in an attempt to provide extra tutoring to both of you. Frankly, you need it. Of all the students enrolled in this section of

Beginning Psychology the two of you are the least well prepared for college level work."

Stif looked down. He hadn't expected just another lecture. This was hurtful to his hypertrophied ego. He could see that the waist button of his trousers was undone and his zipper was partly unzipped. He looked at Professor Greenleigh. Her eyes also seemed to focus on the disordered state of his clothing.

In Bronislaw Malinowski's epoch making study *The Sex Lives of Savages*, first published more than a hundred years ago but still relevant to understanding patterns of human sexual behavior today, the author remarked that at certain times of the year the women of the Trobriand Islands attack the men with whom they desire to have sexual relations. Greenleigh had read Malinowski. She had a much thumbed paperback copy in her desk and a leather bound volume at home in her library. Some parts of Malinowski's work are subject to dispute or are clearly outdated. Large areas, however, have remained within the canon of generally accepted anthropological and psychological knowledge.

It was not that Greenleigh was physically attracted to Stif to any significant degree. At first she thought he was cute in a funny sort of way, but his oddball behavior had definitely detracted from this appreciation. And then, there was that night in the old car ... As a pedagogue, as a psychologist, as a member of the faculty of Peabody State University, she now knew that she must find within the impressive body of scientific lore stored in her doctoral mind a way of controlling this student, so as to lead him to correct patterns of social interaction. She pulled his shorts down in a motion so brusque that she herself was surprised. She grasped his thing, the appendage responsible for so much of the dysfunction in our society. She stroked and pulled it until, barely ten minutes later, a nauseating whitish discharge shot through the air.

"Okay, so you're getting along pretty good with Greenie in Psych." Buz was talking to Stif back at the dump as they compared notes about their separate class experiences. The television was playing, although the sound was turned to a lower level than the usual eighty-five decibels. It was a hilarious game show, just the sort of thing that Stif loved to watch while he relaxed with a few six packs of beer. Remarkably, he was not yet developing a bulge around his lower abdomen. In this he was unlike most heavy drinkers of beer. It might have been due to the fact that he was still gaining height, thus increasing his ultimate chances for a professional basketball career. Stif thought so. "I had one hell of a hard time with Professor Di Vaggio in English," Buz declared.

"Oh? What the fuck did you try this time?"

"Nothing. She asked me to stay after class in order to 'discuss the situation'. That was one thing. When we were the only ones in the room she looked at me really intense-like and she asked me plain out if you and me were homosexuals."

"What!" Stif choked on a swallow of beer. "She thought we were fuckin' queers? What the hell brought that on?"

"The usual, probably. She's getting pretty old now so she has to make up excuses in her own mind about why she doesn't have any regular boyfriends. It lets her off the hook if she thinks she gets rejected because all the guys she sees are faggots. Besides, I sort of hinted at it before, at least about you."

"The hell with her! I never sucked any guy's dick and I don't want to!" Stif pounded on the unraveling carpet of the living room floor. Mentally he admitted that there had been one or two exceptions to this rule, but that happened to a lot of guys in their early years. It was the result of inebriation and confusion, and it didn't mean anything.

"She said we demonstrated, what did she call it? 'The classic characteristics of a homosexual couple'. We were always together, had few friends of 'the other sex', that sort of thing."

"She's more fuckin' crazy than I thought she was."

"It didn't help when you tried to do her up brown that time after class. She got the idea that was your usual method."

"You told me to!" Stif shouted. "You said I'd have more success with the rear approach, since I did it that way with Greenie before and she really dug it. But it was a mistake that time with Greenie! And what you told me to do with Vaggie was, what the hell do you call it now, a *fallacy*."

"Okay! Cool down." Buz opened a beer and took a top sip. He burped. Then he let it out. "I told her we were a fag couple. It's a lot easier if that's what she thinks. Now she can't claim we're 'sexual aggressors against women', that sort of thing."

"What! Maybe you're a pansy, but I sure in hell aren't. You tell her that, or I will! This isn't the first time you besmirched my honor with that crap."

"Shees! You're pretty dumb when it come to dealing with people. I told her we were a gay couple because I knew that she'd have to be sympathetic if she thought that, since it's faculty rules and they all think that way anyway. I thought maybe it would help get us off this Castration Discourse class. It's pretty gross."

"Uh. Yeah. That's right. Sorry. Pretty smart of you to think of that. So what happened? Do we still gotta go to Castration?"

"Mm. No change yet as far as that. Anyway, she got a thrill out of it when I fucked her. Then she started all over again, even though I didn't really feel like a second go. Maybe she thought she was doing therapy on me, you know, helping me be sexually normal. Mr. Urdangarin from the Spanish Department came into the classroom when we were half way through."

Stif took a jolt. "Fuck! What'd he say to all that?"

"He just said, 'excuse me' and walked back out. Darsellia said it was normal faculty ethics. They're pretty cool about that sort of thing."

Stif slouched further down as he relaxed on the living room floor. Now his head was resting on the outer edge of the old sofa. He put one beer down and picked up another. "Then we still got to do that Castration crap class with Brackle. Okay. I guess it's not all that much worse than the other stuff, after all. It's not what a lot of bozos think it is. It's sorta like daycare. Artesta's kinda nice in some ways and she likes me. You really can't blame her too much anyway for her weird theories. She spent a lotta time with Hambrick. That guy could castrate anybody's brains out."

"I heard from one of Dave's friends that after the Administration guys looked at the videos from the parking lot incident and told Brackle about 'em, she invited Davis to her house and asked him to fuck her on the bed where she used to sleep with Ham."

Despite everything, Stif found this disturbing. "I don't know if that's right at all. I mean, you gotta have some respect for a corpse, after all. Especially if he's your husband or fuck partner or whatever. I mean, what would you say if Darsellia did the twist on your grave with some other guy? Like Davis."`

"I'd say, 'poor Davis'." Buz was standing, looking at the television and drinking beer. Now he took a broader view of the subject. "Anyway, if Artie really did that with Davis, 'cause it's just a rumor, it would probably have some sort of theoretical explanation, like out of linguistics. I think she would say something like 'contempt and desecration are the ultimate respect', since they 'abstract an individual from the corrupt role that society forces him to devolve into, thereby restoring a layer of authentic meaning'. So she did old Ham a favor, or it would have been a favor if he was still alive. There's something in our psychology book like that. I read a few chapters ahead just to see what was in it."

"Wow! You really know how to get off with that hyper-structionism stuff, or whatever it is." Stif gawked at his friend for an instant before he refilled his mouth with beer.

"Post structuralism. I read about it while you were stowing away the beer and watching TV last night. That's another problem. If we're going to make it through Old Piss, get our degrees, and then get good jobs that'll make us popular with a lot of girls, you're going to have to start hitting the books. You got an 'F' on your last College Mathematics quiz."

College Mathematics, taught by Professor Carruthers, was the most difficult class for both roommates. It wasn't all just "word crap", as Stif would have put it, like the other courses. Buz was doing better than his roommate. He could graph the equation for a line or a parabola and he could solve equations for one variable, but he still didn't at all get that stuff about a "quadratic equation" and "solving for two variables". So far Buz had been pulling a C- average in Math, and Stif had at least managed a D+, due to constant coaching by Buz and copying from his quizzes. Stif's latest test scores showed he was slipping into clear flunkout territory.

That evening they were relaxing in the living room of the dump, as usual. They didn't have enough cash to go out to a beer joint, and Stif was already consuming more than the recommended maximum anyway. Buz brought up the math class problem. Stif returned with a passionate objection. "I can't pay attention in class, man! Cruddie keeps staring at me and it gives me the creeps." "Cruddie", an affectionate term used by students for Professor Carruthers.

"It's probably just because of that big bush of red hair you got. You should get it cut short. This way it makes you look like Bozo the Clown."

"No, man. Old Cruddie's a pansy and he's after me. I'm sure of it. He's just waiting to put the make on me and it's driving me up the wall, so naturally I can't concentrate in class."

Buz rubbed his chin. He pulled in a small swallow of beer. "Well, maybe you should do it with him. Then you'd probably get an 'A' in math."

"Fuck you, man! There's no way I'm going to let some

old faculty freak bugger me. I'd flunk out of a million classes first."

"Okay." Buz laughed. "I was just joking, man. Although I think you're wrong about Cruddie. The problem is you're drinking too much beer, you're getting real vague in the head, so naturally you can't study at night or remember anything about the lectures in class."

"Alright. Maybe I am going at it a bit hard." Stif put his can of beer down on the floor at a distance of at least three feet. "I'll try an' listen up better in class from now on."

"But hey. Look at it again." Buz smiled to himself. Teasing his roomie might be a way of bringing him around to a more serious state of mind. "Really, it's not totally off as an idea. Why *don't* you go see Carruthers in his office some time like when they're closing up? You know, get to know him a lot better?"

"Fuck that! I told you, I'm not getting near Cruddie for all the A+'s in China. Forget that shit!" Stif picked up his beer again and drained it at a swallow.

Buz threw his head back and laughed from the guts. Then he headed toward the bedroom. "I was just kidding again, man. No, just hit the books for real, that's what you have to do and then you won't have to bend over backwards for Cruddie."

"Culture serves as a screen." Artesta Brackle was giving her late afternoon Castration Discourse class an update on the latest research discoveries. She was wearing a large white t-shirt above her tapered jeans. There was a message printed on the front of the t-shirt: "I Am Gay and So Are You". Everyone knew that she wasn't, or at least probably wasn't, and that it was just a way of expressing solidarity or shocking people or something like that, or that maybe it referred to the latest scientific study just mentioned on the news that said researchers had discovered that everybody was really Gay. She continued. "The widespread criticism of sexism, patriarchy, domination and inequality in books, magazines, television and internet are a way of deluding us into thinking that our society condemns gender imbalance and genital driven hierarchy. That is totally untrue. Our society is built on the principle of genital elitism. Genital elitism penetrates every nook. Everything from language to toilets to the sexual division of labor is based on it." The class, almost all of it, applauded. The transgender person was confused. Stif wanted to stand on the seat of his desk and shout "hurrah!", but he knew that, as so often, Buz was close by and ready to act fast to prevent imbecility.

"Is sexuality the meaning of our existence? Is sexual anatomy destiny? Is copulation the sole reason for our lives?"

Stif nodded vigorously but said nothing. An athletic type raised his hand.

"I think sexuality can be part of life. I think it has to be."

"'I think sexuality can be part of life'," Artesta mimicked for the benefit of those who might not have heard. "To me that still sounds very much like the dominant belief that an individual's position in society must be based on her or his role in reproduction." Arta backed up and sat down on top of her desk. She looked out at her class with a smile both benign and serious. Her rear was well formed, but not excessively developed.

This was the view from where Stif and Buz sat. "When we look at a person, do we notice first what that person might or might not have between their legs? If that is what we are doing, then we are in a sense castrating that person. We are reducing that person to secondary status if the person does not appear to be flaunting a penis and pair of testicles."

Stif nodded again, but not too vigorously. He wasn't clear on what old Brackie was trying to say. It seemed like maybe a basic anatomy lesson.

Artesta was still smiling. She leaned back as she sat on top of the desk, clasping her hands in front of her knees to maintain balance. She was not aggressive or hostile to anyone. She only wanted to help establish a true and fair basis of understanding and living together for all persons in our society. "Let's be honest with ourselves and with each other. When we have an intention to practice the physical function of sex, are we dismissing an attempt to reach the real individual with whom we are confronted? And what is the objective importance of sex? Why reproduce in a world already desperately overpopulated and under-privileged? Why does our society, in the actual way in which it functions, discard individual signals of humanity in order to maintain formal gender divisions? The answers to these questions will lead us to confront the reality of reproduction-order caste divisions."

Stif was nodding off. All of this stuff was part of the current class assignment in Brackle's textbook, *Discourses of Domination and Discourses of Liberation: The Unequal Personality in Society*. Buz had forced him to read it between beer breaks the night before. Stif woke up with a sudden jerk. "Fuck Sexist Sex!" he shouted. This was a slogan that appeared on signs carried by demonstrators in a photograph that illustrated the cover of Brackle's textbook.

"I'm glad you're paying attention." Artesta spoke in a loud voice, then laughed, at the same time giving Stif one of those penetrating gazes. Now things were totally clear to Stif. Artesta was in love with him.

The mailbox had some letters in it. Buz always collected the mail. He checked the box on the way back from Abarrotes. He and Stif had come to fear the post person. If there was a letter in an official looking envelope, it was always trouble. This time was not an exception. There were two letters, one addressed to Sydney Snedley and one to Bernard Miller. They were from the Dean's office.

"Dear Mr. Miller,

Due to the fact that your grade point average for the courses in which you are enrolled at Peabody State University is below the required level (an overall grade point average of C is acceptable, although this may include individual course grades of D+. Grade point averages lower than C are not acceptable), you are required to engage in our tutorial program. You must attend two hours of tutorial each week for each class in which your grades have failed to reach the accepted level. Contact the Peabody Tutorial Center in Jackson Hall room 342 to engage with the Learning in Action Program (LEAP). Tutorial fees are twenty-five dollars per hour, except for economically disadvantaged students, who may qualify for a reduction."

Stif's (Sydney's) letter was identical. Buz (Bernard) brought the bad news back to the dump, where his roommate was typically enjoying a highly comic late daytime television show. With his eyes bolted to the TV screen, Stif laughed, drank from a can of beer, laughed again, drank again. At least he was enjoying himself while he could.

"Cut it, man. I got some mean orders from the commander in chief." He was serious.

"What?" Stif's hilarity declined through successive stages. "What's that? Can't you wait till after the program? It's a real pisser."

"We got do the tutorial." He waved the letters at Stif. "Because we're both below average. I mean, in our grades. That'll take lots of extra time and money."

"Tutorial," Stif repeated, still watching the screen, but not so happily. "Yeah, that's right. They told us about that when we enrolled. You're getting a C. What the hell do they want?"

"I got a C- average. That's below the acceptable level. And you got a D+ average. That's way below."

"Okay. But why can't we like Tudor each other?" Stif thought about what this might envolve. It could be fun. Sort of like charades in fancy dress at a party.

"Tutor, not Tudor. Tudor means something that happened in the Middle Ages. That's where your fucking brain's stuck."

"All right. Let me see the letter." Stif read. He read slowly. That was one of his academic problems. Twenty minutes later, he looked up at Buz, who was working on a beer, his first of the day. "So why can't we be 'economically disadvantaged'? My old man was a painter. I mean, before he took off somewhere."

"That's your old man, not you. Besides, painters can make a lot of money, if they work instead of boozing it up all the time. You have a student loan and you still have over fifteen thousand in credit at the bank. That disqualifies you for being disadvantaged. I read that in the Peabody College Catalogue. Same for me."

Stif looked morosely at his can of beer. "Nothing ever goes right for me." He was getting teary. It wasn't the alcohol, at least not entirely.

"Look at it this way. It could be a blessing in disguise. If we do tutoring--and the student loan will pay for it— we'll do better in our courses. That'll look a lot better when we get our degrees and start sending resumes to the big companies to get good jobs. Besides, it's more than likely we'll get women tutors, since most students at PSU are women and they do better in grades. So we'll have a chance to get to know them."

"Really? We get Tudored by girls? Great! Where do we sign up?" Stif drained his beer and opened another. This called for a celebration.

The Peabody Tutorial Center in Jackson Hall was one of those warm, welcoming places that tried to make everybody feel at home. The reception office, where you first made contact with clerks and filled out forms, was decorated with photographs and posters of great revolutionary figures. Fixed to the wall were images of Che, of course, and Fidel, Ho Chi Minh, Sitting Bull, Chompy and Malcolm X. Above the reception counter there was a large banner with two opposed photographs.

One was of Pancho Villa and the other of Richard Nixon. "Do You Want to Be This or This?" was the caption between the two pictures. The Center was not involved in politics. Their job was to help students who were doing poorly in their classes. Of course, politics could not be entirely divorced from the learning process, because political issues explained the disadvantaged condition of many students, but neither was it allowed to monopolize the syllabus. A young woman was behind the counter. She wasn't at all bad looking. This was Stif's first impression. She was short and a bit stocky, maybe somewhat overweight, but her well developed breasts made up for everything. She was Afro.

Stif rushed up to the counter while Buz was still trailing somewhere near the elevator. "Hi! I'm Sydney Snedley, but you can just call me Stif. That's what everyone else does. I'm here to be Tudored. Do we do it here or is there some other place nearby?" Stif kept looking at her chest. He also looked into a passage that led from behind the reception counter toward what must be several small rooms.

"Can you all wait one minute?" The reception clerk— probably a part-time student employee—walked down the corridor and went into one of the small rooms.

"She's probably looking for available space. You know, for just the two of us," Stif told his roommate in a breathless voice.

"You're crazy. They're just going to bring you up to speed in Psychology and Native American and Math. You've been looking at *Playboy* too much. Why didn't you let me do the talking? I just stopped to talk to a girl from English class."

The receptionist—her name was Diwanda—came

back with an unsmiling older woman. "I am Ms. Friggins," she said. Ms. Friggins looked about a hundred and twenty years old, with her shriveled body and the deep cracks in her wrinkled, drooping face. Stif was overly influenced by mere physical appearances. But, what else did he have to go by at a first meeting? "I have checked your referral from the Dean's office. Are you Snedley?" Ms. Friggins looked at the wild red clown hair.

Snedley nodded. He didn't want to speak. What if this Friggy woman tried to be his Tudor?

"You will need tutorials in all of your classes, since you are earning a grade below C in all of them. With the exception of Castration Discourse. Professor Brackle does her own tutorials. And you have been dropped from English 1A for this semester. For your other three classes, we will arrange appropriate student tutors for you from our list of qualified assistants."

"Oh." This was clearly a disappointment. Stif had been hoping that it would be just between him and Diwanda. He was too discouraged to continue looking at Diwanda's frontal development. He checked out the floor, which was covered with equidistant black and white linoleum squares all of the same size.

"And you are Miller?" Ms. Friggins turned to Buz. She clearly did not approve of either student. A couple of plain out flunks who had probably been too lazy to do their assignments or to go to class. The Center rarely had any success with this type, but they had to try. "Our computer files note that you are both at the same address and that you have both been sent tutorial letters. You, Miller, will need tutorials only in Native American and College Math. Your grades are not quite as bad as Snedley's."

"My mother graduated from Peabody," Buz explained.

"Our tutorials are arranged in six week segments, with two hours of tutoring each week for each class in which the student has not achieved an acceptable grade. Payment for the entire tutorial is required in advance. Two hours per week for six weeks. That is twelve hours for each deficient course, to be charged at twenty-five dollars per hour. You will each owe $300.00 for each tutored class." Ms. Friggins turned to go. She had almost reached the inner corridor when Stif called out in a loud voice.

"Hey! Thank you!" What a relief to Stif that he was not going to be "Frigged".

Ms. Friggins stopped in her slow path for at least seven seconds, but she did not turn around.

"Can we give our Student Loan numbers for payment?" Buz asked Diwanda.

"Sure can. But there's a 4% surcharge for using Student Loans for paying the tutorial charges."

"That's nothin'," Stif boasted.

Buz took a debit of $608.00 off his bank loan balance. Stif was taken down for $912.00.

"Now." Diwanda was back behind the counter. "Who can we give you to?" She was looking at Stif. "Since you got all your low grades in elementary level classes, all of the tutors are qualified to help. Now if you needed some help in Advanced Physics it'd be different."

Stif laughed at this clearly ridiculous notion. Diwanda, God bless her, had a sense of humor in addition to her other assets.

"Hmm." Diwanda concentrated on a page of the appointment book. The Tutorial Office wouldn't be fully computerized for another six months. Funding problems. "I think I can assign you to Hinckley. He's had experience with rock bottom students and he does real good with them."

"Umm. No. I don't think so." Stif was on the verge of panic. A guy? What the hell for? "You see, we live in a real rough neighborhood and the Tudoring has to be late at night at my place, since I work after class in a cardboard mill," he lied. "It would be dangerous for a guy to have to walk through our neighborhood way after dark."

"Oh. Well, if you're available for tutoring on week days in the early afternoon, I can give you to Lorraine. She's a third year Education major."

"Fantastic!"

"I'll put you down for Lorraine for the three classes that you need help on. If you put in the work you need to do, you'll get turned around in no time."

Stif began to rub himself between the legs. He could hardly wait to start the Tudoring with Lorraine! This type of behavior in public—the rubbing—was no longer considered indecent or subject to official sanctions in any way—very little was—but there was still a widespread if quiet prejudice against the practice. Buz grabbed Stif's arm and kept it tightly engaged.

"Then Mr. Miller. You're down in your grades in two classes. We could give you to Hinckley, unless you work at that cardboard factory too." Sarcastic tone, which Buz twigged to but Stif did not.

This time Stif nudged Buz. "Don't get into that fag stuff, man, it's not worth it," he whispered.

"I work weekends at a restaurant," Buz said. Another lie. He wanted to prove that Stif's fears about the tutoring process were fantastically mistaken. "Yeah, Hinckley would be okay, I guess. I don't know anything about him."

"He sympathizes a lot with the lower achievers."

Stif backed away from his roommate. He gave Buz a funny look.

Diwanda wrote on two slips of paper and handed them to Stif and Buz. "Call your tutors at these phone numbers to set up times and places for you all's get-togethers." She turned and walked back into the recesses of the corridor. Stif did a double take at her rapid exit. What was wrong? Probably she had something to do for, or with, Friggins. She did not strike Stif as completely normal. "That Diwanda's pretty efficient, but she's sort of a cold potato. Anyway, I think maybe her family was field workers not all that long ago so she's trying to make up for it by acting real snooty."

"You mean cotton," Buz barely whispered.

They took the elevator down to the entrance level of Jackson Hall. "What did you do that for, man? You want to get into something with a guy when you could have a girl like Lorraine? That's goin' off queer big time." Stif disapproved on moral as well as aesthetic grounds.

Buz looked at the elevator ceiling for a few seconds. He sighed in exasperation. "You really are nuts. This is for tutoring, helping us study, and nothing else. You already took Lorraine, so there wasn't any reason why I shouldn't sign up with Hinckley. They're just going to fill us in on the ABC's, so to speak. Neither of us is doing too well because we didn't have much preparation at Drakesville High. At Drakesville, you got a B if you could keep the seat warm. That's how we got our high school diplomas. If you think your tutorials are gonna be a big romance thing with Lorraine, you've got trouble coming."

"Of course it's like mainly for studying," Stif brushed off the objection. "That doesn't mean we can't be friends with the Tudors. I mean, we're all students together, right?" They walked. Direction: the parking lot. "Anyway, if you'd rather snuggle up with Hinckley, it's not my business at all. Everybody's all equal." Stif put his hand in front of his mouth to stage stifle the obvious laughter.

Buz gave his former friend a knock in the middle of the back with his fist. "You fucking mental case!"

Stif stood back and raised his fists. "C'mon man. I'm ready to take you on!"

"Ah, cool it." Buz could have floored his buddy in two seconds. Stif was taller, but much less solid. That would have got them nowhere. Buz opened the passenger door of the Fiat and got in. "Forget it. Look, I'll buy you an extra six pack tonight to make up for the hit. Sorry."

"Sounds good to me." Stif cranked up the engine, releasing a huge cloud of pollution into the already badly dilapidated environment. "You know, you're not such a total asshole at all when you want to be."

Stif knew that Lorraine would be everything he had hoped for and dreamed of. Making first contact was a bit awkward. On the telephone, he pushed the sequence of numbers that Diwanda had given him at the Tutorial Center. A young female voice answered.

Stif was almost breathless. "Hi! This is Stif."

Three minutes of silence followed. He repeated. "I'm Stif!"

"I'm afraid you have the wrong number."

"Uh-uh. They gave it to me at the Tudoring center. They said you were gonna help me in my school courses."

"Are you Sydney Snedley?"

"Yeah! Yeah! That's me. Just call me Stif. See, that's the name my mom always uses."

"I'm Lorraine Watsunga. We will have to arrange a schedule for your tutorial hours. Ms. Friggins said that you are available in the post noon hours."

"Anytime, baby, anytime."

"What time would be more convenient for you?" Lorraine's voice had dropped twenty degrees in temperature.

"How 'bout tonight around nine? We could meet somewhere, then come back to my place later to talk. I'll get the dump cleaned up real good for you."

"That is too late in the evening. As a rule I don't do tutorials after six o'clock. And it will have to be at the Peabody Library, in the Talk Center."

"Oh. Okay. I see your point of view. So, how about tonight?"

"It is already almost seven o'clock."

Stif couldn't think of an answer to this one.

"Since your course work is bordering on very unacceptable, I suggest we begin as soon as possible. Can you be at the Library at two o'clock tomorrow afternoon?"

"No problem. That way I can get out of College Math class."

"You should continue to attend your classes as before. Otherwise the tutorials will be of limited advantage to you."

"Right. But see, my math teacher is some kind of fag

and I think he's giving me the look, so I wouldn't mind missing out on that stuff once in a while."

There was a frustrated sigh from the other end of digital space. "I'll see you tomorrow at two, but in the future we will have to arrange your tutorial hours so that you will not miss class time."

"Yeah. I know, because grades are real important."

"Tomorrow in the Library Talk Center at two o'clock."

"Great! I'm way over six feet and I have red hair. You can't miss me."

Stif was lying in front of the TV, his head resting on the sofa, when Buz returned from Abarrotes. That silly, almost imbecile smile could not have resulted from the mere five empty beer cans that lay on the living room floor.

"What's up?"

"You were wrong, dude. I just talked to Lorraine and, man, it's just love off the bat on both sides."

"If you fuck up on this one, your whole education is dead in the water. Play it cool. You have to have that extra tutoring if you want to stay in school and get your degree. If something on the personal side really does happen, it's not a problem. Just don't push it. Don't make wild assumptions about your tutor."

"No man. I could hear it in her voice. She's really hot on me. Maybe she heard about my basketball career already."

Buz went into the kitchen and put the sack of groceries in the refrigerator. He came back with an open can of beer. "Okay. But get caught up in your classes. If you drop out you'll be asking people 'you want fries with that?' for the rest of your life."

"How about you? You call Hinckley?"

"Yeah. We're meeting in the cafeteria Wednesdays and Fridays for two hours each day. Two hours for each of the two classes I'm low in. I think a coffee will help me concentrate."

Stif was going to say, "I hope you two will be very happy together", but he thought better of it.

Lorraine was so terrific that Stif knew from the start that he had found a permanent girl friend. When he walked into the Library he saw a girl sitting alone at a table. She had dark blond hair and a sort of brunette complexion. In front of her was a pile of books. He saw her checking her wristwatch. Stif sat down next to her, not across from her.

"Hi Lorraine! I just knew it was you. You look really great!"

"Mm. Hello Snedley." Lorraine barely looked up at him. She glanced at some papers that she picked up from the table. "I have reports from your teachers and from the Dean's Office. It seems you need help most in ... uh ... it would be College Mathematics. You dropped from English IA for certain reasons, so you'll have to take it next semester with another teacher. I suggest you enroll in Mr. Streithalter's class. He is very good with beginners. Then you have a report from your Native American instructor. You have a bare D+, so you'll need quite a bit of extra studying there too, as well as in Beginning Psychology." She looked up at Stif. He was smiling as before. There was a dreamy look in his eyes. She looked away. "The Dean's report shows that you are enrolled in a class called Castration Discourse. What is that exactly?"

"Oh that. It's nothing, really. I mean, it's not what you think. See, it's just this course that Professor Brackle thought up to teach us how all kinds of people are oppressed in our society because they're different and that kind of thing."

"But what sort of things happen in the class?" Lorraine was disturbed by the course title, like a lot of Peabody students. She wanted to be entirely reassured so that she could drop a suspicion based on nothing more than the unusual course name. She was sure that Peabody could not have a class that was really nasty. After all, she had been at PSU for three years and she had earned an A average. Her teachers had all been very capable, likeable and socio-politically engaged.

"Oh. Well, I just started the class. It's really sort of fun, kind of like when you were in daycare. Artesta's like a big fun mom." Stif looked at Lorraine's neckline. She was wearing a dress and the tops of her breasts were in clear view. They weren't large, like Diwanda's, but they were very well formed and firm looking. "Gosh, Lorraine. How'd you like to go on a date after class? I got my own car and we could go anywhere." Stif was thinking of the drive-in and one of those dark residential streets near the old downtown.

"You can call me Ms. Watsunga. Our contacts will have to be for tutoring purposes only. Ms. Friggins is very strict on that question."

"Um. Okay. D'you want a coke? I can get you one from the snack bar."

"No. Let's look at your Psychology text." Ms.

Watsunga picked up a copy of Doctor Greenleigh's *Discourses of Domination and Discourses of Liberation: the Unequal Personality in Our Society.* "This is a good text. I've been looking through it. It's not the one I had when I took Psych, but it seems highly interesting." She leafed to Chapter Four. "Do you understand what is meant by 'varying impulses to non-conventional methods of interpersonal intercourse'?"

"Yeah. Oh yeah. I got that part." Stif nodded, smiled. The breasts.

"What does it mean?"

"It means, well, as far I understand it, sort of doing it, you know, the rear end method."

"The what?" Lorraine looked directly at him. She was not smiling. She was shocked. Even so, she was really beautiful, sort of Oriental looking.

"Well, you know. It's what Gays do in bed, and some other people too."

"This text passage refers to means of communication and interpersonal involvement, not sexual intercourse."

"Oh. I guess I missed that. No wonder I got the question wrong on the mid-term. Greenie spent a lot of class time making sure that we knew all about the anal approach. Maybe that's how I got confused."

"Yes. Did you read chapter four, the chapter on 'Alternate Ways of Personal Interaction'?"

"Most of it, yeah. I think so."

"I think you did not understand it." Ms. Watsunga looked through the pile of textbooks in front of her. "It will not be possible, Snedley, for me take you line for line and word for word through all of your texts. You are going to have to put in a good deal of work if you want to catch up in your classes.

Tomorrow is Wednesday. Let's meet again on Thursday. I want you to re-read chapter four in your Psychology book and chapter," Lorraine looked at her papers again, "two in Native American. As far as College Mathematics, you might as well start at chapter one. So that's at least four chapters in two days. Do you think you can handle that?"

"No problem." Stif looked again at her neckline. "I'm really motivated."

"I hope." Ms. Watsunga stood up. She held the textbooks in front of her chest between her folded arms. "Goodbye for now."

"Hinckley's an okay guy. He knows what he's talking about and he was able to clue me in on my weak points in Math and English. He just has one semester to go and he'll get his Bachelor's Degree in French. Only one thing bothers me. He keeps trying to put his arm around my shoulder, you know, to show that he's a real good buddy, probably." Buz was telling about his experience with his appointed tutor. Stif put his hand over his mouth to stifle a laugh.

"Yeah. Lorraine's real brainy, too, but outside of that she has a pair of tits you wouldn't believe. I mean, they're not humongous or anything, but they're just totally perfect. She didn't try to put her arm around my shoulders, though. I think at this point she's playing hard to get. I guess that's the usual sort of thing, except if you're real hard up like Di Vaggio and Greenleigh. I'm trying to get Lorraine to go on a date with me. You know, direct to the hamburger drive-in, then to some side street, that sort of thing." Stif took a large suck from his can of beer. He puffed his chest out.

"Fine. Just don't do anything dumb. And remember to save some time for studying. Hinckley told me to re-read a couple of chapters in the Math book and the Native American book. I already started on it. I think I missed a whole lot the first time around. Hinck's a real whiz at algebra, and he sure knows a lot about history, you know, oppression, people's rights, revolutions, that sort of thing."

"Sounds okay." Stif grinned to himself. He was glad he didn't get stuck with Hinck. It was better not to say anything, but he really came out ahead of Buz on the tutoring project. He tossed his empty can into a corner of the living room and started on another one. "Lorraine asked me to read three chapters between now and Thursday. I guess I'll start tomorrow. I got too much to do tonight." He burped for emphasis.

"The interaction of human sexual physiology and structures of class and gender inequality." It was late Wednesday afternoon and the Castration Discourse class had just begun. Artesta Brackle was talking to the students. There were only five now. One of the guys had dropped out. He had run away to join the navy. "Typical male pattern behavior is determined by a hormone secretion called testosterone. This is a drug that induces aggression, violence and a drive to dominance. Watch." Artesta flipped the light switch and the classroom, since it was underground, turned completely dark. Then she pushed a button. A video began to play on a screen mounted against the blackboard. In the video two large moose—they may have been elk—fought by locking horns and twisting their heads from side to side. They separated then met head on again a dozen times. It was a gruesome scene. Stif began to feel nauseous. He grabbed Buz's arm in a desperate groping for reassurance. The moose could kill each other and splatter pounds of blood and flesh everywhere. In the background of the video screen a herd of moose or elk cowered. Probably they were females. No horns. Then Artesta stopped the video. She turned the lights back on.

"The effects of testosterone are partially controlled in human society by cultural inhibitions, by the repression of behavior that is harmful to the prospects of group survival. This does not prevent patterns essentially similar to that which we have just seen in the moose mating ritual from taking place. Human males, driven by excessive levels of hormone excretion, follow the same patterns of combat and display, the same drive to attain sexual domination of females. The result is a situation in which those who are not dominant males are marginalized in their human development and psychically and physically victimized."

The transgender person, Tril, raised a hand. She spoke softly and tearily. She had been emotionally triggered. "Isn't there any treatment available?"

"There is. Several therapeutic paths are being investigated. In the lab section of this course we are experimenting with a form of physical therapy that can reduce testosterone secretions to a level that is less likely to drive susceptible persons to harmful aggression." Artesta turned out the lights again. The video was back on. Now gigantic hippopotamuses were fighting it out in some primeval swamp. Stif held Buz's hand. He watched in anguish. Only the light from the video revealed to others in the class, notably Artesta, how Stif's features were twisted by an infantile anxiety.

"So what's y=x+7?" Stif was reading the math text and scratching his head. "I don't get how letters can be, like, equal to each other."

"They're not." Buz pointed to the equation. "It says that y is equal to x *plus* seven. X can be any number. So whatever x is, y is seven more."

"Oh." Confusion spread on Stif's face. "Then they're not equal after all, right?"

Now Buz was starting to doubt his own understanding of elementary algebra, actually pre-algebra, which wasn't well developed at all. "Stop trying to make it a lot harder than it really is. The point is that you take a number and you find it on the x-axis of the number field, then you add seven to it and you find *that* number on the y-axis. You look for the intersection indicated by both numbers and you mark it with a dot. What you get, when you get a lot of dots together, is the graph of a line."

"Oh. Okay. I get it a little now." Stif looked at the text page again. "Why the hell don't they just draw a line in the first place without going through all that other crap?"

Buz slapped his own face and pulled his hand downward in a gesture of futility. "Man, you *are* dumb. I mean, for real. An equation is a way of describing a curve—it can be a line or anything else—in mathematical symbols. What you draw on the number field using the equation is geometry, it's a shape. See?" Buz pointed again to the text.

"Oh, yeah. Okay, you're right. I never done too well in math. I'm a lot gooder in English."

Buz started to hum. He didn't want to give himself an opportunity of answering sharply. This would further discourage Stif, who was not a high flyer in morale outside of basketball. For the first time he had definite doubts about whether the university project was going to work out for Stif. You had to have a C average to graduate from Old Piss. They pushed you into tutoring when you were under a C, probably to impress the Feds, the money guys, after all those rumors in the newspapers about PSU being a "fake university". If they put in a lot of effort, if Buz and Lorraine pushed hard, they just might be able to shove the dolt over the finish line. It was iffy.

"Okay. Solve the equation for y if x is 3."

Stif thought. He drank from his beer. "Y is 7 more? So if x is 3, then y is ten."

"Right! Right! Now you're catching on. Brilliant, man. At this rate you'll make Einstein look like moron in no time."

Stif opened another can of beer. "I gotta cool off a little. My brain's starting to overheat."

It was Thursday afternoon in the Library Talk Center. Stif and Lorraine had met for tutoring. Stif put his arm around Lorraine's shoulders, just to show that they were friends. Lorraine brushed it off with a two second delay.

"Look, Sydney. I think you're a nice guy in some ways, but this is strictly for business. You're far behind in all of your classes and if you don't begin to concentrate on your academic work you're certain to fail."

"I know. The Dean sent me a letter. But I don't see why we can't concentrate and be friends at the same time."

"All right. Let's say we're friends. We're good friends. Now let's get down to work. Did you read the chapter in Psychology?"

"Sure I did. That makes twice. I'm starting to know whole parts of it by heart."

"What are 'varying impulses to alternate methods of intercourse'?"

Stif—Sydney—thought for a moment. He should know this one. "It doesn't have anything to do with that anal stuff, I'm positive about that. Oh yeah. It means something about how you want to know people, but you're scared to just go up and say hello because your parents were a bunch of neurotic rats, so you figure out other ways of starting up a conversation."

"That's not exactly correct, but you're heading in the right direction. Intercourse in the sense in which the word is used in the text means interaction between individuals. There is beyond doubt a sexual dimension, although the persons involved in an interaction may be unaware of it. The sexual impulse, the libido, is probably acting through other types of interpersonal behavior. This is called *masking*. At some point, however, the sex factor will expose itself. It will become clear to all the persons involved. The sex factor is *visualized* through exposure. Do you understand this concept?"

Stif nodded. "Yeah. Seems pretty clear." He was *visualizing* Lorraine's breasts through the *exposure*.

"Now you really did it. I always thought you were dumb, man, but I never realized you were some kind of psycho." Buz was holding a letter in his hand. He was standing in the living room of the dump while Stif, as usual, sprawled on the floor amidst a clutter of beer cans.

"What are you talking about? I didn't do anything." Stif looked at the floor. He might have been counting empty beer cans as a math exercise.

"This is a letter from the Dean's Office. Another one. It says that Lorraine Watsunga has filed a complaint against you."

"Lorraine! Let me see that." Stif tried to grab the letter from Buz's hand. "Me and her are real good friends. She even said so."

"She made a complaint to the Dean. She said that you were guilty of sexual aggression toward her. She said that you behaved in an obscene manner toward her and that you tried to induce her to engage in sexual acts during a tutorial session."

"What? No, that's really nuts. That's some kind of mistake. It's a *fallacy*."

"'According to the complaint lodged by Ms. Watsunga,'" Buz read from the letter, "you exposed your sexual organs to her while you were seated in a car parked in the University parking lot."

"Oh, that. You see, since the Talk Center was really crowded and noisy that day, I asked Lorraine if we could move to the Fiat to study. It's a lot more quiet there, away from all the blab."

"That doesn't explain the part about 'exposing your sexual organs'!" Buz was angry this time. He made no effort to contain it. After all that he had done to try to get his friend Stif a university education, helping him at every turn, guiding him, advising him, protecting him, Stif had done something that was criminal, felonious and expellable.

"Um." Stif was contrite. He even put his beer can down. "It started with something she was talking about during the Tudoring session on psychology. See, she told me that interpersonal relations were always motivated in some way by a sexual angle. She said that the sex factor was frequently 'visualized through exposure'. I naturally thought she meant that if I really liked her I'd do something like that, so she could *visualize* it after I *exposed* it."

Buz hit himself on the head with the palm of his hand. "I don't understand at all what you're talking about."

"It was in our Psych text. You know, the one Greenleigh wrote, *Discourses of Domination and Discourses of Liberation: the Unequal Personality in Society.* See, the book says that there's a sexual factor in every relationship. It has to be *visualized* through *exposure.* Lorraine made a real point out of it. So of course I thought I'd give it a try. After all, we were all alone in my car, we weren't in Grand Central Station."

"You're just lucky Peabody is a really liberal school, maybe too liberal." Buz looked again at the letter. "They're going to give you another chance. This is your third. First there was that anal intercourse gambit with Di Vaggio. Then there's the fact that you're flunking out because you spend all your time drinking beer and watching TV and hardly ever study. Now you were waving your big dumb wanger at Ms. Watsunga, who was trying to tutor you."

Stif started to whimper. "Lorraine said we were good friends. She said the sex factor had to be 'exposed' so it could be 'visualized'."

"That part of Greenleigh's text is not supposed to be taken literally. It's on the level of *concepts* and *symbolism.* It doesn't at all mean flapping your dick at a tutor. Maybe you really knew that and you were just trying to sneak a base run."

"Uh-uh. Honest, Buz. How the hell would I know

that? When she was talking about it, she seemed, you know, straight out."

"Okay. Anyway, like I said, they're still giving you another chance. Of course, you are never to see Ms. Watsunga again. If you happen to pass by her on campus, just look the other way. 'She will receive the full fee for her planned tutoring services as compensation for your outrageous behavior. Nine hundred dollars will be debited from your student loan.' That's what the Dean's letter says. Then, you will have to continue in the tutoring program, this time with Hinckley. Third, the Dean's Office says that since you are already enrolled in Artesta Brackle's Castration Discourse class because of that backend deal with Di Vaggio, 'you will be required in addition to participate in one-on-one lab sessions'. That's a kind of therapy supposed to suppress really bad sexual behavior. If you refuse to participate, 'the matter of your behavior toward Ms. Watsunga will be referred to police authorities.' That's how the letter ends up."

"No. I don't think that's a good idea at all, calling the police in. I'll do the lab and Hinckley. It couldn't be all that terrible. Didn't you say Hinckley was a nice guy?"

"Yeah. If anything, he's too friendly."

Stif picked up his beer and took a long suck from the sharp tab hole. "Man! If I'da knewn a college degree was so fuckin' complicated, I'da stayed ignorant!"

"I never used the word fag." Another letter arrived two days later. It was addressed to Bernard Miller. "How could the jerk do this to me?" Buz was nearly in tears.

"What's going on now? Who'd you call a fag?" Stif was sitting on the living room floor studying Greenleigh's

Discourses of Domination and Discourses of Liberation: the Unequal Personality in Society. Only one beer can was visible on the floor space around him.

"Nobody! This is a letter from the Dean's Office. It says Hinckley filed a complaint against me for something."

"What'd you do?" Stif was curious. He craned his head toward the letter.

"Whatever happened to the presumption of innocence? I didn't do fuckin' nothing!" Buz let his arm and the letter drop to his side. "Okay. What Hinckley said, what he told the Dean's office, was that I physically abused him and used derogatory expressions that were of a 'homophobic nature'."

"Why the hell did you do that? You're supposed to be the one with all the brains." Stif put the textbook away. He went to retrieve another beer from the refrigerator. College was a bitch. You had to try to get some relief from the shit.

"I *didn't!* That's just what he fuckin' claims. He's wrong. Okay, so what happened is that I was in a tutoring session with Hinckley and he sort of had his arm around my waist, like the better to look at the book we were both studying at the same time, but I threw him off, 'cause I don't like guys getting that close to me. It doesn't feel right. I said something like, 'get off me, you freak'. He says I said 'fag', but it's not true. Maybe it's because he's hard of hearing. He wears a hearing aid, you know."

Stif nodded. "It was a misunderstanding, like with me and Lorraine. Happens to everybody. How come Hinckley's hard of hearing?"

"He told me something about it. He's about thirty. He said that when he was twenty-two or so he was in a rock band and they really blew the fuses on volume, cause that's what the fans wanted, so now he's about fifty percent deaf. Anyway, just because of that stuff, the push and the hard of hearing thing, the Dean's Office wants me to volunteer for the lab session in Brackle's Castration Discourse class, since I'm already enrolled in the classroom section because of what Greenleigh told them about that romp in the Fiat. They say it would be 'an appropriate therapy measure'. Otherwise they go to the police and claim I committed 'homophobic violence'."

"Haw! See?" Stif smirked in self-satisfaction. "You got caught in the same fuckin' bullshit trap as I did and I didn't even do anything very much. When I was a kid my mom always said it was okay for guys to beat off. She said it was normal."

"You're not a kid now. And that doesn't mean in front of a college tutor." Now Buz went to collect a beer from the kitchen. He heard Stif yell after him.

"But Lorraine and me were in love! At least I was."

Buz was back in the living room. He had a beer in each hand. He handed one to Stif. That made three open ones. "Well I wasn't, not with Hinckley. Look pal, we're in this together. We'll just have to play along with them, since they got everything stacked against us. Like I told you from the start, you got to put up with a lot of shit to get through college, but it's worth it in the end. Anyway, like you said, maybe the lab thing won't be so bad." Buz sucked in a significant portion of beer.

Suddenly Stif smiled. He had an idea. "Why don't we both do an appeal? The letter they sent me said I had a right to appeal, didn't it? You could do the same thing."

"Naw. You always lose on those. That's the general

opinion on campus. The Dean and his assistants are judge, jury and executioner when you file an appeal against them. And you're suspended while the appeal goes on. Then they call in the police afterwards and you're really in trouble."

"What's in this lab session stuff anyway? I've heard some weird rumors about it." Now Stif was worried. The cheerful assumed optimism about the class was gone. He rubbed himself between the legs. "I don't want to lose everything. I'm too young to be a unique."

"I'm not sure, but it has to be okay. Peabody is a respected university. It's dedicated to 'educating our nation's youth'. They couldn't go way out on a limb with something really perverted."

Stif stayed after class when Dr. Greenleigh's Psychology hour ended. Buz wasn't there because he was still banned from the class due to that incident in the car with the professor, which was the supposed cause of her complaint to the Dean. Stif had a question to ask. Greenleigh ought to know. She knew everything about sex, that is, from the psychological, sociological and anthropological points of view. As luck had it, the lecture for that day concerned a subject related to the question he wanted to ask. That would make it easier. The professor had gone on for forty-five minutes about a tribe living in some group of islands somewhere off the north east coast of New Guinea. The important point, the take-home message, was that the men of the tribe, before they were allowed to engage in sexual relations with the women of that cultural group, were forced to strip naked and were beaten by female members of the village, sometimes even being partially castrated in the process. Malinowski himself had observed this cultural practice. It was understood as a way of placating the dominant female spirit, which was believed to be opposed to sexual relations between men and women on grounds that were poorly understood by anthropologists but that sociologists and economists believed to be related to the role assigned to women in that society (essentially digging, planting, weeding, and harvesting yams and cooking them for their recognized male associates.) Since the men would be supported by their partners (it is important to avoid using terms such as "wife" that are derived from Eurocentric societies to describe the institutions of very distinct cultures) for the indefinite future, it was economically necessary that the process of collecting a female helper be made forbidding for the men. Otherwise the supply would quickly dry up and some of the men would be forced to support themselves, which was considered degrading and shameful. There was a ritual that took place near the end of the "pre-marital" ceremony. After hours of chanting and dancing the male's foreskin was pierced by a sharp stick that had been left in the fire until it was glowing red. This ritual symbolized a reversal of sex roles, because now the male was "penetrated", including with a good deal of the pain and other undesirable results that could accompany the female role in the sexual process. It completed the ceremonial appeasing of the female spirit.

After the lecture, the students, except Stif, had filed out of the classroom silently, looking dazed and miserable, but enlightened. As she watched them leave Professor Greenleigh knew that she had got the point across. Now she smiled as she sat at her desk. Stif came up.

"Hi." Stif gave his best smile. "Fantastic lecture you gave, Dr. Greenleigh. Wow. I never knew anthropology was so interesting. It really explains a whole bunch of stuff we never knew about before."

Greenleigh beamed in contentment. She considered Stif not quite a friend—he was hardly her equal intellectually, as well as being an associate of the unsatisfactory Buz—but as a student she understood. He was educationally underdeveloped to an extraordinary degree. However, he retained a primitive somatic strength. There was that ride in his old car, just one incident among many others during her career at Peabody, but it had unveiled, that is, exposed, an important part of his personality. She had not reported his role in that event to the school authorities, since it was an authentic and highly personal expression (unlike his friend Buz, who, she believed, had purposefully taken advantage to force a sex encounter). He possessed a genuineness that so-called "primitive" peoples were often said to possess. Well, not his personality, since persons no longer had personalities (according to currently received theory, minds were only a staging area for a large number of fleeting and intersecting discourses that were grouped in a way that could not form what had traditionally been considered "the personality"), but many of his psychological mechanisms were genuine, that is, naïve and largely undetermined. Stif was too primitive to be held responsible.

"Do you have a specific request or question, Sydney?" She had discovered from the class roster that this was his personal name.

"Yeah. I got a friend who has a problem, sort of a psychological problem." Stif had had the brainstorm of trying to enlist Dr. Greenleigh's help in subtracting himself and Buz from Artesta's feared lab sessions, even though Greenie herself was the plaintiff in Buz's case. He hadn't let Buz in on his plan to approach Prof. Greenie, since he would obviously have vetoed the idea, lacking as he was in creative thinking.

Talifa assumed an attentive posture. "Yes?" Stif was a boy who needed a good deal of prodding in most areas.

"Well, it's sort of like this. I have this friend that has to take a course that has this lab session, a one-on-one lab session that's sort of embarrassing. You have to sit in a lab room and then there's some kind of therapy procedure that's supposed to remove sexual aggression or something like that. This friend is scared about it. Could you, like, talk to Dr Brackle—she's the teacher of the course—and get her to change the assignment to like maybe a term paper or an essay or writing a hundred times on the blackboard or something?"

Talifa frowned. "You are referring to your friend Miller." Buz had been cashiered from her College Psychology course not for turning down another invitation to an anthropology film, but because of his rude, sexist and vulgar behavior during the trip to the first documentary. It was socially unacceptable.

"Um. Well, it's not only him."

"I have access to your academic records. I know that both you and Miller have been required to enroll in Castration Discourse and in the lab session."

Talifa didn't beat around the bush. Stif looked at his shoes. He was ashamed of his enrollment in "the course". Even the name of the course was embarrassing. "It's not really what a lot of people think. It's all about how certain people in our society are being denied their full rights sexually." Stif paused for a second. "That's what it seems like to me so far."

"Then what is your concern?"

"It's the lab part. This friend of mine and me both have to take it. Nobody seems to know exactly what it is and there's all these strange rumors you hear from some of the students."

Dr. Greenleigh—Talifa—Professor Greenleigh put her hand on Stif's shoulder. He noticed again that her breasts were well developed and not badly shaped. It was a good thing nobody could take notes on what was happening inside your mind—or could they? "Your anxiety is misplaced, although this anxiety is entirely to be expected. In our society all matters concerning the sexual aspect of human life are anxiogenic. In fact, Dr. Brackle has fully informed members of the Psychology Department about the course, its content and organization, including the lab sessions. It is an excellent course and has been short listed for an award from the Association of North American Psychology Departments. Dr. Brackle herself is internationally acknowledged as a seminal thinker."

"Oh." Stif was still unsure but he couldn't think how to express it. His gaze shifted from his feet to Talifa's breasts and back again. "But see, we're kind of anxio-, anxio-something about it, well, I guess it's mainly the course title and the rumors about it."

Professor Greenleigh laughed. Her neat, small and well preserved teeth were displayed favorably. "Always that castration fear. Freud was right. We will discuss the Oedipus complex later in our class. Freud's conclusions, although substantially altered by more recent research on a number of points, have been shown to be correct in several important areas of clinical investigation. Males, especially younger males, are frequently subject to a fear of losing their male potency, which is equated with the loss of male genitalia. This results from a fear of the father, who is thought of as threatening castration. For the immature male, beginning in early childhood, the father is seen as blocking the way to the sex object, that is, the vagina of the mother, and as preventing the realization of the sex aim, which is usually genital penetration. These fears are irrational. They are products of your sub-conscious insecurity. They are primeval fears. The curriculum and methods of Dr. Brackle's lab course have been approved by the Department, the University and the Association. They are entirely benign and beneficial to the student. In fact, the course is designed to help remove the source of those fears."

"Oh. Okay." Stif was visibly relieved. Now he concentrated on her breasts. There wasn't any need to keep on looking at his shoes.

"Psychology is a science of enlightenment. It helps to open our minds and our feelings to ourselves so that we understand why we think, act and feel as we do. Even an introductory college course can help us change."

"Yeah." Stif was grinning with relief. "Too bad Buz got kicked out of Psychology. Anyway, I'll try to transfer some of the enlightenment to him."

"Excellent." Dr. Greenleigh winced at the word "Buz". Buz had behaved very badly, worse by far than most of the others. He had taken advantage of a weak moment and then refused to offer any reciprocity, such as beginning a longer relationship with her. "Excuse me, but now I have to prepare for my next class."

"Oh, yeah, sure. Sorry. Thanks for the explanation. It really cleared up a whole lot of complexes."

When she was alone in the classroom, Professor Greenleigh chuckled to herself. She hadn't been perfectly ingenuous in her description of the lab course. But then those two twerps deserved it after that disgraceful "hay ride" they had taken her on. Anyway, she had heard that they were really a couple of closet gays.

During their first tutoring sessions Stif was able to interact positively with Hinckley, who had replaced the mistreated Ms. Matsunga. Stif was eager to please, because he believed Hinckley had influence with the higher ups, with the Psychology faculty, and maybe even with the Dean, since the chief disciplinary officer of the University had chosen him to replace Lorraine Watsunga as Stif's tutor, and there were probably a lot of other tutors he might have picked, since Peabody was full of flunkers and needed an equal number of tutors.

Hinckley's first name was Henry. Stif was astonished. He had never known anyone named Henry before. The tutor preferred to be called "Buck" or "Bo". They met for their lesson in the Talk Center of the campus Library. Buck smiled and they shook hands. He was not a bad looking guy at all. About thirty years old, thick dark brown hair and a trim heard on his cheeks. Stif sat opposite the tutor at a Library table. Buck suggested that they not talk about the problem that he, as a tutor, had had with Buz. "It may have been partly a misunderstanding, but it was very serious nevertheless. It would be better if we did not refer to the matter, since it would distract from effective tutoring."

"Yeah. Okay." Stif thought that there wasn't anything to say anyway. Buz just got a little out of control.

"Well, where do you want to start?" Hinckley was smiling. "The whole world is before you."

"I guess, since Lorraine and me did most of our studying about my Psychology class, we ought to try some English or Native American."

"Excellent." Hinckley took up the textbook for the course called Native American Space after the Catastrophe: 1607 to the Present. He opened to the first chapter. He looked briefly at the page, then turned to Stif. "How would you describe the first encounters of the European conquerors with the Native American peoples?"

"I guess they must have been pretty hairy."

Hinck laughed. "Yes. They must have been that. But how would you describe them with a term that expresses a definite concept?"

Stif was trying to cooperate. He had only skimmed the first chapters of the text, and the class sessions with poor old Hambrick Biggins had been so traumatic that he had repressed the memory of the class subject matter. He remembered the shouting and insults. "Interpersonal interaction," Stif tried.

Hinck laughed again. He had an easy laugh. He was an easy going guy. Stif thought about what Buz had said about him, but that hardly mattered now with the lab session hanging over their heads. "That's from your psychology course. I was thinking of the word *imperialism*. Imperialism describes the attempt of one country or nation to impose itself on other countries in order to appropriate for its own sole benefit the resources and the labor that belong rightfully to the original inhabitants of the colonized land. A colony is what results from a successful imposition of imperialism. This country is a colony that was created by the interlopers from another continent, with disastrous results for the original inhabitants."

"Hm. Yeah. I remember that part. Hambrick went on pretty heavy about it."

"Professor Biggins? Yes, that was one of his areas of professional focus. It's a shame he was driven to suicide by problematic personal relations. He was a brilliant scholar."

It was murder, Stif knew. The whole campus knew it by now. It was best to stick to the official version, though. Stif and Buz were already on the Administration shit list. If they didn't behave now they'd never graduate. And if they didn't graduate, they'd never be able to pay back their Student Loans (there was about twelve thousand owing for each of them already, since the bank had debited an entire year's tuition in advance, plus costs and commissions.) Buz had drilled these facts into Stif's normally insouciant head. "Imperialism," Stif repeated. "Yeah. Now I get the concept. It's like if I take over your apartment and then make you take out the garbage."

"Exactly. Although, it is very much more complex than what is suggested by your clever comparison."

Suddenly—it might have been because of Hinckley's relatively formal speech, which reminded him of Lorraine—Stif began to cry. He was thinking of her. They had been so close. It really had been love, at least on his part. "Sorry, Mr. Hinckley." Stif wiped his eyes with his shirt sleeve, then blew his nose on the same. "For a real short time I was thinking of a friend who used to help me with class stuff."

"Call me Buck, please. You are referring to Ms. Watsunga? You used to meet here, I think."

Stif nodded.

"And you were actually very fond of her."

Stif nodded again. He sniffled, cried some more.

"This venue is obviously unfavorable for you emotionally. I sympathize with your feelings, which are evidence of a finely developed sensitivity. I think you were judged too harshly, although we all must abide by the decisions of the Dean's Office. I would suggest moving to a different study venue. Can you think of a place?"

"Beer joint," Stif blurted out. Hinckley was tempted, but he quickly discarded the idea. The Dean's Office would have considered this a major transgression, if they heard of it. Comparatively, Peabody was not very advanced as a university, but it was an institution and it insisted with all its force on control, surveillance and discipline. Read Foucault. And things were not likely to change before the revolution.

"Not practical. The light is always dim in those places. We will have to consult passages of your textbooks."

"How 'bout my car? It's parked in the school lot. There's still plenty of light out and it's real quiet and alone in that corner of the parking area."

They walked along the college paths. "I sympathize with you, and with your roommate too, despite the incidents," Buck messaged softly. "You've both got behind in your studies, and probably you have not applied yourselves adequately, but I think you are sincere and determined students. In all likelihood, your pre-college preparation was poor and of course there are many distractions that can keep you from concentrating on your course work. You're a bit younger than Buz, aren't you?"

"About two years," Stif lied. He was older by four months.

They stood outside the old Fiat. Stif took the car keys out of his pocket. He opened the back door of the car. "Let's get in backwards. There's more room."

Back in the dump Buz was reading the Syllabus and Schedule for Castration Discourse, which had been handed out to students by Professor Brackle at the first meeting of the class. The class met for one and a half hours each week on Wednesdays at four o'clock. Lab sessions were held at five-thirty, just after the regular class meeting. The lab room was in the basement of Sigmund Freud Hall, just behind the classroom. During C.D. class Buz had noticed that the door was always kept locked, and that there was a small window in the upper part of the door with crisscrossing wires in it. Buz was sitting on the living room sofa. He was careful to avoid contact with the protruding sofa springs. Stif was taking a break. He was watching a television show, some sort of adventure story about people who dressed in animal skin bikinis and travelled by swinging on vines from one tree to another.

"Wow," Stif marveled. His speech was slurred. He was already on his tenth beer. Studying books put a lot of psychological pressure on him and he needed the relief. "How'd you of liked to get around like those guys? Seems like it'd be a kick and a half, man."

"Yeah. Cool. But listen. According to orders from the Dean's Office, we both have to sign up for at least one session of C.D. lab. The therapist will decide whether we need further treatment. The fall semester ends in about six weeks and we have to get this done if we want to pass the C.D. course we signed up for and stay enrolled at Peabody."

"Okay," Stif agreed vaguely. "Ha! Ha! Ha!" Stif was laughing at a comic television commercial in which a dog piloted a motorboat across a lake toward a giant pile of a particular brand of dog food. Stif was fingering a chain necklace that he now wore. It looked like gold. A gift from Hinckley. "Buck's a cool guy," Stif had explained to account for the jewelry. "At least in some ways." He had to be careful when sitting down.

Buz tried to ignore this. It was better not to be too curious. They had to make definite course plans. "Either you or me will have to reserve the C.D. lab course for next Wednesday. They only take one student for each session, since it's a one-on-one learning experience. That's what the C.D. teaching assistant told me." The C.D.T.A. was a third year psychology major called De Hooper. Reports had it that he looked at you with these small eyes that appeared to be evaluating you as a fascinating specimen. He was supposed to be a genius. That's what everyone said. He was already working on his planned senior psychology thesis on Foucault. He could read French and was able to get at Fouc's work in the original language. There was all this stuff in it about the history of clinics, behavior control and discipline, that sort of thing. "I think you should go first."

"Me? No, you ought to do it. You're the guy with the brains. Then you could clue me in on how to avoid the pitfalls."

"The reason I think you should take the lab course first is that you're good friends with Hinckley and he's a friend of De Hooper's. If Hoop tries anything real experimental on you, you could complain to Hinck. He gave you a gold chain, didn't he? On the other hand, Hinckley filed a complaint against me. That's why I'm on the lab list in the first place."

"Yeah." With one hand, Stif felt the fine filigree of the necklace. "Okay." He opened another can of beer. "I guess it really couldn't be too bad. I'll make sure De Hoop knows I'm a friend of Hinck's."

"Right. We have to take every advantage we can if we want to get to the goal. Once we both have a B.A. from Peabody State, then we can choose any jobs. Starting with at least six figures."

It was six-thirty, Wednesday evening. Stif walked slowly toward the parking lot where the Fiat was resting as usual. He felt a good deal of discomfort after the C.D. lab course session. De Hooper was an odd sort of guy. Stif didn't know if he was queer or whether he was just sort of crazy.

At the beginning of the therapy session, Hoop had explained the theory. Stif was seated on a sort of examination table in a small windowless room in the lab area. He was wearing something that resembled a hospital gown. This was to allow freer movement of his body during the therapy exercises, he was told. He was given a plastic cup filled with a "calmative solution" at the start of the session. It sort of zoned you out, he found.

"The problem," De Hooper began, "is that an excess of testosterone can induce behavior that is aggressive and even violent. It can also influence the brain in a more general way, making it susceptible to a kind of thinking that propagates gender biases." Hoop was a good deal shorter than Stif, but he was much stockier. He had a heavy build and wide shoulders. Probably, like a lot of other people, he would not have made a good basketball player. As far as his appearance, you immediately noticed a lot of dark, wiry hair in front of his ears and below them on his cheeks. His mouth, nose and eyes were arranged in an irregular pattern, with his mouth very broad above a protruding jaw and small dark eyes looking over the bridge of a thick nose. He had a low voice. The overall impression was somewhat disagreeable. It was those small, intently focusing eyes that you had to try to avoid. Otherwise he seemed friendly and sympathetic. "Did you read the chapters in Artesta's book on the subject? Her *Castration: Ending Male Dominance*? It's a brilliant work, even more advanced than the textbook she wrote."

"Yeah, I read it. I didn't understand all of the things she talked about, but I think I got the main gist." Stif was alarmed when he noticed that he was developing an erection under the thin hospital gown. It had nothing to do with sexuality. It was a spontaneous erection. Still, it could give the wrong idea.

De Hoop was staring at the spontaneous biological effect. His small intense eyes were focused like lasers on the point pushing against cotton fabric. He nodded. "It's a difficult text and C.D. is not at all an easy course. There are many focuses in it that are still being debated in the specialist quarterlies. The main material, though, is well grounded. Many persons in our society receive less than equal treatment, sometimes very harsh treatment, due to gender classifying. It has been widely demonstrated by research studies that high levels of blood testosterone are one factor in producing gender insensitivity and aggression."

"Yeah, yeah. I remember that part." Stif kept looking at the walls and wondering whether he was going to get some sort of massage. It often helped basketball players after an intense workout.

"And of course you know that testosterone is produced principally in the testicles."

Yeah, Stif knew this. They had that much even in high school biology at Drakesville. So what?

T.A. De Hooper took an object out of the pocket of his white lab coat. It was a small ring made of soft plastic. "This is a device that has produced positive effects in the great majority of persons being treated."

Stif walked slowly and with an odd gait in which his legs were far apart, like a cowboy used to long hours on horseback. He eased himself behind the steering wheel of the Fiat. He started the engine. The rocking motion caused by a badly tuned engine provided a sensation like a massage that temporarily eased the discomfort. Fortunately, he probably wouldn't have to sign up for a second lab session. De Hooper told him that the first treatment is successful in well over half of all cases. They would observe his behavior in order to confirm the positive effect. Hinckley himself had already recommended privately that Stif receive no more than one treatment, or at most two, but ideally one, because of the possible side effects of more aggressive therapy, including impotence.

He decided not to tell Buz about the details of the therapy. If he told Buz, he would probably drop out of school immediately even if it meant working at a hamburger joint for all eternity, and then Stif would be the only one to suffer the misery of the "Hoop" treatment and its possible consequences. Misery loves company. Stif had only a vague idea of what had happened, since he was almost dozing when the session began, but his guess was confirmed by later research on the Library computer. De Hoop had fitted a plastic ring above his testicles. This was in fact a device frequently used in sado-masochistic circles. It cut off the blood supply to the testes and could lead to full or partial necrosis of the tissues involved, possibly resulting in sterility and impotence, depending on the length of time the ring was left in place.

It hadn't hurt at the time, because of the medicine Hoop had given him, "a relaxant". This had produced a dazed and insensate condition for as long as the treatment lasted.

Stif was lying flat on his back on the living room floor. His head was raised just enough to drink beer without swallowing the wrong way and to allow his eyes to focus on the TV screen, although from a lower angle than usual.

"How'd the session go?" Buz asked. He had already noticed that his friend seemed not to have suffered any obvious ill effects.

"Oh, not too bad." At the same time Stif winced and rubbed the sore place. Buz interpreted this as just another indiscrete example of pre-masturbation. "It didn't last long. That De Hooper guy gave me a lecture. He sort of puts you through a hoop, but I'm still breathing." Stif took a long, consoling pull on his beer. He felt little discomfort now, as long as he didn't move too quickly.

Buz laughed. "Okay, so you got through that one. Now you're fixed. From here, you just go straight ahead and soon you'll finish your first semester classes with twelve units to your credit. Right on schedule."

Small tears formed in the corners of Stif's eyes. Buz interpreted this as a maudlin condition resulting from excessive beer consumption and the joy caused by the knowledge of a successful semester. In fact, Stif was trying to decide whether he should tell his mother about it. That is, about the "fix". If he was really "fixed", he wouldn't be able to have grandchildren. That is, children who would be grandchildren for her. Maybe she ought to know right away so she could get used to the idea. Even worse, of course, Stif wondered whether he could still get it on with women. If he couldn't like, get it up, then he might as well be one of those transgender intersex persons who marched in funny clothes in San Francisco. It was Buz's fault. Buz had talked him into going to that lab session. He ought to have known that there would be more to it than massage. The goddamn textbook practically told you about it!

The next morning in the shower Buz noticed that his roommate's erection was only partial and that his ejaculation was watery and even contained some blood. "You've been beating at it too hard, man. Let up a little or you're gonna jerk your nuts clean off."

Stif didn't respond to this joke. He got out of the shower and stood in the middle of the flood plain of water caused by the lack of a shower curtain. He dried himself with the stained and stiff towel. He looked at Buz, who was still soaping and singing merrily. Buz had a shorter member, but testicles that were larger, for now, anyway.

Buz noticed that Stif, not dressed yet, was looking at himself in the bathroom mirror while he applied dabs to his face from a small glass bottle that obviously contained cosmetic make-up. "What the heck? I always knew you were kind of weird, but now it looks like you went totally around the bend. Make-up? It isn't even Mardi Gras yet. Not that that would make it okay."

Stif shrugged. "You're not in with the new thinking. A lot of guys wear make-up now. It makes you look better, so people react more friendly to you. Hambrick wore make-up."

"Hambrick's dead," Buz recalled. "Besides, he only did it because he liked to do things that humiliated people, including himself."

"Yeah, that part's true. I guess he probably stuffed his face till he weighed three hundred pounds just to get even with himself because of something about history. Anyway, there was an article in the Daily Peabody yesterday. It said guys on campus were using make-up, even borrowing their girlfriends' make-up, because it was the new culture thing. And cause it made them look younger and girls are going for guys who look younger now."

"Well, okay. How about some lipstick? I could borrow some from Mrs. Jones upstairs. D'you think dark maroon would match your make-up?"

"Fuck you! I'll pick out my own shade of lipstick." Stif put on his clothes, taking care to pull his shorts up slowly. He wasn't going to tell Buz that he had a tutoring session with Hinckley that afternoon, hence the make-up.

On the way to the campus—Stif asked Buz to drive—they talked about classes.

Stif spoke as he looked out the car window at the passing rows of dilapidated and decayed wooden houses. He felt dreamy. He wanted somehow to make Buz feel that the C.D. course wasn't so bad after all, except for that little lab experience, where it was all over pretty quick. That was sort of the way he felt now. He started with English. "Since that run in with Di Vaggio, I'm out of English IA for the semester, but I can take it next term. Lorraine said I should sign up for Mr. Streithalter's section, since it's easier, he's barely past the 1A stage himself, since he got his degree from some nowhere school in eastern Idaho, but I don't see why I gotta take English at all. I speak it pretty damn good already, right?"

"I think you could polish it up a bit. Anyway, you wouldn't have got all that much out of Vaggy's class. I'm still in it and all we do is read these stories about pimps and fast food workers. Vaggy doesn't care about grammar. She says 'all usages are equal'. We have to 'oppose elite class possession of language' by 'substituting ways of speaking in diversity'. It makes writing essays real easy and everybody gets an A, but I don't think it'll help out writing a job experience summary for an employer." Buz.

Stif perked up a bit. "Doesn't sound bad. If only I didn't of tried to do her up brown, I'd still be signed up. That was one of your smart ideas."

"Yeah, well, you were having a real problem doing it the ordinary method and that was pissing her off and making things hard for everybody in class." Buz concentrated on the road. There were lots of potholes and junk that you had to drive around. "Maybe you'll have better luck with Streithalter."

Stif missed the double entendre completely. Then he thought for a moment. He had another idea. Now was the time to put in a plug for C.D., for Buz going to C.D. "In a way, I think it's not so bad after all that we both have to take C.D. We get three units for it and it's only an hour and a half of class per week for six weeks. And usually you only have to go to one lab session.

"Artesta's a smart old bird, you gotta give credit where it's due. She's the one who wrote the book for the class, the one called *Castration: Ending Male Domination*. I sorta looked at it and it's not too easy to understand, but it's not at all about what some people think. It tells you a lot of important things about what's going on all over. You know, like how too much testosterone can lead to violent behavior and genderist attitudes so all kinds of people get their equality transgressed over. Artesta Brackle's the one who first came up with the theory on it."

"Wow, you really swallowed the whole wad." Buz stopped the car to let a bunch of kids cross in the middle of a block. A few threw light objects at the Fiat. "I mean, most professors can make up word crap like that as they go along, like when Brackle's book says, 'no text can have any stable, definite or discoverable meaning. The reader is the only author'. It says nothing means shit. And it sounds real classy. That's why I memorized it, even though, overall, I think we're in a for real brainwashing program. Yeah, though, you got a point. Brackle's got brains, there's no way around it. But I think it's true about those other rumors, that her brains got perverted as crap as a result of her relationship with old Professor

Biggins. It must have been hell doing it with that sack of potatoes on top of you. No wonder she's gotta have revenge on the world."

"Everybody says Ham couldn't do much. He was like a impotentate." Stif suddenly winced and held himself between the legs. Was it possible he too wouldn't be able "to do much" anymore? Tears started to collect in the corners of his eyes. He checked his face in the rearview mirror to see if his makeup was running.

Buz nodded. "It's true, I guess, that C.D.'s a real intellectual class. Although, to tell you my take on it, I think it's kind of scary down there in the basement of Freud. It feels like a scene from one of those mad psychiatrist movies."

"So, did you sign up for the lab session yet? Time's running out, like you said."

Buz brought the car to a screeching stop at a red light on Jefferson Boulevard. "Uh, not yet. I'll do it tomorrow, after class."

"There's really not a whole lot to worry about. It's all fixed real quick." Stif looked at his own reflection in the passenger side rearview window. He looked nice. Almost pretty. In fact, quite pretty.

Wednesday had come around again. The last class of the day for both roommates was C.D., Artesta Brackle's award-winning educational project. *Timesnews* had run another feature article on it just a week ago. "Changing Minds, Changing Behavior". It would be reprinted for use in thousands of high school and college classes.

Stif and Buz sat at the back of the classroom to take advantage of the relative isolation. Artesta was sitting in the front of the classroom, on top of the teacher's desk as students entered. Stif tried to sit on Buz's lap for additional protection. Buz shoved him off. "Ouch!" Stif rubbed himself where it still hurt. You didn't have to worry about being indiscrete in C.D. Even in-class masturbation was considered acceptable and normal, especially when Artesta turned off the classroom lights in order to show video sequences. Stif would not have gone that far, not yet anyway. "You hurt me, you big moron!"

Finally, the hour come round at last, Artesta stood up from the top of the teacher's desk, where she had been resting her well-formed although incipiently massive derriere. "I want to ask every student in my class a question. Think about it before answering. The question is this: if you could have every kind of success in life, in career goals, personal relations and sex enjoyment, but to obtain it you would have to switch sexes, would you accept? Raise your hands if you would be favorable to such an exchange." Two hands went up immediately, the transgender person and the large woman called Dumbo by some. Then another hand went up. One of the guys. One of the guys who still was one of the guys. Then another.

Buz panicked when he discovered that only he and Stif had not raised their hands. It was going to get Arta swooping down on them. He looked over at Stif. His roommate's hand was now raised, although at half-mast, as if he were ashamed of something.

"I'm just playing along," Stif whispered. "For protection."

Artesta walked slowly along the rows of student desks. The students were smiling. Most of them were smiling, although it might have been only a protective adaptation. Buz was definitely not in a joyous mood. He had left himself wide open by not saluting. But how could he not? He wasn't going to play ball with that trans-stuff, no matter how alone he was.

Professor Brackle continued her line of march. Buz looked at his open textbook. He appeared to be searching for answers. His nose almost touched the book paper. "Is gender assignment a qualitative marker? Does it alter the essential experience of life?" She was standing in front of Buz's desk.

Head down, Buz silently mouthed phrases from the text. Stif answered, out of a sense of comradeship and help and a feeling that he had no more to lose. "He's looking for the answer in our book. He wants to get it right."

"Let him answer. Bernard? Do you have an answer to these questions?"

"Umm. I'm not sure." Buz looked up but would not meet the Professor's gaze. "It's an important question, real complicated."

"It is an important question. I would just like to remind some of you that your response to these questions is one of the reasons that you are in this class today."

Stif bent over at his seat and covered his lap with crossed arms. Artesta reached over and patted him on the shoulder. She knew he had already been through C.D. lab. She observed carefully to note any signs of discomfort. "You're pulling an A so far in this class," she told Stif and smiled with real sympathy. "You can be proud." He regretted there might be something else he would not be pulling.

"Mr. Miller. Have you reached a conclusion?"

"I think that, yes, it could make a difference in a lot of ways. Gender, that is. I think it changes a lot of things, not necessarily for better or worse but just different."

"This is what is called Classic Gender Identity Syndrome (CGIS). It can bring with it a host of subjective assumptions. To make those assumptions evident and to change them into an appreciation of gender and sex that is unbiased is a major purpose of this class." Artesta turned and walked toward the front of the class. "By the way," she told the group, "Mr. De Hooper will be out sick for at least a week. I will be conducting the lab sessions until his recovery."

In fact, De Hooper had suffered a serious genital injury during an exploratory sado-masochistic session with a non-student friend. He had been hospitalized.

"Bernard, could you stay after class this afternoon? There is something on your assignment schedule that has not been completed."

Genderism is probably the worst atrocity of the century. For many advanced thinkers, it makes the other dangers threatening our common humanity look petty in comparison. Anti-genderism is not what is commonly referred to in the information media as "anti-sexism". Anti-sexism is only part of the complex of behavior patterns denounced by anti-genderism. Some researchers have gone so far as to maintain that the so-called movement opposed to sexism is itself part of the enormous network of legal, cultural, political, economic and philosophical wrongs that form the nebulous of *genderism*. Anti-sexism denounces inequality of treatment according to sexual identity. At the same time, it inevitably reaffirms the existence of a binary difference inhering in biological gender. The ideology of anti-genderism demands an end to all notions of sexual differentiation in every area of human, animal and vegetable life, including, of course, the erroneous idea of anatomical differences. It promises a new era of universal justice, equality, happiness and pleasure. Dr. Brackle always emphasized these points during the initial discussion phase of the lab sessions that she operated.

Buz agreed to get his lab session over with that Wednesday, the first day of Mr. De Hooper's unfortunate absence due to sickness. It was disagreeable and obnoxious, even more so because Artie seemed to have it in for him now, but, as he constantly reminded Stiff, you had to put up with a lot of shit if you wanted to get to the goal.

In a small room inside the lab area behind the C.D. classroom, Artesta offered him several pills, "to induce a relaxed and receptive state." For some crazy reason she asked him to put on a certain type of gown that reminded Buz of the time he had to have his tonsils taken out. Certain medications, the Professor said, could facilitate the learning process: several recent studies had confirmed that a certain palliative that was usually given in liquid form was less effective than tablets. It seemed to Buz that he almost lost consciousness just when the Professor was finishing her long discourse on the subject of genderism and its many avatars. He was nearly asleep, until the very last part.

Stif was waiting in the Fiat. He was searching in the rearview mirror when he finally saw Buz approaching the car. Buz was walking with that same cowboy gait. Poor guy. Stif felt guilty. Maybe he should have warned his friend, but wasn't the whole college thing Buz's idea anyway? Shouldn't they have to share the negative experiences too? Anyway, didn't they have to go through with it in order to insure their enrollment, eventual degrees and long term futures?

Buz opened the passenger door and eased himself on to the front seat of the car. He looked confused, angry, and in a good deal of physical pain. At first Buz wasn't sure that Stif had undergone the same lab experience that he had just endured, but when he remembered the details of Stif's behavior in the last few days, all doubt dropped.

Stif started the Fiat and drove away. He thought of saying something conventional like, "how'd it go?" or "not too bad, was it?" but this would have been an obvious red flag.

As they pulled up on the grassless lawn that constituted the front yard and parking lot of the building where the dump was located, Stif finally ventured, "I found a few aspirins help."

"Fuck you, man. You knew about it!"

Buz was dragging so badly that Stif tried to support him at the shoulder as he crossed the living room. He got a hard push in return for his efforts. Buz made it to the bedroom, lowered himself slowly onto the mattress, turned to face the wall and fell asleep.

Buz must have got it worse, Stif thought when he was back in the living room. Buz had had to face the creator of the lab course, the brilliant Professor Brackle, seminal thinker and innovative practitioner, and not some two bit assistant like the perverse Mr. Hoop. Still, life had to go on. Stif armed himself with an open can of beer and prepared to face the television.

Two hours later, in the midst of a respectable clutter

of empty cans, Stif was bravely laughing at a sitcom when Buz reappeared. "Oh, hi. Try a shower with warm water. I did and it helped a lot."

Buz went wordlessly into the kitchen and came back drinking from a plastic carton of milk. He went toward the bedroom. He walked slowly, carefully measuring every step.

The next day was an at home day. Buz was in no shape to go to class and Stif felt obliged to stay home to provide whatever help he could. Sometime after midday Buz got up from the bedroom mattress and walked into the living room. He was moving more normally now. Perhaps the injury had already healed, at least somewhat. But when he let himself down on top of an arm of the sofa with a painful grunt, it was cleared that he was still in a lot of pain.

Buz sat silently for several minutes. He glanced at the idiotic program now showing on the telescreen, then stared intensely at Stif, who was sitting at his usual place on the floor in front of the machine. "You set me up for this," he said quietly but firmly.

"Huh? No. Uh-uh." Stif shook his head.

"You went first, so you knew what went on in the lab sessions and you didn't warn me."

"No. I mean, I didn't know either. I mean, I thought you knew already." Stif looked frantically around the room.

"You let me walk right into that lab session and you knew Brackle would try to smash my balls."

"I didn't know what to do, man. I didn't know they'd try the same thing on you. You talked me into going through with that lab session. You said we had to do all this crappy stuff at Peabody, to get our diplomas and graduate, all that junk."

"If I had any idea of the kind of thing Brackle was up to behind that locked door I never would have let you sign up for the lab session and I never would have gone myself. They said it was a sort of individualized counseling and some special exercises."

"Yeah, me too. They told me the same." Stif smiled. It looked like they were reaching an agreement on collective peace.

"Bullshit. You already went through the session and you knew exactly what they did there. You didn't warn me." Buz was getting angrier as he talked on. His voice was louder, harsher. "We were friends all the way through high school and we were in this college project together. I had to pull you with both hands just to get you this far, and for your own good."

"I thought you knew all about it already. It wasn't really all that bad. I feel almost recovered now."

"You were in real pain after your lab session but you didn't say a word."

"Well, it's sort of an embarrassing thing to talk about, having your nuts crunched."

"So why the hell didn't you let me know! You fucked me over, you fuckin' bitch!"

"Well, I mean, I had Hooper. I mean, I'm sorry. I don't think he gives the same treatment as Brackle. He likes to go easier, at least at first."

Buz had it with talk. He had reached a level of anger that could not be diffused by any amount of phony discussion. Although it cost him a good deal of pain in the groin area, he landed a quick hard kick to Stif's chest.

Stif rolled to one side. The blow had taken the air out of him, but he stood up and hit his former buddy in the jaw with his fist. Buz staggered and almost collapsed. He shot back with a right to the side of Stif's head.

"You fucking bastard!"

"Fuck you, you shithead creep!"

After half a dozen blows by each, Buz lay on the living room floor clutching his lower abdomen and groaning. Stif ran out the door.

Stif walked in the neighborhood streets. He felt like a ghost, like his body had been left behind somewhere and his mind was just wandering alone. Okay, Buz had a right to be mad as hell. Still, Buz had betrayed their friendship. Yeah, it was wrong not to tell, but he was a victim, too, maybe more than Buz, who had the brilliant idea of going to Old Piss in the first place. And he felt betrayed. Without any warning, the bastard had given him a hard kick in the chest. It was still sore. There was no reason to do it like that, kind of a sneak attack. Guys fight, but there's something about being buddies, too. You don't just off and whack a pal without any warning. Brackle and the Dean and Hooper had suckered them both into the "therapy session" where the real goal was something that was "effectively almost a partial emasculation", as their text had described a supposedly benign treatment for Classic Gender Identity Syndrome (CGIS). So that they would become more obedient and do and say and think just what they were told. The objective was to lower their "excessive testosterone levels, the ultimate source of aggression, conflict and unruly behavior". The text had explained all about it, but in a vague way. There was even a reference in Brackle's book about "articles in specialist quarterlies" and "hopeful experimental results", all that crap. Stif had read it, afterwards, at least partly.

He walked on. Since Stif had always travelled to and from the dump in the car, he had, up until now, no real idea of how run down and low class the neighborhood was. Trash filled the streets and the yards. Windows were smashed and repaired with cardboard. Old sofas filled porches and blocked sidewalks. People were living in their cars. Children ran about screaming, trying to destroy fences, trees, houses and each other. But they always seemed to have enough money to buy snacks and drinks loaded with sugar.

It was true. He hadn't let Buz in on the secret. He had let his friend walk right into what was almost a sort of "partial castration as therapy" session because he didn't want to be the only one to suffer humiliation and possibly permanent damage because of "the treatment". It was pretty crappy behavior. It almost put him in the same league with Brackle, Hooper and Hinckley. Now he knew where he was going. He walked into Abarrotes. His eyes immediately found what he was looking for. A pint of whiskey from the shelves behind the checkout counter. He also picked up a large bag of taco chips and some sort of green sauce in a plastic tub. He paid the man behind the counter with his last twenty dollar bill and took the change. Subsistence withdrawals from the Loan were limited to three hundred and fifty-eight dollars a month. It was already the twenty-sixth or twenty-eighth of the month.

He was heading back to the dump. He knew he had

to go back. He had to check to see if Buz was okay, that bastard who had caused it all but hadn't deserved what he got. Stif cracked open the pint and took a first short sip. He didn't like it. He much preferred beer, but the case called for strong medicine. Whiskey fueled tears rolled down his cheeks.

Buz was not in the living room. Stif peeked inside the bedroom and saw him lying on the mattress, on his back. He was probably awake, unless you could sleep with your eyes open. Stif went back to his customary spot in the living room, where he could rest his back against the lower part of the sofa and have a clear view of the television, itself resting on the floor. The screen showed that some sort of disaster had happened on campus, an explosion or murder. Police were bustling about in their heavy padded shirts, squad cars were twirling dozens of lights in all directions. Camera crews were taking it all in. Stif switched channels. Life could be awful. Why look at it for entertainment?

Stif took a strong suck from the pint bottle. Now he decided to make the ultimate sacrifice that one pal can make for another. On the feet of a cat (Stif had often been both praised and ridiculed for his feline movements), he crept into the bedroom. Buz was awake. Crouching, Stif moved close to the mattress. He put the bottle of whiskey on the floor close to the edge of the mattress. Then he rested his thin bottom on a corner that was not covered by the blanket.

"It's my fault," he managed to snivel between sobs. He stared at the wall with its faded green paint. He didn't want Buz to see that he was crying. It was obvious, but at least he didn't want Buz to think that he wanted to be seen crying. "I didn't tell you on purpose. I didn't want to be the only one."

"The only eunuch?" Buz asked in a toneless voice.

"I don't think the effect lasts forever, at least not completely. It's already starting to come back for me. I can almost get a hard on now."

Buz ignored this. "Can you imagine if we can't get it on with girls again, ever again, forever?" Buz had the pint bottle in his hand. He drank, although he didn't like whiskey either. He didn't really even like beer all that much, at least not as much as Stif did. "I mean, what if we can't do any fucking thing at all again except try to wank it off soft?"

Stif didn't have an answer to this one. He was just glad to see that his buddy was talking to him again. He put his arm on Buz's shoulder. Maybe they should give it a try now. Wanking it off soft. Or at least maybe he, Stif, should. He could show how much he had recovered already. Stif rejected this idea. It was gross and uncouth and maybe even perverted, and his friend Buz was nothing if not polite and well mannered.

The bottle went back to Stif. Stif swallowed dry, then poured at least an ounce into this mouth. He coughed, gasped. "That would be fuckin' awful. I suppose then we'd have to become monks and I'm not even a Catholic yet. Lorraine is. Maybe she could give me catechism lessons or something."

"You're not supposed to see Lorraine any more. If you do, they might make you go through the treatment again." Buz winced in pain and he grabbed an area below his solar plexus.

"Yeah. Well, if not Lorraine, then maybe one of her

friends. Anyway, I don't think the effect is permanent. I remember Hinckley told me that treatment to control *machismo syndrome* oughtn't to, well, I think he said *degenderize*. I didn't have any idea of what he was talking about at the time."

"Forewarned is forewise," Buz said in a low, hopeless voice.

Stif pressed the whiskey bottle on his friend again. "Here, this'll make you feel a lot better."

Buz took another small sip. "Just get me a beer from the refrigerator. If I drink a few beers at least I'll know whether I can still piss."

"Sure. Anything for you, buddy."

Five days later, including the weekend and Monday through Wednesday, they were back at the Peabody State University campus. Buz still believed in the value of their education at Peabody, in spite of the experience they had just gone through and even though, at this point, he knew that the PSU curriculum was mainly a kind of swindle with some mayhem thrown in. Stif, as always, could be led by the nose. The afternoon class was College Mathematics. Buz skipped his morning English class. He felt he couldn't face Di Vaggio right now. She probably knew about "the treatment". Faculty had all kinds of secret records on you.

The lecture given by Professor Carruthers made it clear that they were way behind the others in the class syllabus. Now the rest of the class had finished studying quadratic equations. They were starting on differentials and integrals. Neither Buz nor Stif had used their convalescent time to keep up on assignments. They stared uncomprehendingly as the teacher drew graphs and wrote equations on the blackboard. It was a different language.

"I gotta get started on the math book again," Buz said in a low voice. "Maybe I can pick up on this. I don't remember studying any of this stuff before."

Stif stared at the blackboard. His mouth hung open. His skill in figures had bogged down badly years ago during junior high school division and multiplication. "Yeah. How many chapters behind are we?"

Buz flipped through textbook pages. "Four, maybe six." He frantically rechecked previous chapters.

Then there was a pop quiz. The professor handed out sheets of paper printed with ten questions.

Buz and Stif looked at the questions with full non-understanding. Stif was trying to read his quiz sheet upside down. Buz re-orientated the page for him, not that it made any difference as far as comprehension. After twenty minutes the quiz papers were called in. Buz and Stiff signed their quiz sheets. Otherwise they were blank.

In the campus cafeteria, Buz took a deep pull on a large paper cup containing coffee. "At least I can still piss. I suppose I ought to be grateful for that."

"Yeah," Stif agreed with an earnest series of nods of his head. Like most people, he was unable to recognize satire.

Neither spoke for several minutes. Stif sucked loudly on his coffee. He knew that this was bad manners, his mother had even made a point of it, but at least it was a diversion. He wanted to put off thinking about *it*. "It" was the fact that it was Wednesday and they were expected to attend their Castration Discourse class that afternoon, even after having "successfully" completed the lab sessions.

"I think we got a right to skip it," Stif finally said. "I mean, after the crap they put us through, nobody sane would go back."

Buz felt the same about the Course, but he also knew that grades and credits had to be maintained, otherwise they would get the boot as flunkers and they'd have to start paying their Loans back right away, and without any chance of getting good paying jobs. He was still committed to higher education. "I think we at least ought to sit through it. Anyway, it's not the lab session. It's just the word crap. I'd say hell no to any more lab sessions, but we should try to get the course credits that we have coming. Let's sit as far from the lab door as possible. If Brackle and Hooper try any funny stuff, we'll know what to do."

They walked with a funereal gait to the basement of Sigmund Freud Hall. A crowd was gathering outside the classroom door. Only police and other officials were entering and exiting. "Wow! What the hell happened now?" Stif was silently hoping that Brackle had attempted actual murder and might at that very moment be publicly displayed on all the media.

Tril, the transgender student was standing next to them. Tril had been the first to arrive and had heard all the rumors and even seen a few peculiar things. "It's that Mr. De Hooper, the lab assistant. I didn't like him from the first. He always gave me this really weird look like he wanted to cut … anyway, the police took him away. I saw him in handcuffs. He looked like he just stepped out of some horror film. There was blood on his head and hands. I'm not kidding. Real blood! I can tell the difference from ketchup, blood's darker and more sort of oozy." Tril, the trans person, was a good friend. Tril liked to help people. That's just the way Tril was.

Stif raised himself to his full six feet three and a half inches and tried to see above the heads of the crowd into the classroom. It was totally wrecked up inside, with something that looked, at least to him, like ketchup smeared around. "Wow." Stif was not in the least aware that he was again repeating a cliche exclamation and he would not have cared anyway. "Did Hooper actually try to murder Artesta? I mean, Hambrick got done in something like the same way."

"No dear." Tril shook her head at this off the wall suggestion. "Professor Brackle has not yet arrived. I don't think she'll come. Here, that is. The police probably telephoned her and told her what they found. Ricky was the first one on the scene and he called campus security right away on his phone." Ricky was one of the students attending Brackle's C.D. lecture class at the insistence of the Dean's Office, as a result of some obscure tussle in a women's dorm shower area. He was also fond of transgender students. Not because they were better or worse than any other students, but just because they were different, or maybe not even different.

Before long the details of the media event were assembled and the University student body and faculty, plus maintenance personnel and cafeteria staff, were shocked and amazed. No one had been murdered. There had evidently been a serious injury, but the victim was expected to recover and perhaps be even better than before. Ricky, the Dean's student, had gone into the empty classroom. He had discovered that the door to the lab area was ajar. It had not been properly shut and had swung open. Many of the doors in Freud were like that. Out of curiosity—since conflicting rumors about the lab zone were circulating on campus—he peeked in, then walked in. A lab session cubicle abounded in blood. There was blood on the floor. There was blood on Mr. De Hooper. There was blood on someone lying on an examination table. On the floor were two small objects that forensic experts later identified as human testicles.

The next day's edition of the campus newspaper, The Daily Peabody, contained no mention of the "event", as cautious reporters called it. They always tried to maintain the Peabody image, for the better advantage of students and teachers alike, and for the good of the entire learning community. Self-censorship was futile, however, as the internet and television sources were already full of it. Of the "story". Mr. De Hooper and a non-student friend had gone too far in their erotic research on the subject of machist aggression. Hoop had actually proceeded to a real life orchidectomy. "Trag", as the victim was referred to in the media, since his last name was at first unknown, although it was later found to be tattooed on several parts of his body, was expected to recover. He told police investigators that he regretted the event, although he would probably have sought something along the same lines from a licensed surgeon eventually anyway. He was a transitioning transsexual, M-F. It had been voluntary on Trag's part.

Professor Brackle used the following week—since

she was relieved from her normal teaching load due to the emotional distress that she had suffered as a result of the events, which occurred in the lab area associated with one of her classes, although she had not been present—to prepare an article for *The New Advance*, a professional psychology periodical. In her article, which was well received by the psychology community and other interested persons, she maintained that the unexpected event was highly regrettable and could never be repeated because of increased security measures at the Peabody facility, but that it was an "explicit demonstration of the reality in which the aims of *machismo* are captured by its broadcast intentions through a process of undenied self-fulfillment lying among pre-developed contradictions."

Faculty tended to ignore the occurrence, although there were five letters as well as two articles from Peabody Profs published in the next edition of *The New Advance*. They took up the thesis articulated by Professor Brackle, challenging it in part but on the whole completing it and recognizing its incisive analysis and seminal significance.

Trag was out of the hospital after four days of treatment. Trag said he felt basically okay, only a bit lighter.

Another letter came from the Dean's Office. At first Buz did not even want to open it. The Dean's Office always sent bad news. It might be best just to pack up and hightail it out of town. Curiosity got the better of him. What could they want this time? It turned out to be a benign communication. It explained that "due to technical problems all the class sections of Castration Discourse have been suspended. The Discourse classroom and the adjoining lab area in the basement floor of Sigmund Freud Hall are currently being remodeled. Students enrolled in Castration Discourse will be able to finish the course and receive full academic credit. In consultation with Professor Brackle, enrolled students are offered the following alternatives as a substitute to attendance in the remaining part of the scheduled C.D. classes.

1) Submit a paper of at least three hundred words but not more than five hundred words on the theme, "Opposing Machist Violence: Why Radical Solutions are Often Necessary", or on Transgender discrimination.

2) Create, if possible in collaboration with other C.D. students, a program to sensitize the larger student body and the general public to the themes of Doctor Brackle's course. Suggestions: meetings, brochures, teach-ins, one- on-one discussions with non-enrolled persons, banners, posters, letters and postings to communication forums.

3) Marches, sing-ins, demonstrations, occupations and simulation of death in costumes.

4) Suggest an alternative activity that brings the C.D. curriculum into focus or helps generalize its concepts among a wider group.

It is the hope of the Dean's Office that all Castration Discourse students will be able to obtain full credit for their course work. Our best wishes to you in your future academic career."

It wasn't so bad after all. Feelings of gratitude toward the Dean's Office flooded Buz's heart. Stif would no doubt receive an identical letter the next day. He showed his letter to Stif, who was watching an info program on the telescreen.

"Hey. That's great. So we get full credit for that shitty course after all. Cheers!" Stif drained his beer, which only had a sip or two left anyway.

"Not exactly," Buz explained in a more sober tone. "We have to do one of the three suggested substitute activities or propose something else. That's what the letter says. I think I'll try to do a paper."

"Mm," Stif replied. He was staring at the television after returning from the kitchen with another beer. "They're having a discussion about violence on the Peabody campus," he pointed at the screen where four talking heads were wagging. "Everybody's opposed to it, but they can't agree how to stop it."

"What are you going to do to complete class credit for C.D.?"

"I don't know. Haven't thought about it much yet. How long do we have to do it in?"

"It says in a postscript that the alternate projects must be completed before the end of the current semester. That gives us about six weeks." He handed the letter to his friend, who spent about fifteen minutes reading it and turning it over in various directions.

"Uh, I think I'll go for simulated death in costume." Stif nodded in recognition of the wisdom of his own choice. "Sounds like a kick, sorta like Halloween."

"You can't do just the simulated death thing. It has

to be accompanied by marches, sing-ins, occupations and demonstrations, or at least some of them."

"Oh. Okay, I'll look at it later. I can't really sing too great. Hey, but listen. I heard something really awesome on TV. De Hooper is going to have to do a hundred hours of community work. At least that's what the D.A. wants. He's going to plead guilty to committing 'unlicensed medical procedures'. What a bummer! For him, I mean. Although you can't say he doesn't have it coming."

Buz scratched his chin. He was trying to grow a beard. Not a huge beard that fell straggling to his chest like the politically involved often sported, but a beard just long enough to emphasize maleness. "What about Artesta? No charges, I suppose."

"No." Stif took a moderate drink from his current beer. "The University is offering her an out of court settlement of two hundred thousand."

"She has to pay Peabody two hundred thousand?" Buz was shocked by this. "They ought to make her pay it to us. We're the victims."

"No. That's what they're going to pay her. To make up for all the psychological trauma and shit she suffered from."

"She wasn't even in class that day!"

"They say that makes it worse." Stif turned his full attention back to the screen. "Anyway, it's in her faculty contract. Since they interrupted her assigned course 'for reasons extraneous to the process of teaching', they have to pay her back big time. It was on the TV." Stif took a big advance on his beer. "With all the time off she's got coming, she'll probably go to Jamaica and get a real good tan and stuff."

Now Buz sought the relief that could be provided by a can of beer, but he drank slowly. This was partly just to give a good example to Stif. "Anyway, I'm going to try to catch up in math now." He walked in the direction of the bedroom. "That stuff's so hard to understand it almost makes you want to get castrated instead."

"I'm not taking pills anymore for the pain." It was late morning and Stif was explaining to Buz that he had recovered very substantially from the treatment inflicted on him in the lab area of C.D. by Mr. De Hooper. They were in the shower. "See. I can get it almost up completely." A few minutes later he was able to add breathlessly, "and there's only about thirty percent less sperm."

Buz turned away with an expression of disgust and began to soap his hair. "Fine. I'm still in too much pain to try out some kind of fag number like that. And I wish you'd cut that stuff out before they make us transfer to San Francisco. Anyway, I had Brackle for lab, remember, and she's a 'more thorough practitioner'."

Dried off, but still naked, Stif was eating a breakfast tortilla in the living room. He was experimenting with the idea of holding a tortilla in such a way that it was cupped in the center so that beer could be poured through it into his mouth. It didn't work out too well. Excessive foam prevented an accurate evaluation of the amount of beer lodged in the cupped pocket, leading to considerable spillage onto the living room floor.

Buz, dressed for class, stood watching his roommate. "Now you're doing beer for breakfast? How much are you drinking per day?" Stif's intake had been a concern for Buz for some time, but it was a delicate subject and he had put off talking about it. He didn't want to appear prudish or disciplinarian, like the people at the Dean's Office. Beer was the only or one of the only two ways of finding relief from school stress available to his roommate.

"Umm," Stif gave the question some honest thought. He counted on his fingers. "Only about nine and a half beers a day, I suppose. Maybe less on weekends."

"That's a lot. In fact, I think it's too much. You and me are still pretty young, but that doesn't mean we can't be alcoholics. On the telescreen and in our psychology book they say you should never drink more than one four ounce glass of wine a day, and not every day. After that it affects your behavior, your moral judgment, your liver and kidney function and even your brain. Your mind slows down so that you can't really think clear about your intake."

Stif scratched his head. "Really?" He stared into space, trying to give these new claims due consideration. Finally he said, "I don't really like wine anyway. It's kind of bitter and fruity at the same time."

"Yeah. So start thinking about cutting down on alcohol. Last night I was studying the math book and drinking beer at the same time and it was a slow go. I mean, I found myself re-reading the same explanation six times and I still didn't get it."

"Maybe you're right." Stif threw away the tortilla and drank the remaining beer directly from the can. "I'll start cutting back real soon."

Buz drove. He was almost as efficient at keeping the old Fiat running as Stif now. He knew how to keep the engine going during stops by pressing the accelerator with his foot, and at the same time putting the clutch in and keeping the gear shift in neutral. He could wiggle the steering wheel to compensate for the left pull tendency of the ill-mounted front suspension in order to stay on course. "Not bad, huh?" He looked at Stif for a word of approval about his driving.

Stif was asleep. The open can of beer he was holding on his lap was spilling large amounts onto his jeans.

Then they were at the University parking lot. Buz shook his roommate by the shoulder until Stif regained a sort of dopey consciousness. "You can't go to class like that. Look at yourself. Your jeans are drenched in beer. And you smell like a barroom at two a.m." Stif looked at his soggy lap with astonishment and terror.

"What class do we got?"

"You missed this morning's Psych class since I forgot to remind you about it (and I wasn't thinking about it because I got kicked out of Psychology for not wanting to take Greenleigh on another hayride), so it's Math. And it's an important lecture. Dr. Carruthers is going to explain again about integrals and derivatives. I asked him to give it another go. The book isn't too much help. Too technical."

"Well what the hell can we do now?" Stif looked at his watch. "There's not enough time left to go home and change. Besides, my other pants are worse."

"Okay, what we do is, find some friend from class and borrow some clothes for you, just for the day."

They walked toward the quad. Three minutes later they ran into Tril, the post-surgery transgender student from their C.D. class. They had struck up a friendship with Tril during the three completed sessions of Brackle's classroom lectures. Tril was really an okay person. And she lived close by in student housing on campus. Buz explained the problem.

"Our buddy Stif here had a real shock on the way to campus. We almost ran over a dog that ran out into the middle of the street. Stif was so upset by it that he spilled a whole cup of coffee on his pants."

Tril was deeply concerned. "Was the dog all right? I just love animals."

"The dog wasn't hit. The problem is that we have an important math class in about fifteen minutes and Stif can't go to class in soggy jeans. It'd be too embarrassing and there's not enough time for him to go home to change clothes. You couldn't lend him a pair of trousers just for today, could you? You two are about the same size, although he's a bit taller." Buz spoke and Stif looked beseechingly at their friend. Tril was wearing tight chartreuse trousers with the zipper in back.

"Well, I guess I could. Let's go up to my dorm room and I'll see what I have. I have to check out my wardrobe." Tril was a real friend. She would always help you out if you had any kind of balls-up. Her voice was definitely feminine but it had a sort of gravelly background at the same time.

They took the elevator to floor eleven of Malcolm X Hall, one of the ten campus student dormitories. "I feel sorry about what happened to Trag," she commented as they ascended slowly, floor by floor. "I heard all about it on the news. Hinckley introduced me to him. He was so sweet. He wore the wrong shade of makeup, though. He's really a fairly dark brunette. And I think he concentrated too much on the anatomical side of gender. Maybe that was the problem. They've put him in a mental ward for a twenty day observation period and I know he's going to hate that. He really loves his freedom."

At last they landed at floor eleven. Tril led the way down the hall. Like all the Peabody dorms, Malcolm was unisex. Many doors of the tiny student rooms were open and they could see women and guys resting, sleeping, studying books, working at computers and doing other things alone or in groups. Several sound systems were going at once and the varieties of rap, rock and punk blended in the corridor.

"It gets kind of wild here sometimes. Campus security was here three times last night, but it wasn't serious. Just fights and shouting and loud music and things like that. I don't like it when they start doing sex right in the hallway. It's really gross."

Tril opened a door and entered a tiny room. Buz and Stif followed. They looked at the room in astonished awe. The walls were covered with posters of movie stars and rock bands. Books, clothes, magazines and odd objects made of plastic covered most of the floor. There was an unmade bed, really just a mattress. Tril pointed at it. "I try to keep things neat but it usually gets away from me. I got up late for class this morning. Not as late as my roomie." She pointed to another mattress on the floor. Its occupant was stretched out and covered with blankets. They could hear snoring. Two feet and part of a head protruded from opposite ends of the blanket cover. If they hadn't known better (Davis was way too macho to room with a trans), Stif and Buz would have guessed that it was Davis. Same shape, same size, hair, color.

"That's Davy, my roommate. He got real stinko last night on drugs and booze. He'll probably be out cold until after five o'clock. Fortunately for him he doesn't have to go to class, since he's a big sports star, or so he says. He used to live near the old Abarrotes store, but he put in for an emergency dorm housing assignment. He says the campus police are a lot more easy going than the Peabody city bunch. I don't know, but I think it had to do with some wild drug parties."

Stif nodded. Lucky guy. Not everybody got the same privileges.

"By the way, my full sympathies to you two for the hard time you had in C.D. lab. Everybody in the class heard about it. I know it can be very painful, although I'm exempt from C.D. lab for certain reasons, so I'm not too likely to have the experience, if you know what I mean." Tril laughed in an embarrassed way. "It's just what I've heard from some others. But you get over it and then you're better than before because you don't have so many of those negative urges. Hinckley told me about it. He used to be friends with that horrible Hooper."

Time was running out. Buz checked out the clothes on the floor. Nothing seemed to be appropriate for Stif. "Thanks for the information, but you said you had a pair of pants you could lend Stif. Class starts in about ten minutes now."

"Oh, of course!" Tril looked Stif up and down. "What side do you dress on, honey?"

"Back of the room," Stiff answered. He hadn't understood the question.

"Okay." Tril went to the small closet and rifled through disordered piles. "Try this on." She handed Stif a pair of tapered, close-fitting, yellowish trousers with the zipper in back.

Stif took off his soggy jeans. Tril stared in fascination at his underwear. The borrowed pants didn't fit. Stif had put the back of the pants in front so that it would zip up in the more common way. The back was now too tight and the front ballooned in loose cloth.

"No go, sweetie. You'll have to wear them zipper backside. All my pants are like that."

Stif stood contemplating a void. He couldn't do that. Everyone would think he was a ... he didn't know exactly how to say it politely, but like those people who did floor shows in San Francisco. "Don't you have anything else at all?" he pleaded in final desperation.

Tril pointed to a pile on the bottom shelf of the closet. "Just a lot of old skirts I hardly wear anymore."

Seen from the closest possible distance, destiny has no characteristics that can be called remarkable. Stif chose a gray one. A gray skirt. It would call less attention in class and on the way to class. He put it on and adjusted it to his waist. He looked at himself in the long mirror attached to the closet door. It wasn't really so horrible at all. Anyone might think that it was a kilt and that he was celebrating some kind of Scottish holiday.

Tril threw up her hands in admiration. "Honey, you look darling, really, I mean it. You are so cute."

Stif looked in the mirror again. Tril had a point. Wearing a dress was sort of weird for a guy, unless you interpreted it as some kind of national costume, but it certainly didn't look that bad in *itself.* It showed off his athletic legs to good effect. Unfortunately, he hadn't shaved.

Buz gave his friend a look that combined disapproval and regretful acceptance of the inevitable. But it was better than having a zipper over your ass, which would give people the wrong idea. Anyway, guys sometimes wore skirts now. It was part of the new intersex look that the television media liked to talk about. "Let's get going! We're almost late already. It'll make a bad impression on Professor Carruthers if we come in late," he explained to Tril. "I personally asked him to go over something from the last math class again."

They were off. But first Tril gave Stif a kiss on the cheek. "You're just too pretty. Come back later and we can experiment with make-up."

Buz and Stif ran for the elevator. They didn't hear a groan coming from the unconscious Davie.

Class had already started when they went in. Fortunately, Carruthers was writing at the blackboard and they were able take seats in the back of the classroom without being noticed. With chalk, Carruthers drew the famous Cartesian field with its two intersecting axes, the abscissa and the ordinate. Then he drew the graph of a simple equation. Finally he filled in the space beneath the curve with chalk crosshatching.

"Derivative yields the slope of the curve at any point," he explained. "Integral gives us the area under the curve within fixed limits."

Carruthers was a small man with dark hair. He must have been around forty or thirty. Tril, who had a thing about brunettes, and about "daddy" figures, would have gone for him. Stif certainly didn't, although he was convinced that Cruddie had been giving him the eyeball routine. He had regular features, although they were too small and bunched up on his tan face. You could tell from the way he taught the class that he loved his subject. Hardly anyone else did.

Buz was staring at the blackboard and taking notes. He copied the equation onto a page of his notebook. He made a small replica of the graph. He took down the Professor's words.

Stif's jaw was hanging open in amazement at the drawings and the professor's explanation. From time to time he looked down and smoothed his skirt. It hardly went down to his knees.

The lecture went on. Even beginning calculus was complicated, in fact almost incomprehensible to those without a background in algebra. They had had a course in algebra at Drakesville High, but it must have been dumbed down to infinity. Stif was still trying to take in x=y. He took a pull on his can of beer from time to time. He had secretly borrowed a couple from Tril's dorm room refrigerator when she was bending over the piles of clothes in her closet, just to relax a bit latter. He had opened one very discretely under his math class desk. Buz hadn't noticed. He was too preoccupied with the stuff Cruddie was putting on the blackboard.

The professor at last turned to the seated students. He asked a question. "Mr. Miller. I believe you requested this demonstration. First, let's see how well you have studied our text assignment for this class meeting. How do we find the *second* derivative of the graph of an equation?"

Carruthers and the class turned to look at Buz Miller as he sat at a desk, pondering his notebook, at the back of the classroom. They also took in the oddly dressed occupant of the adjacent desk, Sydney "Stif" Snerdley. The two were always together. There was something between them. Buz thought about the professor's question. He had read something about it in the textbook yesterday, but what? He was about to panic. Then he looked at his roommate. For several minutes he believed that he was hallucinating or that he was dreaming or that he was back in the dump imagining that he was in math class. Stif was sipping from a beer can right in the middle of math class! He was using his other hand to try to stretch his skirt below his knees.

Buz grabbed the can away from Stif. Professor Carruthers frowned in wrath. He had triggered to a scene of "totally unacceptable behavior". Drinking was strictly prohibited on campus, except in the Faculty Lounge! It was completely taboo during class sessions. When Buz looked again, Stif had another beer in his hand. He had been carrying two. Several students used their cell phones to take pictures. Buz and Stif, each with a can in his hand. Stif stood up to escape Buz's attempt to grab his second beer. Cell phones caught images of Stif with a beer can in his hand, standing against a background of desks and blackboards, and wearing a skirt. Next to him, and also holding a beer, was Buz.

An enraged Buz headed for the Fiat. He was homebound and hell with the rest. Let that drag queen drunk fend for himself! Stif followed. He wanted to explain. He walked more slowly in the unfamiliar outfit. He noticed the approving stares of students and faculty and others as he walked steadily and gracefully in the borrowed kilt. He still held the offending beer can in his hand. He wasn't thirsty now, but he hadn't thought of disposing of it. The campus crowd laughed, but it seemed a laugh of appreciation. They laughed at an appearance that was outlandish but also imaginative. A few, especially some of the older faculty men, seemed highly appreciative of the aesthetic qualities that Tril had also admired.

When he saw that Buz was behind the driver's seat of the Fiat and that he had started the long, noisy process of igniting the engine, Stif broke into a run. To reach full speed he had to hold his skirt up to mid-thigh level.

"Hold on! Wait up, motherfucker! That's my fucking car you're driving off in!"

Stif reached the passenger door but found that it was locked. Buz had kept possession of the only set of keys. The Fiat started to move. Stif climbed up on the hood. Hah! Buz wouldn't dare drive off with someone lying on top of the car hood. "Let me in, you freak! It's your fault! You made me into a fucking drag queen for the whole fucking school to watch! Just so we wouldn't miss fucking math class!"

The Fiat started to accelerate. It must have been going about twenty-five or thirty m.p.h. when Stif was spun off by the conjoint effects of inertia and acceleration, two physics concepts that Dr. Carruthers had briefly touched on in last week's class meeting.

Stif was left lying face down in the parking lot. When he raised himself to a kneeling position and checked himself out, he noticed that his face was covered with a sticky liquid. Blood! Now he could see it on his hand. His face had been grazed by the half-paved parking lot surface. Red drops were falling on his skirt. He got up and started to walk. It was a good three miles home to the dump, but where else could he go? If he stayed on campus he might be questioned by Security. They would suspect that he was the victim of some sort of assault. They would bring him, skirt clad, bleeding from the face, to their office for a full interrogation. The humiliation! Although, without all that blood, he might not have made such a bad impression at all.

Two hours later Stif stumbled into the living room of the dump. All through downtown Peabody he had suffered the harsh and revolted looks of those small town hicks. Just because of the blood, and the skirt. In the neighborhood he had been followed for blocks by shouting kids. Now he went to the bathroom and looked at himself in the cracked mirror above the wash basin. Most of the blood had dried. His face didn't look too badly damaged. There were some large but superficial scratches on one cheek. He washed off the dried blood. The scratches bled more. He tamped the red places with the dirty bathroom towel.

The Fiat wasn't back yet. Buz was not in the bedroom. That bastard! He had ruined Stif. How could he ever face Peabody again, when he had walked for miles through town as a sort of wounded transvestite Frankenstein? Stif would never forgive him for this. He went to the kitchen. There were only four beers left. He took two and went back to the living room, where the TV was still flickering, forgotten in the morning rush to class. What a fool he had been!

Two hours later Buz drove up in the lurching Fiat. He walked into the apartment and headed to the bedroom. He had someone in tow. He passed Stif without a word.

The girl gave Stif an interested look, then turned away with a grimace when she noticed the scabbed cheek.

Buz and the girl were occupied in the bedroom for about an hour. Stif kept getting up to peek in at their activities through the partly open bedroom door (it couldn't be completely closed because of the warped door frame), although, out of a sense of decency, he stayed mainly in the living room. Not bad. The girl. She and Buz almost tore the mattress apart jumping and tossing at one another. They must have gone for two times, but it was hard to tell because the whole thing went on non-stop and was continually punctuated by moans and grunts of pleasure. Then the girl, dressed again, walked out of the bedroom. As she moved across the living room she put some folded banknotes into her purse. She took Stif in again.

"How you, baby? You got you'self bruised up pretty good. How that happen?"

"Math class," Stif explained.

"Oh. I know about that stuff. I been through the high school. Yeah, that'd bleed you dry, all that mumbo-jumbo. Anyway, you a friend of Buz?"

"Used to be." Stif looked away.

"Uh-huh. Well, anytime you want a little party, just drive down to Jefferson Street, near the mall. Close to that big ol' willow tree on the corner. And you know something? You'd be kinda cute without all that blood an' stuff on your face."

"Thanks. Everybody says so."

"It don't matter if you like wearin' skirts and things like that. I got lots of weird friends. Bye now." She blew kisses from the doorway.

Stif looked out the living room window and saw her

march jauntily down the street. She was walking back to work. Or going home. Probably it wouldn't be a long trip. She doubtless lived in the same neighborhood.

In the bedroom there was silence. Stif walked to the doorway. Buz was stretched out naked on the mattress, turned onto his back. He was sleeping. His penis was only partly detumesced and it was smeared with stains. Stif was shocked. Before, in moments of ejaculation, they had always been in the shower or in the dark. He walked over to the mattress and kicked it. Buz stirred.

"If my mother knew that was the type of person you were, she would never have let me move in with you!"

Buz sat up in bed. He was suddenly lucid. "Because I like real women and not some kind of fag substitute, is that it?"

Stif started to snivel. Soon large tears were rolling down his face, dissolving the coagulated blood. "You brought home a prostitute! That's something my mom would never forgive me for. I mean, that's why she kicked my dad out."

"Look, buddy, you wrecked our college education just about for certain. They're gonna kick our asses out of school. You let me walk into that C.D. lab mayhem when you knew all about what they did, but I wanted to keep on in school anyway. And now this. What the hell got into you drinking beer in math class? The dress business wouldn't have been a problem, but there's no way they're going to forget about alcohol in class. And I already told you the class was real important and that I asked Crudders to repeat the lecture. You decide to bring a couple of beers along anyway."

"I was too nervous. You made me put on a skirt like

some kind of fucking drag queen. I needed a beer to keep cool or I'd of freaked out. I thought I could hide the beer under the desk."

"Maybe you didn't notice, but a lot of guys wear skirts around campus. There's nothing wrong with it. It's a whole movement. Anyway, I believe it was *your* choice."

"I can't take a lot of pressure. Mom used to help me but she's not here." Repeated snivels.

"But now you really blew it. All our hopes for higher education and a good job are down the toilet. No one except a total moron would even think of drinking beer in math class. That's going way too far. The Administration's got a strong anti-alcohol policy and I think they're right."

His face drenched in tears and blood stains, Stif sobbed openly. After ten minutes he sniffled back the last tears and wiped his face on his shirt sleeve. "It was all your idea from the start. I didn't think I could do this college stuff. I barely didn't flunk out of high school. But it was that skirt business that drove me around the bend and it was your idea! Otherwise I don't think I'd of been stupid enough to drink in class. Another thing that caused it is that me and Lorraine were in love, but she had other ideas. I was really pushed out of shape as far as emotions when she complained to the Dean about me. So naturally I got to drinking a lot of beer lately. Anybody could've talked me into any crazy shit at all like wearing a skirt or anything else. Besides, you and me were close friends, then you dragged that whore up here!"

"Well, let me tell you frankly. The truth is, I really don't like guys for that kind of thing."

"Me neither! I thought Lorraine was perfect for me, or anyway one of her friends."

"At least take that fucking skirt off!"

"You mean now?" Although shocked at the idea of disrobing while not alone, Stif turned his back to his roommate, then unbuttoned and unzipped the borrowed skirt and let it fall to the floor. He bent down and picked up a soiled pair of jeans from the bedroom floor. They were Buz's. He put them on anyway. Actually, they were not all that dirty. Stif looked down to admire them. The problem was that they were several inches too short. He either had to adjust the trouser waist down to his crotch or leave his long ankles uncovered.

Buz headed for the bathroom. There was no sense wasting time arguing around and around with Snedley. He felt he had to take a wash up after being with a prostitute, although she really seemed like a nice girl. Soon the shower was going full flood. Buz sang for a few minutes, repeating the lyrics of a hit rap song. "Fuck fuck fuck fuck you baby". Now in the living room, Stif heard the singing and remembered that in English 1A, when he had still been allowed to attend classes, Di Vaggio had told her students that this particular rap number was "richly imbued with social, cultural and political significance."

Stif was watching TV when Buz came back to the living room. Stif was on his third and next to last beer. He was glad to see that his roommate, still naked, was now thoroughly clean. Buz's penis was half erect, an artifact of his highly erotic experience with the prostitute, or maybe just too much soaping. Stif tried not to look. It was impolite.

"I'm willing to try it if you are," he told Buz.

"What? What the hell are you talking about?" Buz suspected the worst.

"I'm willing to try going back to school if you are. If they let us."

Buz thought for a minute. "I doubt it. I think what you did was about the limit. Okay, though. If they don't kick us out, I'll go back to class too."

"Hey, Buz," Stif spoke in a softer voice, almost pleading. "Could you go down to the store and get me a couple of six packs? I can't go out with my face all fucked up from what happened in the parking lot. The police might pick me up for brawling."

"You got here from campus without any problem. Sure, I'll go. Let me put some clothes on first. I still got that much decency."

The television was showing a news report about a crowd of Peabody students who, apparently inebriated or under the influence of drugs, had thrown a Baptist TV preacher's wife into a campus fountain. The Governor had arrived to investigate. The hick vote still trumped the student vote. All responsible leaders were denouncing the barbarity of it all, that is, the dunking, except for the President of Peabody State University. He pleaded for comprehension of societal circumstances and mentioned the parallel with adult baptism.

"I'm going to get you some beer just this time, because of everything that happened today. What I think, though, is that you're a real alcoholic now. You always have to have a beer in your hand. That's what made you screw up in Math class." Buz.

Tearing up again, Stif nodded. "I know. I'm going to go dry, I swear it. I just can't start today."

At Abarrotes Buz was paying for the six packs of beer and a few refrigerated burritos when he noticed a pile of newspapers on the checkout counter. They distributed the campus paper, The Daily Peabody, to poor neighborhoods in order to give poor children encouragement to reach for higher education. On the cover was a familiar face. A large photograph showed Stif, dressed in a skirt, holding a can of beer, standing in front of desks and a blackboard. News travelled fast. That had been just hours ago. "Transgender dressing is allowed and even encouraged as an advance in the direction of multi-diversity," the caption read, "but alcoholic beverages are linked to abusive behavior and are absolutely forbidden on campus."

The Castration Discourse class that the roommates had enrolled in under pressure from the Dean's Office was suspended due to the "unfortunate incident" involving unlicensed surgery on Trag in the lab area, but they could still get credit for C.D. Buz was working on a paper that would substitute for the remaining C.D. class sessions and allow him full academic credit. He had read several chapters in Artesta Brackle's best selling paperback *Castration: Ending Male Dominance,* which had been published before the C.D. class text came out. He chose a theme that he knew would guarantee a good grade. The subject would be "How Capitalism Castrates Transgender Persons in Our Society". The idea was that Trans people, because they are frequently rejected by our society as being "other", that is, not conforming to accepted social and gender patterns, were condemned to occupy the lowest places in the social-economic pyramid. With few exceptions, they were confined to minimum wage service jobs, when they were not simply warehoused on welfare subsistence. Hence they were left financially and socially bereft, powerless, castrated. Buz had the idea of developing this theme by using anecdotes about Transgender persons he had known (Tril told them about how (s)he had "worked his ass off" one summer selling encyclopedias door to door in San Francisco but no one would buy from him/her even in S.F, because he/she was trans!) and a few statistics he had picked up from Brackle's paperback. That ought to be enough to swing at least a B for the paper, maybe better if Artie was in a good mood. After all, it was the idea that counted, not the writing style (Buz knew that was a weak point for him). And anyway, putting in more effort might not pay, since they didn't know if they'd still be enrolled in PSU after the Dean's Office took up the question of Stif's (and Buz's) dumb beer-in-class performance.

In the meantime, Buz thought about their Native American class. They had already missed the last two meetings. Luckily, Ham's young replacement was too laid back to take attendance or they might have got a lot of flak from the Student Loan guys. Well, okay, it hardly mattered if you missed a few classes of N.A. There, you were judged on how you shouted. That seemed to be almost a general rule at Peabody. Still, you had to put in an appearance some time. Buz couldn't remember when their next N.A. test was scheduled. As for Math, they ought to hold off for awhile, especially since Cruddie was really pissed at Stif, despite having some sort of crush on him. That picture of Stif on the cover of the Daily Peabody had made Cruddie a campus laughing stock. Stif could still go to Greenleigh's Psych class, where his current notoriety might gain sympathy and interest from a psychological point of view. And Buz could attend Vaggy's English 1A section, and both were required to attend Castration Discourse, so that ought to keep them plodding along with at least some hope of finishing the semester with full credit.

"Maybe I ought to go back to campus and give Tril her skirt back." Stif was wearing freshly laundered jeans and he looked almost normal, except for a large scab on one side of his face, the result of that parking lot misunderstanding.

"I guess. I'll go with you. I could use some air. I've been working my ass off trying to write about castration." In fact, Buz was afraid that Stif might stumble into yet another incident, one completely beyond repair.

"Okay. Maybe we could invite Tril for a cup of coffee in the cafeteria, sort of as a thank you. She's really nice."

"Don't get romantic. You're supposed to be in love with Lorraine, remember."

Stif looked confused. "That's right. Although it's kind of difficult, since I'm not supposed to even go near her because of what happened in the Fiat."

"Oh, yeah, the masturbation business. What the hell got into you anyway?"

"My mom always said there was nothing wrong with it. I thought it would be a good way to break the ice." Stif looked away. "I gotta stop at a pharmacy on the way to campus. I have to get some sort of bandage for my face. It doesn't look too hot with this huge scab right on my best side."

"Why is that your best side?"

"I don't know. That's what Lorraine said."

They pulled into the parking lot of Pharmaload, a large drugstore with outlets all over the state and in some other states. Buz stayed behind the wheel while Stif went in. Buz did most of the driving now. Stif said he was still too nervous because of the several dramatic events of the last few weeks to chance a spree behind the wheel.

Stif was in the store for at least twenty-five minutes. Buz looked at the passing women. Whatever its faults, Peabody certainly had a good supply of attractive women. Once again, he was glad that this sexist thought would remain strictly inside his head, unless Brackle had invented some sort of thought control machine.

Finally Stif emerged from the Pharmaload store and got into the front passenger's seat of the Fiat.

"What the hell took you? I thought maybe they were giving you some kind of over-the-counter plastic surgery." Buz laughed.

"Nothing." Stif sounded hurt. He looked away. Buz could see that the scab was less noticeable. It was covered, like the rest of his face, with a heavy layer of cosmetics.

Malcolm X, the towering campus dorm, was noticeable from a good distance. A large red neon star on the roof flashed on and off even in the daytime. As they walked along the path that led through the quad to the high rise dormitory, curious or disturbed but sometimes impressed students stared at Stif. The large scab was much less visible, but Buz's impression was that all that make-up made his buddy look like a really insecure transvestite prostitute.

Then they were in the tower elevator. Buz looked closely at his pal in the electric light as the elevator started its slow climb. "You've got way too much make-up on, dude. And it isn't spread even on your face. It looks weird."

"No I don't. I mean, a little. The druggist said it was the best way to cover up a facial blemish. It doesn't look as obvious as a big bandage."

"Yeah, but with that stuff all over your face you look sort of like a …"

"Drag queen," Stif finished the sentence.

"I wasn't going to put it like that, but yeah."

Stif said nothing for at least two minutes, then blurted it. "I read we were supposed to encourage the transgender style. It helps liberate all of us."

Before Buz could answer, and he was thinking of something along the lines of, "that's only if you *are* a drag queen", the elevator came to a halt and the door opened. Outside, on the landing, there was a huge commotion. Several paramedics were pushing a gurney. On top of the gurney was an unconscious person who looked remarkably like Davis, the basketball star. In the crowd of shouting students that surrounded the medics they recognized Tril.

"Evacuate the elevator," a paramedic ordered.

Stif and Buz got out fast.

The gurney and the paramedics disappeared into the elevator. The doors closed, the box dropped.

Tril rushed to them. "Oh my god! It was just terrible and I saw it all!"

"What happened?" Buz.

"I don't know exactly. I think Davis took some more drugs when he woke up this afternoon and this time he really o.d.'d."

"Wow," Stif sympathized. "That's freakin' awful. Why the hell did he do that?"

Tril thought for several moments. Explaining

the obvious was often more difficult than explaining something complicated. "He just did it, that's all."

The students were finally going back to their rooms. Several were dressed only in underwear. At least two were completely naked. Both Buz and Stif stared until the students disappeared. Tril smirked to show her indifference.

Tril took Stif's head in his/her hands and looked closely at Stif's face. "What do you have on your face, honey? It looks like acne cream."

"It's not. I went to a pharmacy because I had this big scab on my face from an accident and they said this stuff would cover it up." Stif took a small glass bottle out of his pants pocket. The label said, "Lady Di's Rich Surprise".

"Lover," Tril commented, shaking her head, "you got gypped. That's the worst junk on the market. Come inside my room and I'll fix you up." Tril led the way along the dorm hallway through discarded junk and trash. "They had a big party last night, and no one from housekeeping has turned up here yet," she explained. In the room shared by Tril and formerly by Davis, they passed an overflowing plastic garbage container on the edge of the mini-kitchen. It gave off an odd chemical smell. Tril again explained. "Davey bought some real cheap powder and I threw it away last night while he was sleeping, except for a dose I couldn't find because he hid it somewhere. I did it for his own good." Tril wrinkled his/her nose at the harsh smell. "Then, this afternoon, he got out the last ounce or two of the stuff and swallowed it before I could stop him. No wonder he got so cratered out I had to call the medics. They said he was in a coma. I mean, he'll probably be alright, but he'll just go back to doing it again."

Soon they were standing next to a small sink beside the tiny refrigerator. Tril turned the water on and bent Stif's head over the sink. After a few minutes of careful cleansing, Lady Di's Rich Surprise was gone. "Never use the cheap stuff. It's not worth it, honey. Take it from me, I've tried 'em all."

Now Tril brought her friend to a low plastic make-up table and made him sit down on the matching pink plush stool. At the back of the low plastic table was a large mirror that magnified your complexion. "See, hon, first you gotta put on some basic. That covers up all the little holes and lines on your face from zits and stuff like that." Tril opened a large bottle and expertly began to dab Stif's face with just the adequate amount of cosmetic, at the same time touching the scabbed area very gently. "Um. That looks about fairly good. Then you put on your tone coloring." From the table drawer, Tril took out a small bottle about the same size as the Lady Di preparation but much more stylishly designed. "This is 'pure ivory' shade. I think it's about right for your complexion." She dabbed Stif's face with small amounts of the toner, then smoothed it in. Finally she opened a compact and powered Stif's face to prevent oily glare.

"Honey, you are going to be beautiful! I really mean it. You got good bone structure, high cheekbones, and all of that is to your best advantage." Tril worked intensively for several more minutes, completing the job with eyeliner, eye shadow and a small amount of lipstick. "Uh huh. Just perfect."

"Lover, you are never going to be hard up for boyfriends again!" Tril guided Stif's face to a direct confrontation with the mirror. "Sweetie, you are just too gorgeous!"

Stif looked at his image in the make-up table mirror. At first he was confused. He did not recognize himself. Then he started to take it in. Not too bad. Stif looked, mugged a bit at the mirror, turned his head in various directions. He was very attractive, there was no doubt about it. He was almost beautiful. It fact, he thought that if he had not been himself, he might have asked himself for a date and tried to pull a car breakdown stunt in a dark backstreet.

"Stif, buddy," Buz spoke up for the first time. He had been looking on silently but with growing disapproval. Now he realized the full extent of Stif's problem. He held back on the obvious derogatory remarks because he knew that he, Buz, had in some way encouraged what his roommate had become. "We actually came here to give Tril back the skirt you borrowed a few days ago. Give her the skirt."

Stif offered the drab kilt to the humane transgender person.

"No. You keep it. I don't wear them anymore. At least not unless they're really style. That one came from the Salvation Army."

Stif turned back to his reflection. Maybe looking like this, he could stay in C.D. class when it reopened and even be readmitted to English 1A. He used a finger to smooth the make-up on a few small areas of his face.

Buz looked at the mattress that poor Davis had once occupied. With the blankets dragged off you could see that there were pills, packets of powder and even a few syringes left scattered on top.

Tril noticed Buz's stare. "Poor Davey. I really told him to go easy, but he shut me up. He said I was a straight dude without a soul and he wanted to live life to the limit every minute, and to hell with the rest."

Buz nodded in an appropriate gesture of sympathy, then turned to his roommate. "Buddy, there's something I gotta say. You can't walk around campus like that, with all that makeup. I mean, unless you think you're really transgender—and that's all right too, I'm not criticizing it. But you got to decide."

Tril looked at Stif again. She was not quite so satisfied now. "I think Buz has a point. Maybe a little less eye shadow would be better. And that's not exactly your toner shade, you're a bit lighter. Still, I think you're totally beautiful, whatever gender you decide. And like this, you could almost be a Marilyn look alike."

Stif left Tril's dorm bedroom in complete Marilyn-like cosmetics. When they reached the cafeteria he washed it off in the restroom. On the way to the cafeteria Buz had walked a few paces behind him, pretending that they weren't together. Students were laughing. A few yelled out "it's not Mardi Gras yet!" Some of the girls were obviously turned off. A lot of girls didn't like trans-guys. It was like some sort of cultural backlash. By the time they reached the cafeteria Stif had decided that he wasn't convinced about getting into cross appearance. It wasn't really him. He had once been a high school basketball star. He told Buz about his decision when he got back from the restroom. It was a firm choice. "I don't know why I let Tril put all that goop on me. That's not me at all. I didn't want to offend her though by acting too macho."

Tril had refused their invitation for a cup of coffee at the cafeteria. "I just have tons of studying to do. In addition to all my other courses, I have to work out a scenario for 'simulated death in costume' to get C.D. credit." Stif suspected that the real reason for Tril's refusal was a disinclination to appear in public in competition with the new Stif, who was clearly the more attractive of the two.

"I won't do more than a six pack a day, then I'll cut down to four cans, then two, then I'll stop completely." Back in the dump, Stif was relaxing once again in front of the TV. Buz, standing in the middle of the living room, sized up his friend's plan for sobriety. "Okay, I think it's a good idea that you want to stop drinking. But don't fool yourself with that line about cutting back on the booze a little at a time, though. That's what a lot of winos tell themselves . It never happens."

"No, don't worry about that. I'll watch it real close. Besides, I've experimented a couple of times and I think I can understand the math book better after just two beers."

Buz picked up the math book. They had a lot of chapters to get caught up on. "Hey, what the hell did you do to the book, pour beer all over it? It's sticky as hell and it stinks."

"Oh. Sorry. It was an accident, like you had with it, but maybe a little more spilled. I looked up at the TV and my hand turned the wrong way. I think my beer was more full than the one you had."

"Now we won't be able to sell it back to the school bookstore at the end of the semester and that fucker cost a hundred and ten dollars!"

"Sorry. Anyway, the money came out of the Loan, didn't it?"

"That doesn't mean it's free. We gotta pay the Student Loan back some time. Maybe from now on it would be better if I read the textbooks. I'll give you a summary of the important points. That's all you really need to know."

Stif focused on the telescreen. He took a long drink. That signified agreement.

Late that afternoon Stif wandered into the bedroom. Buz was lying on his back on the mattress. He had fallen asleep with the Native American textbook open on his chest. It was turned to a picture of General Custer at the Little Big Horn. "The imperialist invaders consistently worked to exterminate the Native Peoples of North America. Unfortunately for them, it did not always work out the way they planned", read the explanatory note.

"Buz! Wake up, okay? I gotta say something."

The roommate's eyes opened. He sat up on the mattress. "Sure. Go ahead, shoot. What do you want to say?"

"Um, it's sort of personal." It was clear that Stif had already exceeded his self-imposed six beer daily limit. His voice was slurred and his eyes were teary.

"Yeah?"

"Well, it's sort of, like, you know when we had to do those therapy sessions in C.D. lab?"

"Yeah." Buz's voice and expression showed that he was still angry.

"I've been sort of experimenting around. I think I'm about thirty percent down on sperm and my thing won't get full length." His voice cracked plaintively on the last phrase.

Buz had already confirmed these findings for his

own case. He didn't want to admit it. Even having made the experiment would tar you with more than a dab of homosexuality.

"Maybe I'll never completely recover."

"Sit down, bud." Buz made room on the mattress. "They pulled some rotten shit on us, but at least we're still here. I had to put out a bigger effort on that trial run with Sassyline, that's the girl I brought up here, but there was hardly any difference at all in the long run, at least in feeling. Maybe you just have to go at it longer."

Stif leaned back. The head of the mattress was flush against the bedroom wall. "Yeah. I suppose maybe with Lorraine she wouldn't have noticed the difference, or maybe she would have thought like it was more genteel."

Now Buz noticed that Stif was wearing Tril's old skirt. "Take that thing off! I thought you decided that trans business wasn't for you."

"I did. I just wanted to see how I would have looked in the mirror."

Buz also noticed that Stif had rather nice legs, especially since they were now shaved. "Put some pants on, dude! You're starting to lose it big time."

Stif stood up and turned his back to Buz. He slipped off the skirt, half bending his torso in the process. He had also shaved another part of his body.

The next day Buz went to the mailbox early. Their only class that day, besides Psychology, which Buz couldn't attend, was College Mathematics and they decided to lay off for a while, and to study the math text at home, until things calmed down. Cruddie was probably still pissed as shit.

There were two letters in formal white business size envelopes with a printed return address: The Office of the Dean, Peabody State University. Buz felt his stomach drop to his shoes. This was it, the kiss, the goodbye, the shove off. His plan for a higher education and commensurate job opportunities were getting the ax. He knew it. He could sense it. It was the dead end, long delayed after the math class event, but always expected. He opened the letter addressed to Stif first.

Mr. Snerdley,

Testimony from a member of the faculty and from several enrolled students, confirmed by photographic evidence, proves beyond any doubt that you have engaged in the consumption of alcoholic beverages during a scheduled class on the campus of Peabody State University. The rules of the Code of Ethical Behavior (see annex II of the Course Catalog) state that the use of alcohol in any form is forbidden during classes and on the grounds and buildings of Peabody State University without exception. Violations of this rule are to be sanctioned by expulsion from the University. The strictness of the penalties that are prescribed for breaking this fundamental regulation is based on the recognition by Administration authorities of the severe harm that alcohol abuse has caused to the minority, female, and transgender communities and to children of all groups. The policy of Administration is to enforce a rule of zero tolerance in regard to the use of alcohol in our classrooms and facilities. You are hereby given notice of a provisory order of expulsion by decision of the Dean.

You have the right to appeal this decision. If you wish

to appeal, you must file a response within ten days at the Dean's Office, making use of the forms provided for that purpose. You are not to attend any class or to enter the grounds and premises of Peabody State University, except for purposes of making an appeal or of asking for an explanation of the forms and processes of appeal. You are advised, however, that students violating the prohibition of alcohol in class have the option of attending treatment sessions based on experimental therapeutic methods of alcoholism treatment. These sessions have achieved a high degree of success in the cure of substance addiction. Academic credit is available for those attending both the classroom sessions and the associated lab sessions. Substance Discourse (S.D.) is taught by Professor Emerita Artesta Brackle in the basement of Sigmund Freud Hall on campus. Application for enrollment is to be made at the Dean's Office.

Head down, as if accompanied by the chaplain and the warden, Buz walked slowly back from the mailbox. In the living room Stif was at his usual place in front of the flickering screen. A beer can was glued to his right hand. Buz went to the kitchen, opened the fridge and took out a can of Regal Alabama. He popped it open and let the foam spray his face and chest. Then back to the living room. He sat down next to Stif. He showed him the letter.

"What the hell do they want now?" Stif baulked at putting out the effort to read the whole thing. He was a slow reader and not at all inclined to an interest in literature.

"You're expelled. You were caught drinking in class."

"Oh." Stif took a small sip, focused on the screen.

"You are no longer a student at Peabody State! Your college education has been totally terminated!"

"Huh? Why?"

"For your fucking alcoholism!" Buz took the beer can out of his friend's hand. "Just read the letter, will you? It's not Hamlet in braille."

Stif bent over the letter. He read for at least ten minutes. At times his lips moved as he pronounced the words silently. "Then I don't have to go to class anymore." His back slid against the edge of the sofa as he rewarded himself with a sip of beer from an open can that he hadn't entirely drained.

"It's the end! No more college education for you! No more high job prospects! Don't you dig that much? What kind of girl friends are you going to get flipping hamburgers all your life?"

"Just because of that one little beer? I hardly started on it." Stif grabbed his current can back from Buz. Now he was pissed off. Now he understood what it was about. "That's injustice. I'm going to protest till I drop! And I got a lot of important friends at Old Piss! Professor Greenleigh'll stand up for me, I know she will. I stood up for her, in a way." He looked down at his now only seventy percent functional crotch. "How 'bout you? They still letting you going to classes?" Stif was morose, regretful, envious.

"I got the same letter. I just haven't opened it yet."

"We got to fight against this crap to the last breath! C'mon. Let's let 'em know we want our rights back, just like Martin Luther … whoever it was." History was Stif's worst subject.

His buddy's reaction was encouraging to Buz. Now

Stif was rising above the alcohol fumes in his brain. Maybe he would have some other good ideas. Normally Buz's roommate was not a valuable source of intellectual enrichment, but it was possible he had been inspired by their study of the rights struggle in N.A. (Native American). "There's another thing in the letter that I think you didn't notice. If we want to stay at Old Piss, it says we have to take another Discourse class. In the basement at Freud, with individual lab sessions." Buz was hoping that somehow, against all improbable hope, Stif might have a solution to this problem in his beer mellowed but strangely creative brain. Buz waited. He looked at his roommate with encouraging eyes. "With Artesta Brackle!"

"Fuck that." Stif refocused on the screen. Horses were fighting in front of a pile of upturned wagons while Native Americans circled on horseback, firing their rifles and shrieking. "I'll flip burgers."

Buz nodded, partly satisfied. Okay, maybe he had to drag it out of his buddy, but at least Stif was starting to understand the problem. Was there anything else moving in Stif's brain on the subject of higher education? "So that's your last word on our college hopes?" Usually Buz was the problem solver, but he had run out of ideas.

Stif took a moderate sip from a new can. He usually lined up three or four next to him to avoid repeated trips to the kitchen. "I'm not going back to any lab cubicle with a psycho in charge." He defensively hugged his crotch with one hand. "But here's a idea. We'll appeal and do a protest gig at the Dean's Office till they have to give in! Like I said, I got influential friends at PSU. Old Greenie'll back my ass, I'm sure of it. She's like, crazy in love with me."

"Now you got it. I'm a hundred percent with you."

Buz's voice was cracking with emotion. "After all, a college degree is the key to a great future." He remembered this line. It was printed on a banner hanging in the Post Office.

"I know. I'll ask Greenleigh to talk to the Dean for us. She could wear her red skirt, the real short one. And that low neckline shirt she had on when we went to see that movie. She could talk him up alone in his office."

"Won't work." Buz was morose again. "The Dean's gay. He's even on the National Rights Board."

"Shit." Stif knew that this one word comment was repetitive and ineloquent, but ... well, not everyone's Shakespeare.

"Wait. No." Buz had found a possible key, thanks to Stif's suggestion about Doctor Greenleigh. "I think there's just one chance left and I think we have to take it. We've come a long way already and we've put in a lot of effort. It would be a crime against humanity if we let everything drop now without making a last try." Buz sat staring into the distance.

"So what is it?" Stif drank a quarter can in one swallow. He nervously put a finger up his nose. Something was coming.

"Okay. It's nothing really bad, so just relax. What I was thinking is, you could go to the Dean's Office and make a special appeal to the Dean, you know, like you just suggested for old Greenie."

"Why couldn't we both go and make an appeal to the Dean?" Stif now held Buz's half finished beer in his other hand.

"Well, it's because, like I said, the Dean's 'on the Rights Board'. Get it? So if you went in that skirt you got from

Tril and with the makeup you bought to cover up that scab, I think when he saw you he'd be real sympathetic."

"Gays aren't attracted to women, not too much anyway, not in that way," Stif countered with obvious common sense.

"He'll know that you're not really a woman. That's the point. You have to tell him that you're a transgender person and you've been suffering from the pressures of society. So that's why you made the mistake of drinking beer in class just once, because you were too nervous about everyone laughing at you." Buz managed a slight smile. He had squared the circle.

"Then what about you? You'll have to go in drag too."

"No, that wouldn't work. I've got a heavy beard and a muscular build. Tell him that I'm your Gay boyfriend. Say we live together and we're a couple. I grabbed the beer can to protect you from official reaction, but I wasn't drinking any myself. That part's totally true, anyway."

"No. I can't do it." Stif shook his head. "I've sworn off that transgender stuff. You told me I had to decide, remember? And I did."

"Of course you did, and it was never anything serious. You were just going through a confused stage because of C.D. lab, Lorraine and drinking. You won't be going back to drag if you go dressed that way to the Dean's Office, you'd just be using a stratagem to keep us in college."

"I don't know. I don't think I want to wear a skirt anymore. It doesn't feel right."

"I understand. Listen, it'll just be for one afternoon and we'll be way ahead if it works. We'll be college students again and we'll study hard to get real smart and we won't have to take any more individual lab sessions. That part is totally out."

"Okay. But what do you suppose he'll want me to do in his office all alone with him? What if he tries something creepy?"

"He won't. He's the Dean and he could get splattered all over the news media if he tries anything. He'll just like looking at you and maybe putting his arm around you and giving you a little kiss. There's nothing wrong with that." Buz demonstrated. It wasn't bad at all.

"All right. But I refuse to do any fucking striptease."

Unlike last night, Buz thought.

"I don't like this fucking shit at all." Stif was standing in front of the cracked bathroom mirror in the dump. Despite the large discontinuities due to the cracks and missing pieces, he could make out his image with fair accuracy. He had followed Tril's advice on makeup application. First the layer of basic, then the toner, then eye makeup, and finally a dusting and smoothing with a compact pad.

"You're really sort of pretty, I mean, made up like that," Buz admired. "You know, your mother was right. You're not bad looking, even as a guy."

"Thanks. You never said that before."

Stif went back to the living room. Buz noticed that Stif's skirt was askew at the waist. He adjusted it for his buddy, then stepped back to take in the whole effect. He stood musing. "There's only one big problem now. Your hair. No self-respecting girl would show up with that rat's nest on her head. And there's no time for a visit to a hairdresser. You'll have to wear a hat." Buz disappeared into the bedroom. He dug in the closet for a good ten minutes. Then he emerged into broad daylight. "Eureka!" He was holding a dark blue beret. It was French and it dated from the Liberation. His great-uncle had brought it back from France in nineteen forty-six. "Put this on and no one will notice you haven't combed your hair in two weeks."

Stif followed orders. Buz gave the *chapeau* several final tugs and twists to fit it perfectly on Stif's head. "There you go. You look just like Brigitte Bardot."

"Fuck you."

"I mean, just right now, like you're doing it as an actor. Lots of male actors play women's roles for comedy or for special reasons."

They were in the Fiat. Buz drove. As they trundled through the poor streets, then rolled along the wide boulevard, and finally passed through "beautiful downtown Peabody", Stif repeatedly looked at his reflection in the passenger side rearview mirror. At times he seemed pleased and he patted his beret or smoothed his cheeks. He had some doubts, though. On several occasions he looked at his image, squinted, shook his head, tried a hat adjustment.

"Relax. You look great. Don't worry about a thing. The old Dean's going to be charmed out of his wits. Just remember to mention me as your long suffering partner, so I can get back in class too."

Stif brought his hand to his mouth, then noticed that he wasn't holding anything. He looked glum. Something was wrong.

"Okay. Take a pull of this." Buz handed his roomie

a can of beer. He had foreseen the problem. "But don't drink the whole fucking thing. You're on your third this morning already."

Stif gratefully accepted. His face brightened. He looked in the mirror again. He wasn't Brigitte, but he wasn't exactly Frankenstein, either.

The Dean's Office. It was located on the second floor of the large neo-classical Administration Building, which occupied one whole side of the campus quad. At least it wasn't in the basement. They stood outside the building. Crowds of students were passing in the square. A few gave Stif curious looks. Even at multi-cultural Peabody some things stuck out.

"Uh, I can't go in the building with you," Buz spoke in a low voice, his hand reassuringly set on Stif's shoulder. "If they recognized me they'd suspect some sort of collusion. I'll wait right outside, over there near the big oak tree." He pointed. "Afterwards, we'll celebrate, have a bunch of beer. But when we're enrolled again, it's going to be serious study and I'll help you every step of the way. I'll help you kick that alcohol habit, too." He gave Stif a knock of comradely affection on the arm.

"Okay. I'm real scared, though. What if this guy's some kind of wild psycho nut? He could do a lot of damage on me."

"Use this." Buz handed over a jar of Vaseline. It was the jar that Stif had brought back from the drugstore a few days ago and kept near the bedroom mattress, just to ease any sort of irritation. The lid was sticky.

Buz waited alone under the oak tree. After half an hour he started to look at his watch every five minutes. The fact that Stif was taking so long must be a good sign. If he got rejected right away he would be out by now. Buz also experienced certain minor feelings of jealousy. It would be a crime if the Dean took advantage of his friend, more than a kiss or a hug, just so they could be readmitted to school. After all, they had done practically nothing wrong at all. A few sips of beer. Big deal. But the Dean and the school authorities made the rules and they ran the game. You had to play along if you wanted to get anywhere. It was not that Buz was sexually or romantically involved with poor Stif. Not at all. That wasn't Buz's cup of tea and probably not Stif's favorite tipple, either. They were friends and had been friends for years, but that was all there was to it. He felt sorry for Stif. Stif came from a broken home. His old man had been an alcoholic. Except for basketball, his talents were few. His mother had smothered him too much. Now Stif was a drinker too and he was completely unprepared for college level studies. Buz himself wasn't exactly a Rhodes Scholar. Sure, they had played around together sexually a bit, when they were much younger, mainly joint masturbation. That was fairly normal, as he knew from Greenleigh's psychology class textbook. It did not mean that they were ... well, that term wasn't used anymore ... abnormal. At least he, Buz, wasn't. He watched the college girls go by. He was attracted to them. He knew it, felt it. He hadn't got anywhere as far as trying to start a relationship with a girl at Peabody because at this point he had little to offer. He lived in a dump in a poor neighborhood and was financed by a Student Loan. He was only barely scraping by academically. He wasn't bad looking, but he was never going to be recruited as a Hollywood star. He looked at his watch again. Stif had entered the dragon forty-five minutes ago. What the hell was going on?

Minutes passed. Buz hummed, sang a few lines from old rock songs. He stood up, walked around. He approached the Administration Building, peered inside. He could see nothing except a long, ornate flight of stairs and some marble columns.

One hour and ten minutes. Buz was walking back and forth under the oak tree. If Stif wasn't out in another ten minutes he was going in after him. Whatever the Dean wanted to do with him or to him ought to have been over long ago.

An hour and fifteen minutes had passed. Then he saw a bedraggled figure slowly and carefully descending the steps of Administration. It was Stif. His beret was totally off kilter and his shirt hung loose over his skirt in front. Buz rushed up to meet him.

"How'd it go?" He looked at Stif, trying to discover other signs of ill usage.

"Well, not too bad." Stif kept walking, although he apparently had no idea where he was going. Buz kept pace.

"So how'd it go?"

Stif walked. He seemed to be daydreaming. He rubbed himself behind.

"Did you see the Dean?"

"Yeah, I saw him. I got in his office."

"And?"

"At first he was real pissed. He looked up something on his computer screen and he said me and you were a couple of troublemakers and we had offended the sensitivity of other students." As Stif talked he seemed to focus more. "He stared at me for a long time, then he accused me of 'impersonating a transgender person as an act of ridicule', that's how he put it." Stif stopped in his tracks. He rubbed his rear, adjusted his skirt. Students were watching them, smiling, laughing.

"You were supposed to tell him that you *are* a transgender person. That was the whole plan, remember?"

"I did. He wouldn't believe me for a long time, though, because my student records didn't say anything about it. He looked it up. Finally he asked me to take the skirt off to prove that I wasn't just an ordinary guy in drag."

Buz looked back at the Admin Building. "How was that supposed to prove it?"

"I don't know. Later he said there'd be certain signs."

"So what happened?"

Stif began walking again. "I left the Vaseline there." They were leaving the quad, going off to the left in the direction of the parking lot when Stif added, "for somebody who goes for other guys, he was kind of muscular … and, well, sort of developed." He stopped in his tracks. Tears were accumulating under his eyelids. "I never would have fucking done it if I'd known that was going to happen! But you talked me into it!"

"I wanted to get us reinstated in school, for both our futures, upper education and careers, all that. Sure I talked you into it. I didn't tell you to do anything really shitty."

"So why did you want me to put on a fucking skirt? And bring a jar of Vaseline!" Stif shrieked. He was openly crying. His makeup was running.

"Well," Buz's voice now marked his own doubts about the wisdom of the plan. "You know, it was because the Dean was Gay. I thought he'd be lenient with you, that he'd let you off because he'd think you were a good looking trans-, and maybe there'd be a kiss or something. The Vaseline stuff was just to give him the idea that you went for that sort of thing. I never thought he'd try anything in his office, except a kiss, maybe, and a hug."

"It was a hell of a lot more than that!" Stif was walking directly toward the Fiat, in the far corner of the parking lot.

Buz followed. "You mean he … I don't think you should have let him go that far. It wasn't worth it." Not that this was Stif's first time.

Stif got into the passenger's seat. He sat sulking with his arms folded in front of his chest. Then he tried to scratch a gray stain on his skirt with a fingernail.

"Where do you want to go, buddy?" Buz had the keys in the ignition. "Just say the word. Any beer joint in town."

"I don't want any beer," Stif said with quiet resolution.

"You don't want *beer*? What *do* you want?"

"Whiskey."

It was far worse than anything Buz thought at first. Stif was on the brink. He might topple over into the abyss of psychotic collapse at any moment. It was essential to humor him. "You got it."

Buz pulled the Fiat to the curb in front of Abarrotes and disappeared into the little store. He emerged minutes later carrying a brown bag. He drew a bottle out of the bag and showed it to Stif. *Johnny Walker*, a full quart. There were also two large bags of chips and a tub of green sauce. "We'll have a daytime party and forget all about the Dean. That fucker ought to be in

Artesta's Castration Discourse class. And with Artesta as lab monitor."

Stif recovered rapidly. After his second glass of whiskey he was staring intently at the telescreen, taking in as much of the daytime programming as he could understand. Buz sipped from his own glass. He wasn't a whiskey fan, that was certain. He urged chips and dip on Stif. "Have some. You shouldn't drink on an empty stomach." It was amazing, but Stif could drink whiskey almost as fast as he could drink beer.

Thirty minutes later Stif was definitely mellow. He laughed at the programs, at the commercials, at the news announcements. Buz decided to try to find out about the main point.

"So, did you get reinstated?"

"What?"

"Did the Dean agree to let you back in your classes? I hope you remembered to mention my case, too."

Stif drank a long slug of whiskey. "He didn't say."

"What do you mean, 'he didn't say'? That's what you went up there for."

"He said he'd review the matter and come to a conclusion." Stif's eyes were on the entertainment screen. A hand carried chips and dip to his mouth.

"Oh. I guess that's something, at least. What do you think the chances are? Was he in a friendly mood when you left his office?"

"I don't know. He was wiping shit off his dick!" Stif was looking at the telescreen. His voice carried a note of resentment from the experience, although his anger was evaporating along with the whiskey in his glass.

Once again Buz was assaulted by the impression

that his roommate and friend was suffering from deep psychological problems, even if you really had to blame childhood experiences for it, and maybe genetics, too. "You must have noticed something in his voice, his expression, something."

"Oh yeah. He said he was bending over to be friendly to sexual minorities."

He was bending over? Buz decided to drop the subject of reinstatement for now. It did not seem hopeless. Stif had always found it difficult to center his attention on the major points. Maybe it was a defensive mechanism. Old doc Greenleigh had talked about the subject in Psychology while Buz was still enrolled in the class. The vulnerable personality sought protection through various psychological defense mechanisms, including Severe Attention Deficit (SAD).

The next morning would have been the time for their Native American history class, but they were still barred from campus, except for visits to the Dean's Office. Buz woke up late. He found that Stif was already out of bed. He crept to the bedroom door and peeked into the living room. Stif, dressed in jeans and a t-shirt, was at his habitual post in front of the television. He was drinking beer. The whiskey had dried up late yesterday afternoon. Stif was smiling. He took in Buz's presence at a glance, then announced, "there was a big demonstration at Peabody State yesterday. Somebody threw a bag of rotten tomatoes at the head of the Digital Engineering Department. Must've been a real gas! Can't you just see it? The head of the Department, all dignified and all that shit and suddenly he gets it on the noggin with a mass of gooey stinking tomatoes!" Stif laughed till he started to hiccup.

"Yeah. Probably he had it coming. Must have been for 'violating student rights' or something like that." Buz went to check out the kitchen. He came back to the living room. "You had anything to eat yet?"

"Naw. I'm not hungry."

As usual, just thirsty. "I'll make you a tortilla sandwich with cheese. Don't forget, breakfast is the most important meal of the day."

"Oh yeah? Why's that? What the hell's wrong with lunch?"

"I don't know. It's just what they always say. Anyway, now that we've done all that we can to get reinstated at Peabody, I'm going to concentrate on getting you off the juice. You know you have to kick the habit. You'll never get anywhere being a drunk all the time and it'll ruin your health and your looks, too."

"Yeah, I know. I know all that. It's just that I have to come down slow after all the crap they pulled on us at Peabody. I ought to be on some sort of therapy, but I'm afraid to go to the Student Clinic for help with drinking. De Hooper used to work there. He's got a lot of buddies at the Clinic."

Ten minutes later Buz was back. "Here you are, a toasted cheese tortilla sandwich. Just eat it and you'll be back in nutrition city."

Stif chewed slowly, almost unconsciously. He was thinking about something. "Do you suppose, I mean, do you think the Dean really likes some of the students he sees in his office? Or is it all just part of the job?"

Buz stared at his roommate. What the hell was this

about? Now Stif wanted to know if his bugger-rapist really liked him. "Hard to say." Buz was playing it safe. Stif was a psychologically fragile individual. You had to humor him to avoid worse outbreaks. "I guess he might like some of them, sometimes."

"Then, if they let us back into classes, he might be like a friend or something."

Buz thought. He looked at his friend, looked at the ceiling with its peeling layers of paint. Stif was really going off track. The alcoholism was probably to blame, that and the fact that poor Stif might be unconsciously seeking a father substitute, even in the Dean. Stif's old man hit the road when he was about five. Now Buz had two major problems to worry about, in addition to their academic work, assuming they were ever readmitted to class. He was going to have to fight against his roomie's alcoholism and his sexual identity confusion. Why the hell couldn't Stif have been more intelligent and less addictive? That would have helped in all three areas.

They watched television for hours. Buz was not interested in the programs; he was watching only to provide Stif with companionship. He found it hard to understand why large, reputable corporations would sponsor endless quantities of moronic puke. But Stif enjoyed it. He smiled and laughed frequently. Buz opened a beer and took a suck. His mood gradually changed. Maybe the TV shows weren't all that bad really. He was just worried and depressed. The important thing was that the tube helped keep Stif from going off steady.

The screen was showing a film "segment" of costumed crowds and bizarre portable street exhibits. Mardi gras was only weeks away. This was an archive video from last Mardi Gras. "Hey! Wow! Awesome!" Stif enthused. "Man, wouldn't it be a killer to actually be there in New Orleans on Mardi Gras? It'd be a gas and a half, man."

New Orleans. Stif had originally wanted to go there instead of to Peabody. Buz had had to clue him in on the fact that without an education neither of them would have been able to land a decent job in a big city, no matter how great the parties. "Yeah. A lot of fun," Buz humored.

"I think I'd like to dress up like a kind of pirate, like in the movies, maybe with a scarf over my head and a patch over one eye and big baggy pants."

"You sure you wouldn't prefer being a Southern Belle in a white dress and lots of flounces?" This was a cruel remark, but sometimes harshness could serve to bring a wandering spirit back to reality.

"Fuck you, man." Stif studied the telescreen. In fact, he did find those large flounced dresses attractive. Although, in the past society made women wear those things so they would be dependant and psychologically vulnerable. Stif remembered this from Greenie's psych class. With those dresses on, women could hardly work or do anything except show off like an exhibit. "Anyway, they show a lot of class. A girl wearing one of those today would really attract the guys."

Suddenly Buz noticed what his roommate was wearing now. Stif was sitting on the floor, his back was resting against the base of the sofa, and he was wearing that same old skirt he had borrowed from Tril. He must have changed out from his jeans while Buz was in the kitchen cooking breakfast.

"What the hell? Are you going total transvestite on

me now? You said you were going to drop all of that stuff and that it was just a phase or a sort of disguise."

Stif looked in the direction of his lap. "Oh. Yeah. It was the first thing I found after I spilled some beer on my jeans a minute ago. I guess I'm real shaky on account of the problems we're having at Peabody. I don't know where my other pants are right now."

"Take that fuckin' skirt off! Like I said before, there's nothing wrong with it if you're a real transvestual, but if you're an ordinary guy, it's nuts!"

With his rear still resting on the worn and stained living room rug, Stif slowly slipped the skirt from his body. He wasn't wearing underwear. He looked up at Buz in confusion and expectation. His mouth hung open.

Buz didn't want to do it. He did not enjoy it sexually. It seemed that Stif didn't get such a thrill from the actual act either. The reason, the motive, the way Buz thought of it, was to strengthen Stif's self-confidence, to build up his sense of self-value as a partner in our social-sexual community by emphasizing to him that he was wanted, in fact, desired, and to remove the feelings of sexual imposition resulting from his encounter with the Dean. This would lead to restoring Stif's capacity to develop relations with women, his true orientation. Buz remembered this stuff from Greenie's psych text.

Later, Stif was lying on the mattress, stomach down. His elbows were resting on the mattress and his hands were under his chin. He was talking about his basketball achievements. He was naked. His small, youthful buttocks were not quite clean. "I sunk twenty-six points in one game. We were playing Booker Washington and man, they had a tough team! There wasn't a guy on it under seven feet. See, you gotta wait for your time. When there's a clear shot, you go for it. Otherwise you turn and dribble. Twenty-six points. The bleachers were chanting 'Stif! Stif! Stif'! That was a game, fucker."

"Drakesville won?"

"No, we lost ninety-eight to sixty-four, but if the rest of the team'd played like me, we'd've been on our way to the state capital for finals." Stif thought some more. "That wasn't our best game, of course. We floored Maystown eighty-nine to thirty-two. Those guys were a bunch of midgets."

Darkness was coming up. It was up to Buz to get some dinner burritos for them at the store, plus a re-supply of beer. On the way out he stopped to check the mail box. He wasn't surprised to find two white envelopes with the return address of the Dean's Office, Peabody State University. The answer to Stif's direct appeal to the Dean's office. He carried them unopened to Abarrotes and back. He wasn't as optimistic as he had been when he thought up the whole project for Stif to carry out. Probably, this was the final kiss off, the end of it at last, the final confirmation after appeal of the notice of expulsion.

Inside the dump, Buz found Stif dozing in front of the screen. He had been drinking and watching and laughing all day. Naturally he had to rest up a bit. Buz sat down next to his roommate. He opened one of the letters.

Dear Mr. Snerdley,

The Dean's Commission on Discipline has concluded that you have violated the section of the Peabody Code of

Ethical Behavior pertaining to consumption of alcoholic beverages during class sessions on campus. You were observed, and photographed, while in possession of an open container of alcohol during a meeting of the section of College Mathematics in which you were enrolled. Several students and a faculty member with the rank of Professor have signed statements attesting to this fact. Three students have supplied photographic evidence of this violation.

The policy of the Administration of Peabody State University in regard to the consumption of alcohol is extremely strict due to our recognition of the harm that abuse of this substance has caused to women, minorities and children. However, the Dean's Office realizes that the misuse of substances is also a social problem that can be linked to the negative influences of the capitalist economic system and the culture associated with it. For this reason, violators of the Code of Ethical Behavior pertaining to the consumption of alcohol are offered an alternative to expulsion. You have the opportunity to enroll in a section of Substance Discourse with associated lab session. Full academic credit is awarded to students who complete this course. Enquire at the Dean's Office for enrollment procedures. Substance Discourse with lab session is taught by Professor Artesta Brackle. Classes are held in the basement rooms of Sigmund Freud Hall.

Yeah, it was all clear now. Probably the Dean *did* use basically the same letter for just about everything. It saved him a lot of work. Stif had gone through all *that* just for that, a letter that was almost a duplicate of the last one from the Dean's Office. Buz didn't bother to open his own letter. He looked at the TV screen, where smiling, laughing sit-com actors were going through yet another version of the plot, the show, the routine. There was nothing but that. It was destiny. It was why you existed.

"Ha! Ha! Ha!" Stif was awake. Maybe he had only pretended to be passed out, just to see if Buz would try to "take advantage" of him again. He was focusing on the televersion, getting the jokes, taking part, going along with it.

Buz laughed too. It was not a satiric counter-laugh, nor a macabre laugh in death, it was a laugh that tried to join in what little remained. A laugh to reassure and to encourage his friend. When the program stopped and a commercial began, an ad for something totally useless and obnoxious (a brand of sweetened water), he passed the opened letter to Stif. Stif read it, then dropped it on the living room floor. It hardly interrupted his television viewing.

"So? What do you think?"

"It's about what I figured it would be." Stif turned his head toward Buz for the barest moment. "Probably the Dean thinks he's doing me a favor, letting me go for another lab course. Anyway, he told me he had 'limited discretion in extreme cases'."

"It's the same as the first letter after your beer drinking outbreak in math class."

"Not exactly the same. The staff writes up the letters individually every time. The Dean told me. They have to follow the rules laid out in the Code and in the Dean's Instructions, but they try to get the wording a little different, sort of make it more personalized."

"Nice of them."

"Yeah." Stif watched. The remark could have been satiric, or possibly not. Stif was not interested.

"I'm not going through lab again," Buz mumbled. "Nothing's worse than that. Right?"

"Ha! Ha! Ha!" Stif was focusing on the show. "What? Yeah, of course. Me neither. No crazy lab tech's going to grab my balls again. Ha! Ha!" There was a great show playing on the screen. One of the better ones.

The lights were out in the bedroom. Stif seemed unconscious. This was hardly a surprise. He had consumed at least two and a half six packs of beer since breakfast. And all of that while parked in front of the TV. After a few snores that seemed to resonate from partly blocked inner nasal passages, Stif spoke.

"Hey, since we're getting kicked out of Old Piss anyhow, why don't we just blow out of this whole crappy burg? We can go to New Orleans. Mardi Gras's coming up soon. We could get jobs there too, probably eventually."

Buz considered this. He wasn't even going to repeat that it was the end of their university dream—it had really been his dream. It had been more of an illusion than he had thought possible. "Sure. We can pack tomorrow. No point in hanging around stupid Peabody. This whole thing was only 'the appearance of illusion representing itself'. Check out Foucault and Barthes, the references in old Greenie's text."

Stif was really asleep now and probably hadn't heard the last part, which he wouldn't have understood anyway.

The first thing they had to do was to withdraw the cash limit from their Student Loan accounts. That just might keep them going until they could get jobs in New Orleans. The amounts available were between eight hundred and eleven hundred. Eight hundred for Buz and eleven hundred for Stif. These sums represented the allowed loan subsistence cash for the remainder of the term plus the interterm period. These would be the last Student Loan Advances that they would receive, unless the University had already alerted the bank about their expulsion. Then they would get zero.

Stif drove this time. It was a reassertion of his male capability and determination. Buz was impressed. The Fiat barreled through town and pulled into the large downtown parking lot of the Bank of Peabody twenty minutes later. "Let's get our cash out and beat it the hell out of here." Stif.

They shot through the double glass doors of the bank, checked out the space arrangement for a minute, then got into line with other customers waiting to perform transactions at the teller windows.

"If we'd've gone to New Orleans back from before we left Drakesville, we'd a been there for months by now," Stif concluded. Maybe he had read the long inset article on Foucault in Greenie's psychology textbook. He seemed to be able to put things in the most confusing way possible.

"Sure. I should have known you had twenty-twenty hindsight."

The line of customers snaked through several turns of the red marquee-like crowd guards. It was only after ten minutes of waiting in line that Stif noticed that the person in line just ahead of him was Professor DiVaggio. He signaled silently to Buz by pushing against his cheek with his tongue in the direction of the English teacher.

DiVaggio was more observant. She had seen them from the start. After a few oblique glances in their direction, she outed, "I hope the two of you have learned your lesson." She knew they had been through the dread Castration Discourse Lab. "At Peabody we do not exhibit insensitive behavior to others."

"Oh we learned all right," Buz answered with due humility. "I think Stif learned even better than I did."

Stif bobbed his head rapidly in eager agreement. Meanwhile he had been staring at Vaggy's strategic places, those larger developments on a generally thin body. This was sexist discourse, he knew it, and it was Dean's Office territory. Or, it would be, once they discovered a way to find out what you're thinking.

After a while DiVaggio defrosted. She had once like the two, after all. She still thought that there was something about them that was unconventional and refreshing, although not exactly wild. "What are you going to do now? I heard you were both expelled from P.S.U. for drinking in class."

"We're going to New Orleans to find jobs," Buz answered, expressing an enthusiasm that surprised even him.

"We'll be there in time for Mardi Gras," Stif added grinning.

Di Vaggio registered this with jealous reactivity. "I always go to New Orleans for Mardi Gras." Plain informative tone.

"Why don't we meet up there, the three of us, for Carnival?" Again, Stif checked out his old English teacher's areas of gender differentiation. To him, she was now almost an ideal.

DiVaggio brightened. "I would really like to." She gave Stiffy a quick side look of naughty connivance. "Perhaps I can keep you two out of further trouble. Let me know your address when you get established there." Even Peabody Administration didn't care what you did out of town, as long as it didn't get blabbered in the press.

The bank teller called "next!" and Vaggy was off.

Now at the head of the line, Buz and Stif were still waiting while DiVaggio was being paid out with stacks of hundred dollar bills by the teller. Faculty salaries at Peabody started at eighty-five thousand per year. This was peanuts, of course. Generalized faculty resentment about low pay partly explained the harsh, but mainly understandable, deconstruction critiques published by P.S.U. teachers against the "dominant class".

After hours on the road in the Fiat, they stopped for the night at a cheap motel in Meridian, Mississippi. When they started out again in the morning it was plain that Stif was wearing make-up. Later in the day they had to pull into a gas station to refill the car's gas tank. They were only a few miles from Lake Pontchartrain. As Buz hung up the fuel hose, Stif emerged from the gas station restroom. He was wearing the borrowed skirt.

New Orleans was there, in the medium distance, as they crossed the lake on a low bridge. Buz was driving. He thought about arrival. He now had three main problems to deal with: jobs for both of them, Stif's alcoholism, and his homosexuality.

Printed in the United States
By Bookmasters